For my parents.
You are the best anyone could ask for, thank you for having more
faith in me than I have in myself. I love you.

Special Thanks to:

Jack Whisner, Jeff Burgeson, Terri Wilson, Carrie Ingraham, Elaine
Hutchison, Robert Dykes, Celeste Cope, Holly Liles, Jessica
Bowers, Josh Barnwell, Riley Brown, Russell Parman, Jason Keen,
Franklin Ward, Hannah Morgan, Tammy Fathera, Nathan Holt, my
sister, and of course my extended family of favorite cousins–you
know who you are.

A Very Special Thanks to my best friends Dave and Antoinette
Mangan.

2

America's Martyrs

Richard Hodgkinson

America's Martyrs

ISBN: 978-0-6151-9119-5

"What we do for ourselves dies with us. What we do for others and the world remains immortal."

Albert Pike

Prologue:

The camera sat on its tripod, focusing intently on the white drywall at which it had been aimed. Its operator zoomed in and out until he had the distance that he wanted. He lifted his eye from the eyepiece and spoke in Arabic. Soon thereafter, a man brought a short stool over to the wall and placed it neatly in front of the camera before using it as his seat. The lights that had been set up were absorbed by the man's green cargo pants and black sweater, on his head was a dark blue almost black turban covering his entire face. Only his menacing and angry eyes could be seen by the man behind the camera. He spoke gently in Arabic to the camera operator who adjusted the focus slightly before pressing the record button on his machine. Once the operator saw the red light in the corner of his eyepiece, he nodded to the man in front of him.

"Too long our faithful have sacrificed themselves in Allah's name against the imperial west." The man began confidently in perfect English. "Too many of our brothers and sisters have become martyrs in our war for freedom from tyranny. American soldiers kill our people in our very own native lands, lands that belong not to America, Briton or even us, but lands that belong to Allah. Our soldiers have attacked New York and the Pentagon previously, sacrificing themselves in magnificent displays of loyalty to our cause and to Allah. Our soldiers fight the jihad in Iraq, Palestine, and even in this country. They fight with courage, respect, and impunity. Throughout this America has retaliated with atrocities committed against Islam and its people's. On the surface, America is a strong and courageous empire, they are to be feared by those without Allah's spirit on their heels, but America cannot win against Allah's soldiers. America's strength shall be rendered useless by their own laws which they claim to hold in such esteem. America's courage will be used against them in a way never before conceived. Today we will use America's courage to bring our jihad to the people of this country. A country that is fighting a war against Allah that it can never win. America's sacrifice will show that no one is safe from Allah's wrath, and that all infidels everywhere will tremble at Allah's reach." The man's proclamation forced the operator to fight through his own tears while shutting off the camera.

Joe Stinson sat sweating in his car. He was clearly nervous and scared. He looked at his watch with dread, it was almost time.

Joe was the son of a prominent lawyer in Chicago, who was in turn the son of another prominent attorney. Joe was different however, he had married young, and against his father's wishes. His wife had gotten pregnant with their first child while he was in law school and because his parents would not help him with bills; he had been forced to drop out. He had to take a job as a bus driver and since the pay wasn't good he and his family had moved to the lower east side, where they still reside. Joe always regretted his children having to grow up impoverished, especially because he always had so much when he was young. He was also aware of the challenges that his children faced. Caucasian children attending schools that are eighty to eighty five percent minority is never easy, not only are they different, their race is typically seen as the cause of the poverty in the area. For these reasons Joe had grown to feel more and more like a failure in life.

Sitting in the front seat of his car, Joe pondered these things and took a very small comfort in the fact that he was now doing something good for his family. That perhaps now he was being the man that he had not been before. He looked at his watch again. It was time. He wiped the sweat from his brow and exited the car, not bothering to lock the door. He straightened out his long trench coat and walked over to the trunk, which he opened, and removed a brown leather briefcase. He stopped for just a moment after closing the trunk and took a long breath before continuing on.

He walked along the wall of the parking garage until he arrived at a set of stairs that led him up three stories. Once at the top of the stairs he surveyed the area, he had just exited the parking garage onto the main check-in area of O'Hare International Airport, one of the busiest in the world, and he could tell it. The area was packed with people trying to get to their morning flights. This was the busiest time of day for the airport with many flights departing, and security lines backing people out the doors onto the luggage check on the sidewalks. Joe strode across the street when the vehicles allowed, and stopped next to the wall by the automatic door that led to the ticket counters.

He was sweating much more than before. He felt an uncontrollable fear raising from his stomach into his face, but he couldn't stop now. He took a look around at all the people going about their business, checking their bags in, saying goodbye to loved ones, and kissing their children. He felt a great pity for these people, but there was nothing he could do for them, events had been set in motion and he couldn't stop them. He took a deep breath and sat the briefcase down where he was standing, then quickly went through the door.

"Mommy, Mommy," a young girl tugged at her mother's coat. "That man forgot his suitcase." She said pointing so that her mother could see. The mother looked up and saw the briefcase sitting alone and the door closing behind a man in a trench coat. She nudged her husband.

"Jim, that man just left that briefcase." She told him. He looked suspiciously at it, and knowing what all the security at the airport was for, he became nervous.

"Wait here," he told her. "I'll be right back." He began looking around and saw a police officer walking down the sidewalk. "Sir, sir?" He waved to cop down. "I'm sorry, someone just left that briefcase there." He informed. The police officer thanked him for letting him know and started toward the briefcase while speaking into his radio.

Joe Stinson maneuvered himself well into the lobby of the airport, which was filled with people. Swimming in his own sweat, he looked around at the huge crowd. He placed his hand on the collar of his coat, holding both ends together while he unbuttoned it. He took a deep breath, said the lord's prayer and released the collars. The coat opened to reveal a vest filled with thick squares of plastic explosive wrapped in yellow paper. Joe reached up with his right hand, closed his eyes and flipped a switch on the front of the vest. A tenth of a second later a shockwave sent the glass windows encasing the lobby outward with the velocity of a million bullets immediately followed by suffocating smoke.

"Mom!" the precocious six year old yelled. "Becca stole my pink barrettes and now I can't find them!"

"Calleigh don't worry, there are more in your room." Her mother stated calmly. "And your sister didn't steal them. She was just playing with them." She said before going back to cooking her eggs. Her statement however, caused the young girl to march into the kitchen and make a proclamation of her own.

"I have to have them! I can't go to school without them! Find them!" Calleigh ordered in the meanest tone the child could muster. This caused her mother to stop stirring the eggs, and turn her eyes then her head toward the little girl. The child knew she'd made a mistake and stopped in her tracks.

"What have I told you about that tone young lady?" She said in a surprisingly calm yet scary tone. The young girl's eyes suddenly changed from defiance to capitulation. "What did I tell you about that tone?" The mother ordered slightly louder than the first time.

"That young ladies don't talk like that." The girl said in a whisper.

"What?" The mother ordered again, raising her spatula up and down.

"That young ladies don't talk like that." The girl said at a normal volume.

"Good, now go and get your sister, breakfast is almost ready." The mother commanded.

"But what about my barrettes? I can't go to school without them, I was going to show them to Emily, and Isabella." Calleigh argued.

"You can wear the green ones and I'm sure we'll find the others when you get home."

"But those are ugly, I want the pink ones." The girl tried one last time.

"Go now." The mother commanded, waiving her spatula towards the stairs in the living room. Her daughter reluctantly obeyed. "Dylan," the mother yelled to her eight year old son in the living room, "are you finished with your writing?"

"No Mom. I hate cursive!" The boy announced. "Why do I have to do this anyway?"

"Because you have to practice, and practice makes perfect." The mother told him virtually automatically. "Come on in here so you can eat breakfast. You can practice it some more after school." With those words the boy got up from the coffee table he was sitting at and ran into the kitchen, jumping into a chair without breaking stride. "Lewis, breakfast is ready." She yelled to her husband.

Elizabeth Austin or Liz as she was called, sometimes thought she was the busiest woman in the world. The mother of three children and the wife of a Seattle police officer, her responsibilities, and her schedule knew almost no bounds. She was a beautiful woman of thirty-one years, she had light brown hair with natural blonde highlights made by the sun, sparkling green eyes and a smile that made everyone who saw it trip over themselves. In her youth her figure had been better, more streamlined, and curvy, but after three children she was thankful that she hadn't retained more weight. She wished that she had the time to work out, but knew that would never happen. Still, she thought that being five foot six inches and one hundred and thirty five pounds wasn't bad for her circumstances or her age. Plus she knew that it was only uphill from here.

Her husband Lewis loved her with all of his heart and together they had a pretty good marriage, they would fight sometimes but who didn't? They had entered into much more than a romantic relationship when they were married and both knew it. Lewis and Liz had entered into a partnership in all things, raising children, managing finances, advancing Lewis' career, and of course love. Their partnership had always worked for them, and unlike most other cop's marriages, they could say with confidence that their's was not only stable and loving, but almost always in good spirits.

Lewis was upstairs in their bedroom when he heard his wife call to him. He had been dressing for work in his usual suit and tie. While combing his thick black hair in the mirror he had noticed some of it thinning. Lewis was almost a full ten years older than his wife and felt lucky to have found such a young, vibrant, beautiful woman who loved him. He shook off his concern for his hair and walked over to his wife's jewelry cabinet. He opened the door and from a drawer at the top where the children could not reach, he removed his service weapon, a Smith and Wesson automatic, which was locked with a trigger lock as a secondary precaution. He removed his keys from his dresser and fumbled to find the keys to the lock.

"Lewis?" He heard his wife yell, "you're breakfast is getting cold." she said, sitting down a plate for herself and her three children began to eat. Not wanting to anger his wife, Lewis set the keys and pistol down on the dresser and started down the stairs.

Just after he got down the stairs and started for the kitchen he heard a knock at the door. He immediately turned around and went to answer it. Liz looked up from her plate and thought she heard a faint sound coming from outside on the kitchen patio of their house.

"Excuse me," the young Middle Eastern man of about twenty said when Lewis opened the door "my car has broken down and I was wondering if I could use your phone?"

"Sure, stay here, I'll bring it out to you, wait here." Lewis said without hesitating. After he turned to get the phone, two more Arabic men emerged from next to the door and burst in, each pointing pistols at Lewis and yelling for him to get on the floor.

Liz heard the commotion but didn't know what was going on, she began to stand, but was stopped when someone used a two-by-four to break the plate glass window in the kitchen's sliding door.

In a second, four more men had entered the house, violently grabbing Liz and the children.

"I think I'll use it in here." The young man said. The other men grabbed Lewis by the hair and threw him onto the wooden floor, bloodying his head in the process. Before Lewis knew what was happening, his hands had been cuffed behind his back and he was being picked up. The young man who had knocked on the door waited for one last man to enter, then closed the door and locked it with the deadbolt.

Lewis was led into the kitchen, all the while pleading with the men not to hurt his family. When he arrived, he saw his wife and three children being taped to their chairs with duct tape, the children were crying and the tape was being placed over their mouths to silence them. In the back he could see a man closing the blinds to the broken kitchen door. One of the men fastened him to a kitchen chair using the tape.

"Please don't hurt my family, I'll do whatever you want!" He exclaimed. "I'll cooperate with whatever you want me to do, I swear, just don't hurt my family."

"I know." The last man to enter the house told him. The man grabbed the last chair at the table, turned it around and planted himself in it. "Do you know why I am here?" He asked, taking out a Glock pistol and affixing a silencer to it.

"No, but there is no need for that, we'll cooperate." Lewis

told him. Liz's eyes grew wide at the sight of the gun.

"My name is Qudamah bin Salman bin Abdul Aziz Al-Khalifa." The man said in perfect English and with a smile. "You may call me Qudamah." The man told Lewis. "I am fighting for the freedom of my people and sadly your family must be involved."

"Look, I'll do whatever you want, just let my family go, they're no threat to you. They don't have anything to do with your war. Please?" Lewis begged.

"I understand your devotion to your family my friend, I respect that," Qudamah returned, "but regrettably I cannot let them go. Rest assured that we will do everything we can to see that they are set free, I make that promise to you." Qudamah paused for a moment. "I want you to know, that unlike many of my brothers, I know and respect this country, you have courage and I respect that also."

"Then please let my family go, they have done nothing to you, at least my children, they are innocent, even in God's eyes." Lewis begged again, a tear running down his cheek. "Look, I'm a police officer, a Lieutenant in the Seattle Police Department. I might be able to help you, if you let my family go, I'll do everything I can." Lewis continued. Qudamah finished twisting the silencer onto his weapon. "You don't need them, they're useless to you, I'm the one you want, let them go." Qudamah looked intently into Lewis' eyes as though reading his soul. He took a long breath, then after a moment he finally spoke.

"Who said we wanted you?" Qudamah asked nonchalantly. Lewis' eyes shot over to his wife, and a wave of dread flooded his body. A moment later a .45 caliber hollow point entered his left eye.

Chapter 1:

C arey Rent awoke to a ringing telephone. The sound of the ring echoed through his small loft apartment like church bells on a Sunday afternoon. Rent slowly lifted himself out of bed and took the five or six steps that he needed to get into his kitchen. He looked at the caller I.D. on the cheap phone and saw that it said "unknown caller." He shook off some of his sleep and decided he wasn't ready to talk to an unknown caller this early in the day and ignored the phone, instead turning on his small thirteen inch television set. He scratched his lower back and took a few more steps over to his toilet and relieved himself.

On the television was the local news, its anchor recapping the headline story of the morning, apparently several hours ago a suicide bomber had blown himself up at O'Hare International Airport in Chicago. The anchorman soon switched to talking about one of the powerful Senators from the state of California who was an outspoken proponent of the current war on terror, in which the United States was engaged.

"Yesterday, I had the opportunity to speak with Senator Cale, and this is what he had to say about terrorism." The anchorman said just before the screen switched to taped conversation between the two. "Senator," the anchorman began, "you're a Vietnam veteran and former POW, what do you think about the President's policy of holding suspected terrorists without trial?"

"First, we aren't holding anyone without trial so to speak, each detainee immediately goes before a military judge where the evidence against him is presented and the judge determines whether or not we should hold the individual. It may not be a trial in the usual sense, but there is due process here. It's important to remind the American public that we are not doing to these detainee's what was done to myself and others like me by the Vietnamese. It's also important to remember that these people are engaging in a terror campaign against America, and that it's this particular in-fighting amongst us that they are hoping to perpetuate. I think the President's methods in the war on terror have been very successful but we can't forget that we still have much more work to do and we must do that work with the same diligence and determination as we have so far."

Rent watched the senator speak before he picked up a half consumed beer bottle from the night before that he had left on the counter and poured it down the sink. He opened his refrigerator, took out a carton of orange juice, checked the date on it and began drinking.

"Yes, I support a ban on torture, but that ban must have certain exemptions. The reason for that is that we have to acknowledge that there may or will be certain circumstances in which gaining information quickly will be necessary to save American lives. I'm sure everyone will agree that we must do whatever is necessary to safeguard the lives of our citizens and that must be first and foremost..." Rent's attention faltered when he heard the phone ring again. He quickly finished off the carton of orange juice and checked the caller I.D. again. This time he knew the caller and picked up the phone, giving his usual grunt for greeting.

"Carey, it's Mack, did I wake you?"

"Pretty much." Was Rent's quick reply.

"It's almost noon man, what have you been doing?"

"The club doesn't close until two and we don't get everybody out of there until at least three." Rent replied.

"Is that going well? I was kind of worried."

"Yeah it's fine, but working as a bouncer two days a week isn't going to cut it, tell me good news."

"Carey I'm sorry, I spoke with the Department of Commerce and Insurance this morning and they're going to deny your security license application."

"Aww, c'mon I did three months!"

"It was an eighteen month sentence, and you know their

rules."

"How am I supposed to get a decent job?"

"They can't do it Carey, I told you, they aren't going to license anyone with a felony conviction. I'm sorry." Mack paused for a moment, "you need to take the other job."

"So I can live out my days working a register at a gas station and getting robbed nightly, thanks but I told you no."

"Carey, it's a means to an end, just until we find you something better, as your friend I'm telling you, you need to take it, just to stay stable. As your parole officer I'm telling you, you need to take it because it's part of your parole that you take the job."

"Mack tell me there's something better out there, tell me I won't be there for the next twenty-five years?" Rent said in frustration. "Do I have a future anymore?"

"Of course you have a future, you've just fallen on some tough times is all, don't down yourself. Look, I'm going to keep looking, and maybe we can get you in on the docks and I'll keep hounding the license people to get you a waiver. Until then you need to take this job."

"Fine." Rent finally gave in, lacking other options he decided that some money was better than no money.

"Good, be down there at three. I'll tell the manager to expect you. Thanks Carey, and we are going to find you something."

"Yeah, yeah." Rent hung up the phone. He stepped over to

his bed, passing his bathroom mirror on the way. Rent looked old now, older than his thirty-five years should have shown him, but then in the last year he'd been through a lot and he couldn't expect to maintain his youthful good looks forever. He noticed a single gray hair in the sea of brown that covered his head and gave it only a moment's attention before moving on and settling himself on the edge of his bed. The Senator on television was still speaking, and Rent's ear was once again lassoed by his words.

"I can't say that we won't be attacked here in the states again, but what I can say definitively is that the brave and heroic men and women of our intelligence agencies and federal and local law enforcement are doing everything humanly possible to prevent such an attack."

"Doughnut?" Narcotics Detective Jesse Owens inquired in his slight southern accent of the tall, stocky, African American staring through the window blinds of the construction trailer. The man didn't respond, keeping his gaze fixed out the window. "No?" Owens asked again before putting half of a large doughnut in his mouth. "You know," he said, chewing a mouthful, "I figure, I workout about ten hours a week, give or take one or two you know? I do squats, curls, pullups, running, bench press, the works. I especially like the leg press, and you know why I do it?" Owens paused for an answer, but got ignored. "I do it so that I can enjoy this fine delicacy that law enforcement everywhere have been stereotyped to devour." After pausing for a moment longer, Owens took the man's silence as permission to continue. "You see, I just can't bring myself to be different from all the others that gone before me. I figure it's tradition, you know Sarge?"

"Did you get laid last night?" Dave Jackson asked more out of the pain of having to listen to his partner than anything else.

"Not that I recall?" Owens responded, "but you know, that might do you some good, I can have Vice hook you up if you want?" Owens joked.

"Nope, I'm married, I get laid once a month, whether I need it or not. Besides, I'd be very scared of the kind you'd hook me up with, probably from your hometown of hickville, nowhere. Snaggle toothed, always pregnant, and thinks I should to be picking cotton." Jackson returned.

"Suit yourself chief, but it aint fair your playing the race card and and all that. I wasn't one of them that treated nobody bad, hell I aint even flown no rebel flag." Owens asserted. The two had been partners for almost a year and had immediately hit it off with the type of rapport to which they were now engaged. At first, several of the other officers in Jackson's narcotics squad had become quite self-conscious at the quantity and voracity of the racially motivated remarks, however given time, the officers had become accustomed to them, and figured out that underneath the callous insults, that they were actually very good friends.

"You kidding me?" Jackson took the bait. "You've got one on that dilapidated truck you pretend to drive around."

"Yeah, but it's just a little one." Owens exclaimed.

"It's your front license plate." Jackson pointed out.

"Yeah, but nobody looks at front license plates." Owens said, picking up another doughnut.

"I'm surprised you haven't gotten your honky ass kicked for it yet."

"Well, that's why I moved up to the old Pacific Northwest, you guys will tolerate anything." Owens said with a mouthful of doughnut.

"Yeah why is it the south kicked you out again? Something about being able to read and..." Jackson stopped. The expensive Mercedes entering the construction lot catching his eye. He raised his radio and began to speak. "Everybody take your positions, the suspect is on location, I say again, suspect on site, get ready to move." He put the radio back on his belt and spoke to his partner without taking his eyes off the window. "Get on your feet KKK, it's time to go to work." Owens immediately tossed his doughnut in the trash and got out of his chair, pulling his weapon in the process.

Dave Jackson's squad had been working on this bust for two

months, and now it was game day. Jackson's narcotics squad was the point team for the larger, more significant operations in Seattle. This particular scenario had been dropped into their laps by the Coast Guard whom just two and a half months ago arrested several drug smugglers attempting to ship high grade heroin into the United States by way of Canada and the Puget Sound. Along with the arrests came a seizure of over four million dollars worth of drugs, and a tenuous connection to Jackson's current suspect.

Seattle has always been an entertainment boomtown, which along with high grade executives from computer companies makes the city a paradise for those addicted to illegal narcotics. Rock singers, grundge artists, drop of a coin street musicians, corporate Vice Presidents, CEO's, music agents, secretaries, out-of-work programmers, and even a few foreign dignitaries have been known to visit the city, each attempting to at least taste the nirvana it is famous for. This makes for an excellent market in very high priced, low profile drug peddlers who are smart enough not to hawk their products on street corners like common thugs. Jackson's suspect was one such individual, an individual who incidentally, had simultaneously been ratted out to the authorities and seen his inventory dry up with the same arrest, though he didn't know about the former, he was worried sick about the latter.

That was what made him a good target for local law enforcement. The politics of this were simple, the Coast Guard, which is a federal agency, makes a seizure that is worth four million dollars in free publicity in sight of Seattle, which makes the Seattle Police Department look a bit foolish and in need of assistance. The Coast Guard, happy about their new found fame kicks back some of the information they attain after the bust to the SPD because they're good team players. Also because the city leases the land they use in the bay to the federal government at a considerably cheaper rate than they would anyone else, and will continue to do so as long as the city's back gets scratched. A little while later the SPD makes an important, yet seemingly unrelated arrest of a big drug dealer they've been trying to sink their teeth into for quite some time. The Coast Guard comes out looking like seafaring heroes, and the SPD comes out looking competent and efficient, everybody's happy. That is except the drug dealer, who gets ten to fifteen, but then again that's life.

Jackson continued to watch the Mercedes pull up to a black SUV. A tall, lanky, Caucasian in the Mercedes stepped out and dusted off his expensive suit. A moment later, another man got out of the SUV, the two shook hands and began to speak with Jackson listening on the speaker and recording system that his partner had set up in the trailer. The two conversed for a few minutes, mostly about the suspect's ulcer, before getting down to business. The undercover officer opened the back door to the SUV and unzipped two gym bags full of drugs, with the suspect smiling widely. They talked for a few more minutes, mostly haggling price, which had been settled upon before the meeting, however the suspect had decided he was going to try to talk the undercover officer down slightly. The officer didn't budge though and the suspect agreed to get the money.

"All units, get ready to move on my command." Jackson said into his radio. The suspect walked casually to his car while the undercover officer pretended to look around to see if anyone was watching. The squad had a good position at the construction site, they had decided on a secluded area next to the foundation of what was to be a four story building. Though only the concrete frame for the first two floors was up, it provided the privacy that the suspect demanded, while giving plenty of room for the squad to be put into position for the takedown.

At twenty-five yards away, Jackson and Owens were the closest in the construction trailer. There were two more officers hiding in the concrete pillars of the building frame, and two more were pretending to work as part of the construction crew on the other side of the building, they had put their equipment down now, and were at the ready with their weapons drawn. Two patrol cars were also standing by to block the entrance to the site, which was about 50 yards behind the suspect's vehicle. All the bases were covered, now it was time to make their move. Jackson and Owens were watching the suspect intently, Jackson from the window and Owens peaking out the door. When the suspect removed a medium sized leather handbag from his trunk, Owens noticed something.

"Gun, Dave," Owens said more loudly than he intended. "He's got a gun there!"

"Move in, all units go!" Jackson immediately yelled into the radio. Simultaneously, the two officers on the construction crew lifted their weapons and started a mad dash towards the suspect, the two in the building frame came out in the same manner and Jackson and Owens burst through the door. The suspect first noticed Jackson and Owens, and without hesitation, he dropped both the handbag and .38 caliber revolver he was holding and started running for the entrance to the construction site. The undercover officer drew his weapon and gave chase, but it was Owens who proved to be faster than the other officers, tackling the suspect a few feet before he reached the entrance. Putting his lower leg across the suspect's back, while pointing his service Smith and Wesson at the back of the suspect's head. He started giving commands.

"Extend your arms, palms up! Extend your arms, palms up!" He yelled. A second later Jackson and the undercover officers were with him, and a second after that, the other four members of the squad. The patrol cars were the last to arrive, but it only took them a few seconds longer than the others.

"Put your left wrist in the small of your back, do it now!" Owens commanded while holstering his weapon and retrieving his handcuffs. The suspect complied, and a moment later found both his hands cuffed behind his back. "You got any knives or needles?" Owens said, searching the suspect, pulling out his pockets in the process. The suspect nodded to the negative. Owens continued, helping the suspect up when he was finished. "Guess what peach? You're under arrest baby. That's right, you're goin' down to the land of cable TV, internet girlfriends, live-in boyfriends, and free college!"

Rent's shower lasted only with the hot water, which was nearly fifteen minutes, a record for his apartment building. He enjoyed the soothing pace the tapping water provided on his body, for a few moments he actually forgot his life and his predicament. Even though his phone had rang twice while he was showering, he ignored it, opting instead for the peace of solitude. Once the water began to cool, Rent turned it off and stepped out of the small tub in the corner of his tiny loft apartment. Almost the moment the sound of the water abated, his ear was once again caught by his television, which was uncharacteristically carrying more news reports.

"The identity of the gunman is unknown at this time, but unconfirmed reports state that it was a middle aged white male. We'll be right back with full coverage of both the Chicago airport bombing and the apparent shooting spree inside Atlanta's famed underground mall." The anchorman said just before the screen switched to a commercial. Rent grabbed his towel and started drying off while listening to a blurb for something that was supposed to give him an erection. Rent was interested in these happenings but only moderately. He'd been concerned about the war on terror, like every other American ever since it had started, but like most Americans all he could do was pay it lip service. In fact, these apparent attacks weren't of large concern to him at all, they were apparently domestic in origin as reports were coming back from both scenes that the suspects were white males, and the real threat was radical Islamic terrorism wasn't it? To any extent, they didn't effect Rent, who was planning to demean himself to the lowest point in his life today by taking a job so incredibly beneath him that a freckled sixteen year old could do it.

"We have breaking news from our network affiliate!" The anchorman said on the television after they broke into the middle of the third in the series of commercials they had been airing. "For more, we go to our network headquarters in New York." The anchorman promised. The screen switched to another, older anchorman with a solemn look on his face.

"This just in, there has been a bombing at a church led summer camp just outside Salt Lake City, Utah, for more, we go to our own Jane Cawl on the scene in Orem Utah." The screen switched one more time, to a female reporter in casual clothes, which looked very disheveled. "What can you tell us Jane?" The anchorman asked.

"It's a tragic sight down here, we were on site covering the United Mormon Tabernacle's largest summer camp in history, but unfortunately didn't get any footage of the actual attack. What I can tell you is this Jim, about twenty minutes ago as the Reverend Charles Martin Smith was preparing to take the stage for the camp's final luncheon and prayer meeting. Someone drove a pickup truck onto the grounds and hit a tree, after that things got very strange Jim, there was a massive explosion." She told the world.

"My God Jane, are you alright?" The anchorman asked in feigned concern.

"Yes, we are shaken here, but we were shielded by the stage which we were behind preparing our equipment." She said, a little irritated at the interruption to the story which could make her career. "Rescue crews arrived on the scene a few minutes later, but Jim it's a horrible sight. Over two hundred children ranging in age from six to eighteen were sitting at picnic tables out here, and many of them have not survived the explosion. From what we can tell, almost all of them are injured in some way. We are not showing any pictures from the area out of respect for the children and their families. However we have found shrapnel such as ball bearings and industrial sized nails all over the area, leading this reporter to believe that this was not an accident but a planned terrorist attack!"

"Thank you Jane, we'll come back to you in a minute." The anchorman said to his colleague before continuing on. "We now have breaking news from Washington D.C. where the Homeland Security Agency has just announced that they are upgrading the terror alert level from amber to red, and that an attack is imminent. We now take you to that press conference." The screen switched to a podium with an older man standing making a statement.

"We have not determined much about the attacks in Chicago, Atlanta and Utah, but we can tell you definitively that these were planned terror attacks and that there may be more. I'll take a few questions now." All the reporters in the room simultaneously rose their hands. "You." The man pointed at a reporter.

"We have heard that all of the descriptions coming from the scenes are that the suspects are white males, can you elaborate on that." A reporter asked.

"Yes, we have confirmed that the suspects from the Chicago bombing and the Atlanta Shooting spree were both indeed white males. We don't yet know about the bomber in Utah. Next, you?"

"We were told that a briefcase was recovered from the Chicago bombing, can you tell us about that?" Another reporter asked.

"I can't comment on that right now." The man answered. Rent pushed the button on his television set, turning it off. He didn't want to hear anymore, mostly because there was nothing he could do. In another time he would have been on the edge of his seat, but that time in his life was gone now, and all that he had to look forward to was making change in a gas station.

Rent had just finished zipping up his khakis when his phone rang again. It had been a long time since he'd received so many phone calls in one day, and his annoyance grew even further when he again saw that his caller ID said "unknown caller." Thinking that he would vent some of his frustration on a telemarketer he picked up the phone and shouted.

"What do you want?!"

"I want you to answer your phone!" A man with a slight Middle Eastern accent said in perfect English. "I have someone who wants to speak to you." Rent didn't have time to respond before he heard the weeping female voice.

"Carey?" Liz Austin asked. Without his answer she continued. "Carey, they killed Lewis, they shot him in front of the kids." She broke into uncontrolled crying. "They're going to kill us all!" She exclaimed through her tears. Rent began shaking, his mind racing. Qudamah took the phone from Liz and spoke again.

"You can save them, but only if you do exactly as I say. Go to the payphone at the corner of 67th Street and 8th Avenue, under interstate 5. There is a cell taped under it, I will call it in twenty minutes. If you do not answer it, or if you try to alert the authorities, I will fedex you all four of their headless corpses." Qudamah stated just before he pushed the "end call" button on his cell phone.

Chapter 2:

One Police Plaza's halls were uniquely busy on this Friday morning. The terrorist attacks caused alarms across the country and Seattle was no different. Though Seattle hadn't had a terrorist incident yet, when word began arriving of the second terrorist strike in Atlanta, the chief ordered the department to go from terror alert level 4 to terror alert level 3.

Though the rest of the country constantly watched the federal government's color coded terror alert level system, it was up to local municipalities and jurisdictions who operated separate from the federal government to come up with their own systems and policies to handle terrorism. Seattle was no exception, after the September 11th attacks in 2001, the city instituted it's 5 level system. The lowest level on the system was level 5, which meant that there was no threat of a terrorist attack. Level 4, which was what the police department had remained at since the program was instituted, stated that there was a possibility of a terrorist attack and called for increased vigil. Level 3 stated that there was a credible threat of a terrorist attack and called for extra patrols in sensitive areas–mostly business districts—and postings of officers at a list of designated terrorist targets such as the Space Needle, etc. Level 2 stated that a terrorist attack was probable, every officer was to be recalled, and all Lieutenants and below were to be out on the street either patrolling or guarding possible targets. Level 1 was the highest level and meant that the city was under attack by terrorists and to expect more such attacks. It called for the Mayor to have an option to call the federal government for military assistance, and if the situation warranted, a possible declaration of martial law within the city as well as other measures of the same caliber. Of note was that the only person who could change the terror alert level was the Chief of Police and even he had to be in agreement with the Mayor to go to level 1.

After hearing of the shooting at the underground mall in Atlanta, the Chief changed the alert level to 3, but after seeing the bombing in Salt Lake City on the news, the Chief determined that the attacks must have been coordinated. So he again changed the alert system from 3 to 2.

The department itself was split into five precincts: North, West, East, South and Southwest. Of course there was one Chief, but there were also two Deputy Chiefs who oversaw administration and operations, there were also five Assistant Chiefs who ran everything from patrols to emergency preparedness. Assistant Chief Bethany Knox commanded the Criminal Investigations Bureau which consisted of everything from Homicide to Domestic Violence. Also under her jurisdiction were the various narcotics squads, one of which she was waiting for a phone call from.

Knox had just turned 55 years old two weeks before and it showed. A twenty-five year veteran of the police department, she had grown up in Seattle, and even attended the University of Washington Seattle, where she attained a masters degree in Policy Studies of Criminal Justice. She was never an especially good-looking woman, she had always had an odd shaped face, and had for some reason gained wrinkles and gray hair at a very young age. She liked to keep her hair long, as though it womanized her skinny muscular frame. Her lack of good looks didn't prevent her from marrying though. Her husband was a divorce lawyer working in the Seattle area, and together they had two children, one 19 and another 17, both living at home, the oldest attending his mothers alma-mater.

Knox's office had been located on the third floor of Police Plaza however, since the chief had decided to remodel the third floor, her office had been reluctantly relocated to the first floor in the very back of the building. The noise generated from the hallways, especially on this day, caused her to start keeping her door closed. When her desk phone rang she picked it up with haste.

"Assistant Chief Knox," she informed the caller.

"It's Jackson, we've got him." Sergeant David Jackson said into his cell phone.

"Good, any problems?" Knox inquired.

"Well we didn't get any money, he hoped to pass off newspaper, and rob our man." Jackson informed. "We got him without incident, but I don't think much is gonna come of this."

"Why would he do that?" Knox wondered aloud. "That's way too big a risk for him."

"I figure his stock is too low, he's probably losing customers, they're getting desperate now."

"And you think somebody's gonna fill the hole." Knox finished the deduction.

"Somebody always does. We'd better be looking, cause there's going to be a delivery coming in soon."

"I agree. I'll inform harbor and the border patrol, bring him back and we'll see what we can get out of him."

"Ok, but I'm having some trouble out here, we need a dog to go through the car, and a patrol to haul this guy back, but I just lost both the patrol cars assigned to us." Jackson told her.

"That's because the Chief has upgraded us to level 2."

"There's been another attack?" Jackson asked in surprise.

"Salt Lake City, you're going to have to have some of your guys bring him back, we've got to put him in lock-up until this terrorist thing blows over. We're also going to have to loan most of your team out to patrol, can you do the arrest paperwork out there and send it back with your guys?"

"Sure, I have it."

"Good, I want you on one of the high value targets, I don't know which yet, I'll call you back." She said just before putting the phone down. She had just started to return to her paperwork when a knock at her door came. "Come in." She ordered. The door opened and in walked a stout man in a black suit. She immediately stood up. "Assistant Director Bannister, it's good to see you again." She said extending her hand.

"Thank you. It's good to see you too." Terry Bannister said in his slightly gravely voice. "The FAA shut down all the airports, so I'm going to be running northwest FBI operations from here." The FBI Assistant Director stated, he'd been in Seattle for a meeting with the Border Patrol, but now couldn't get back to his home office in Washington D.C..

"Shouldn't you be with your team then?" Knox asked and motioned for him to sit down.

"I am, the Federal Building is a high value target, so when we have a terrorist incident like this we pick up and move. We're going to be conducting operations out of this building now." Bannister informed.

"That's great, we're already hurting for space. Where did they put you?"

"The third floor, I'm actually using your office." Bannister said with a smile. "You've got a great view of the elementary school across the street." He joked. Knox was accustomed to Bannister's wry sense of humor. They'd known each other for quite some time and had developed a friendly rapport.

"Isn't it ironic." Knox returned. "I get the beauty of the concrete wall of our parking garage down here." She said, motioning to her window, outside of which was a thick wall of concrete.

"Well you can have it back when this is over." Bannister assured her.

"Do you think there's going to be an attack in Seattle?" Knox returned to business.

"I don't know." Bannister informed. "I can tell you that we were tracking an important person whom we think may have terror ties here, but our information is very limited at this point. We think that radical Islamic terrorists are somehow or have in someway corrupted people who don't share their ideology, getting them to commit terrorist acts, but we're not sure how, and we don't know why."

"All the descriptions are of white males." Knox observed.

"We know that the Chicago bomber was a Christian, and we found a briefcase with all of his personal documents close to the scene. Likewise for the Atlanta shooter, but his effects were all on him. Whatever is going on, they want us to know these people aren't terrorists."

"Homegrown terrorism?" Knox asked.

"We keep a fairly close eye on that." Bannister had already dismissed the notion. "These people don't have any of the usual links or red flags for that sort of thing."

"Maybe it's some sort of distraction strategy?" Knox wondered.

"We just don't know, I'm being updated every fifteen minutes, when I know more, you'll know more."

"Ok, what can I do for you?" Knox asked.

"I have kind of a sensitive issue," he said, handing her a piece of paper. "I need somebody competent for it."

"Alright," Knox unfolded the paper and read it. "Why me?" She asked when finished.

"My staff is limited here, and all the others are tapped out, they told me that your people are typically the last to be assigned."

"Yeah, I've got just the guys, I'll send them." Knox said.

"Thank you Bethany." Bannister stood up, shook the Assistant Chief's hand and closed the door behind him.

Liz looked around at her location, it wasn't the first time she'd looked around, but it was the first time she did so with the intention of noticing things. She was in some sort of industrial facility, that's all she could determine. She tried to remember what had happened, but her memory of the current day was very confusing because all sense of time had left her.

She could recall that it was after eight when the men broke in, she remembered that much, but she couldn't remember how much time had passed since then. Each time she thought about it the word eternity crept into her mind. She had remained rather calm until they killed her husband, and she only recalled that because it happened so quickly and unexpectedly that it took her a moment to process it.

She tried to forget her husband but couldn't, every time she closed her eyes, the image of the back of his head blowing out onto the wall behind him popped onto the inside of her eyelids as though her mind were a movie projector. Qudamah shot Lewis and he had fallen to his left, taking the chair he was in with him. She remembered that she hadn't screamed until she looked down at his lifeless body at rest on her kitchen floor, blood flowing out of the giant gaping hole in the back of his head like it was coming out of a kitchen faucet. The blood pooling around her dead husband as though it hadn't wanted to be set free. That was when she began screaming uncontrollably, and then that they had gagged her.

She remembered thinking that she was next and the fear of dying sweeping over her until she was awakened by her son Dylan who was choking on his own vomit, which the tape on his mouth prevented him from spitting out. Calleigh the second oldest wet herself and Liz remembered hearing it dripping from the girl's pant leg to the floor. That combined with the sound of the blood inching its way out onto the floor were the sounds she remembered, the men in the house had been moving around, speaking and making sounds, but she couldn't remember hearing them at all. She stared at Dylan even after Qudamah had noticed his distress and removed the tape, spewing vomit all over Dylan's lap and the floor beneath him. He slapped Dylan on the back several times to get him to heave it all up. He gave orders to some of his men, who cut the tape from Dylan and Calleigh, and took them upstairs leaving Liz and her youngest daughter Becca, sitting in the kitchen by the body of their patriarch.

Becca didn't wet herself, she didn't vomit inside her taped mouth, she didn't shed tears, and she didn't move. She just sat there. Quiet. Peaceful. Staring at the body of her father. Liz remembered thinking that perhaps the three year old did not understand what was happening, and that thought brought Liz a mild degree of comfort while she and her child waited to see what was happening to the other two children.

Some time later, to Liz it could have been ten minutes, or two days, the men came back into the room with Dylan and Calleigh, both their mouths sealed with fresh tape. Both had been redressed in clean clothes, and must have been showered because Liz noticed that their hair was wet. Both were holding the hands of one of the men who had assaulted the family. The man nodded and said something that Liz couldn't hear to Qudamah who in turn said something to another man, who cut Liz and Becca free from their chairs.

The family was walked around the back of the house to the driveway where they had been put into a white colored van. Inside, their heads were covered with brown paper bags. The thought of the paper bag brought horror to Liz's mind whenever she thought of it, from the moment the bag covered her, until the moment it was taken off, Liz saw with perfect detail her husband's shooting over and over again. She didn't know how long the ride was, in fact she couldn't even say if it had been long or short. When it was over she remembered being led out of the van and the wind hitting her, but the images she was reliving did not stop. She remembered walking, and tripping on some stairs because she could not see, until she was again fastened to a chair. It was only then that the images stopped with the bag's removal. She remembered not being able to think, that no matter how hard she tried, no thoughts would pop into her head, until just one thought emerged. Her children! Where were they? She didn't know and that terrified her. At some point they had been separated. Worry flooded over her, and that was all she could think about. Without freedom of movement, or even the ability to speak, she descended into the only thing she could do, she wept.

She didn't know how much time she spent crying, only like everything else that had happened in this nightmare, that it seemed to last an eternity. She was in a hallway, there were large pipes running across the ceiling and walls, and men, all Arabic would go up and down the hallway, they seemed to have a purpose, but she didn't know what. None had spoken to her, or even acknowledged her presence until she saw Qudamah come through the door at the end of the hallway with two other men. He had the men unlock the handcuffs holding her arms and feet to the old office chair. They lifted her up out of the chair and took her down the hall through another door, and then another until they got to a room with a steel door and thick lock, which one of the men opened. She remembered thinking first that the room was large, but when she entered it she noticed that it was smaller than it appeared. Her three children were in the room, the tape now gone from their mouths. Dylan sat against the back wall, holding Calleigh in his little arms. Becca sat in the corner of the room, staring at the men and her mother, an emotionless look on her face.

"You will talk to a man named Carey Rent. Do you remember him?" Qudamah had asked. "You will tell him that we have killed your husband and that we will kill you if he doesn't do what we tell him. If you do not, or if you say anything else, I will shoot your boy. Nod if you understand." Liz didn't remember nodding, but she must have because Qudamah ripped the tape from her face, and dialed a number. Apparently there had not been an answer because Qudamah stomped out of the room angrily. After a short period of time, in which Liz had the opportunity to hold her children, the men took her back to her chair until the process repeated itself. Liz couldn't be sure, but she thought it was about the fifth attempt when someone picked up and Qudamah said something, Liz couldn't remember what, then he put the phone by her ear. She said what she had been told and Qudamah took the phone away. When his call was finished, he said something to the men, who led Liz back to her chair and reapplied the cuffs.

That had been some time ago, but Liz couldn't say how long. Her thoughts were broken one last time when Qudamah stepped through the door at the end of the hallway and took his phone out of his pocket when he approached her. She continued to watch Qudamah but he passed her and went into another door in the hallway. She continued to weep, feeling somewhat relieved that he hadn't stopped.

Rent put on a dark green button up short sleeved shirt over his t-shirt before he left. He had to run to get to the highway overpass where the phone was already ringing. It was two blocks from his studio apartment to the pay phones, and Rent thought that something must be wrong with him because he could feel the muscles in his legs tightening up as he ran. He stopped just short of the pay phones to catch his breath and reached under the one where the ring was coming from. He ripped out the cell phone that was taped underneath and opened it.

"I'm here" he said gasping slightly.

"Good," Qudamah told him. "Underneath the other phone is a gun, take it." Rent reached underneath the other pay phone and removed a Sig Sauer P220 handgun in a holster.

"Yeah, I've got it," he said.

"We've called you a cab Mr. Rent, take it to the Regal Arms Hotel next to Bellevue Square, once you are in the lobby I will call you again." Qudamah ordered.

"What do you want me to do?" Rent asked, wanting to find out more about what was happening.

"I want you to save the lives of a mother and three children, to do that you must do what you are told." Qudamah responded, almost expecting the question.

"Wait, I want to talk to Liz, I want to know they're still alive." Rent said into the phone.

"You are not in a position to make demands, if you do so again they will no longer be alive!" Qudamah yelled furiously at him, then pressed a button on his phone. Rent heard the line go dead. Then looked around, his mind racing. He frowned, and started toward the red and white taxicab parked on the corner. He unbuckled his belt and slid the cheap leather holster onto it, pulling his shirt down to conceal it.

"Where to, buddy?" The Moroccan cab driver asked without an accent. Rent didn't reply immediately, he wanted to think a moment longer. He looked through the plexiglass at the rectangular identification card just underneath the vehicle's meter. The card contained the cab driver's picture and his name, which was Kicham Bradley. "Hey bub? You goin' somewhere?" The driver asked again, slightly annoyed. "I been waitin' for a guy named Rent for ten minutes, that's you right bub?" Rent looked up at him, thought for a second longer then responded.

"Yeah, that's me, Bellevue Square." Rent told him, and the cab pulled off.

The man stood over the balcony looking at all the innocent people going about their shopping, impervious to anything going on in the world. He was at one of the largest malls in Seattle. At three stories, the mall contained just about every store imaginable, and at ten till one on a Friday afternoon in the middle of summer, it was bustling with activity. The man was on the second story watching a woman carrying her infant child in a small pack strapped to her chest, roaming about the first floor, she stopped at almost every kiosk, looking at the various items she wanted to buy.

Jason Brewer didn't know her, but he was in fear for her life. He knew the dangerous men that were out today, in fact he was one of them. Brewer had been a family man since he was eighteen years old, when he joined the United States Army. He married his high school sweetheart just two weeks before shipping out to basic training. He could recall with delight how his new wife sent him a letter in his fourth week of training that informed him of an impending birth. He could remember the day his son Adam was born, the child's first steps, and even that he wet his pants the first day of kindergarten. He thought about how his wife carried little Adam, held tightly to her shoulders, when he was an infant. How his wife was overjoyed when he told her that he was being medically discharged from the Army due to a knee injury, and how he felt ashamed of it. How he had gotten a job at a factory but it had closed last year, leaving him without stable income. None of that mattered now, all that mattered to Jason Brewer was his family, and he was going to do whatever he could for them.

He reached up and swatted the sweat from his forehead, but he may as well have been wiping the ocean clean. He decided that the foodcourt area would be best for him and took the escalator down. His breathing was heavy now, he couldn't bear the thought that in a few minutes he would be dead.

In the foodcourt, he reached into his coat and thumbed the fully loaded, fully automatic MAC-10 machine pistol he had been given. Then he removed his hand from it. He looked around, deciding that he should gather himself before doing his deed. He briskly walked into the restroom that was located at the foodcourt and doused his face with water. His mind contemplated whether a more enclosed space would be better. He decided on that and soaked his face and head with a few more handfuls of water. When he was finished he used some paper towels to dry himself and proceeded out.

He emerged in the foodcourt, where he gained the attention of a police officer who had been assigned to patrol the mall due to the raised terror level. The officer immediately noticed that the man was wearing a black trenchcoat in summertime and decided it was worth looking into. Brewer moved out of the foodcourt and into the main shopping area of the mall. The officer followed.

Brewer found a nice spot where he thought he could do what he had been instructed to do, and stood in the middle of the wide hallway with shops lined up on either side. When Brewer stopped, the officer became convinced that something horrible was about to happen and slowed down, nonchalantly unlatching the safety on his holster. Brewer reached into his coat, which caused the officer to grip his weapon inside the holster.

Brewer stopped when he saw the mother and young child

emerge from a store near him. She was too close to miss, and her child was covering her heart with his own frail little body. Brewer gripped the machine pistol tightly, feeling his lungs collapse of all air and his stomach drop. He couldn't do it, he couldn't go through with it. He couldn't take one family in exchange for his own. Brewer removed his hand from his coat and started a forward pace.

The officer that had been watching Brewer felt a great weight lifted from him, and snapped the safety back on his holster. Brewer was still suspicious looking and the officer still intended to follow him, but was overjoyed to see that perhaps his intuition had led him astray. Brewer exited the mall, not knowing he was being followed and immediately went left of the door to the trash dumpster where he quickly deposited his weapon and continued out to the parking lot. The officer exited the door just in time to see Brewer emerge from the dumpster area on the left and continue on. Brewer crossed several rows of parking spots. The officer peered into the dumpster.

Brewer was about to break into tears, he didn't know what to do; he didn't know how he could save his wife and child without taking someone else's. He took out his car keys and put them into the lock. He looked around and saw the officer running towards him frantically yelling into his radio. He thought for an instant about getting into his car and speeding away but felt the officer was too close, so he ran.

The officer followed him through the traffic of a busy

intersection, hoping to gain on him, but even with his bad knee
Brewer was in good shape. The officer, besides wearing a tight belt
which contained a heavy radio, a heavy pistol and several other
items, along with a tightly fitted bulletproof vest was slightly
overweight and not in a position to gain on his suspect. Brewer ran
about a block before he had the opportunity to duck into an alley.
The officer saw him and having arrived several seconds later,
whipped around the corner. In the alley, the officer caught just a
glimpse of Brewer turning into an intersecting alleyway, and
continued to follow. This alley led to another busy street and once
there the officer stopped, catching his breath and looking down both
sides of the street. Not seeing his suspect, he looked down at his
feet, where he found Brewers black trenchcoat. The officer took
another long look down both directions of the street before
informing dispatch that he'd lost his suspect.

Chapter 3:

A single mother, Lynn struggled for the past four years with raising her daughter, providing her with clothing, shelter, and food, all the while attempting to satisfy her own personal appetites. This fight left Lynn very emotionally battered in the last year, the stress of being there for her daughter, giving her the emotional support and love that a little girl needs to grow up and be productive had produced a tired, lonely, woman. Lynn held onto Jamie like she had just fallen off a ship and her daughter was her life jacket. Lynn didn't know what was going on, she didn't know why this was happening, and she didn't really care, all she wanted was for it to be over.

She wasn't sure what time it was when the men broke into her two bedroom apartment. She knew it was very early morning because the sun had not yet crept into the sky, but she didn't remember looking at any clocks. She remembered that there were three men, all with guns. She heard the sound of a gun's slide moving back and forth coming from her roommate's bedroom, and one of the men exiting the room with blood on his jacket and a silencer on his gun. Is that what a silencer sounds like? She remembered thinking it didn't sound at all like it did on television, and then the realization that her best friend and roommate must be dead hit her. It was that realization that broke her from her dream state and caused the fear to set in.

The large metal door to the room that Lynn and Jamie had been in for many hours finally opened and revealed two different men than she had seen before. Lynn sank into the back wall with her daughter. The men grabbed the mother and child, lifted them to their feet and led them out into a hallway. Lynn noticed the pipes running across the ceiling and the dirty concrete floor of the hallway. They were guided through a series of passages and stairways until they got to what Lynn thought was the third floor where they entered another hallway. About halfway down the passage sat an old office chair with an attractive woman of about thirty years sitting, crying.

The men led Lynn and Jamie past the pitiful woman and into another room. This room seemed out of place in this decrepit place. The room itself was large, about the size of a very large office, it contained tables, chairs, laptop computers, and several televisions. One of which was turned to a national cable news network, another to local Seattle broadcasting, and yet another, with a DVD player sitting on top, was not showing anything. To her left, standing over another man who was operating a laptop was Qudamah. He seemed important because one of Lynn's guides stepped over to him and whispered something in his ear. Lynn heard him give an order in another language and one of the men took Jamie's hand from Lynn's, leading the little girl across the room to an empty table where she could not see the blank television.

"Don't take my daughter." Lynn said quietly.

"Don't worry." Qudamah said turning around from the computer and walking over to Lynn. "May I call you Lynn?" He asked politely.

"Yes." Lynn said while the man with her daughter began showing the child a doll.

"Good, sit down please." Lynn complied and sat down in front of the television, Qudamah pulled up a chair and put his foot in the seat of it, then leaning on his raised knee he began to speak to Lynn in a soft, gentle voice. "Lynn, we are freedom fighters here in America." She looked at him and nodded. "Our ideology has nothing to do with you. But we need you Lynn, we need your courage." He paused again for drama, then continued. "We have no need to hurt your daughter. Nor do we have any desire to." He said looking into her eyes. "Do you love your daughter Lynn?"

"Yes." She wept.

"I know you do, that is why we have chosen you." Qudamah said softly. "Allah asks that you prove it. Do you know what that means? That means that you have been chosen for greatness Lynn." Lynn began shivering. "Will you do anything to protect your daughter?"

"Yes." She pledged.

"Good, you are a very courageous woman, worthy of admiration." Qudamah informed. "This may disturb you, but I need for you to see something." He reached over, turning on the television and hitting a button on the DVD player. The screen came to life, and Lynn saw a teenage girl on her knees, with her hands tied behind her back, in a room that looked eerily similar to the room that Lynn and Jamie had been kept in all day. The girl was kneeling on thick clear plastic, and crying uncontrollably. Lynn noticed that the girl had dark black hair like her own, and that she couldn't be older than fifteen or sixteen. A hooded man walked into the frame, a long curved knife in his hand. He stepped over to the girl, positioning himself behind her. He ripped the tape from the girl's mouth, grabbed the back of the girl's hair and lifted his knife to her throat.

Lynn looked away when the man began sawing away at the girl's neck. With a movement of his eyes, Qudamah sent a message to another man in the room who forcefully grabbed Lynn's head with his hands and pointed it at the screen.

"Be strong." Qudamah said gently. The man on the screen yanked the knife across the girl's throat spilling blood all over the room in the video, and even a few drops on the camera lens. Soon the teenage girl's head was completely separated from her body and Lynn watched the lifeless torso drop to the ground. The man held the head high as a symbol of victory, and Qudamah depressed the pause button, leaving that image on the screen, several large drops of blood en route to the plastic sheet covering the floor. Qudamah leaned in, very close to the woman sitting in the chair in front of him. "If you do not do what we ask, what Allah wills, then I will be forced to do this same thing to your daughter." He told Lynn, the mother stared at her daughter in the back of the room, playing with the ragged doll she had been given. "Will you do this?"

"What do you want me to do?" Lynn said, still staring at Jamie. Qudamah extended his hand and motioned for another man to come forward. The man picked up a heavy green vest. The front of which was layered with blocks that were covered with yellow tape, a large, thin wooden box attached to the back containing nails and ball bearings, and a small silver box over the left breast containing a switch on the side and a red button on top.

"It is simple." The man started. Lynn studied the vest that he was holding in front of her. "Flip this switch, then push the button. You will not feel anything." The man said. Lynn looked the vest up and down. Her stare reverted back to her daughter. Qudamah nodded to the man who returned the vest to its original location. Qudamah next told Lynn exactly what he wanted her to do.

"Can you do this?" He asked when he was finished. She didn't reply immediately, she simply stared at her daughter, then glanced back at the television screen one more time before answering.

"Yes, I can do that." She said.

"You have courage beyond most women." Qudamah complimented. "Do you know the church on 5th avenue?"

"Yes." She said.

"When this is done. I will drop your daughter off at that church. They will keep her safe, and she will know what her mother did for her. She will remember her mother with love and gratitude." Qudamah said softly.

"Thank you." Lynn replied, broken.

"Would you like to leave a message for your parents and daughter? There are rules, but I think that they should know how courageous you are, and how much you love them." Qudamah asked.

"Yes," Lynn said softly, accepting her fate, "please."

"Aziz, bring the camera." Qudamah ordered before turning back to Lynn. "I admire you." He comforted.

Jesse Owens watched the tow truck lift the suspect's car up off the ground with a roar, gravel falling out of the treads in the vehicle's tires. They were about done at the construction site and they were waiting for Sergeant Jackson to finish up the arrest paperwork he would be sending back with the two narcotics detectives that were taking the suspect to lock up.

Dave Jackson emerged from the trailer, paperwork in hand and made his way down to the unmarked police car that the detectives were standing next to. He handed the papers to one of the detectives, giving orders to take the suspect to lockup and then to notify dispatch that they were free so that they could receive their new assignment. He informed them of the increase in terror level and suggested they get some lunch because it was unclear when they would get the chance again. He started walking over to Owens, and his cell phone began to ring.

"Jackson," he said into the phone.

"It's me." Knox told him, then started giving him instructions. Jackson took his notebook out. While sitting the notebook on the trunk he began to scribble down notes. "Any questions?" Knox asked after she finished.

"No, but it's going to take a while, we're across town." Jackson informed. Owens approached.

"That's ok, he has two bodyguards. It should be ok until you get there." Knox told him. "Look, keep a sharp eye though, a patrol officer spotted a guy who dumped a fully automatic weapon in a dumpster at the mall downtown, it might have been another attack gone bad."

"Do you know who he was?" Jackson asked.

"Not yet, it just came in, the officer chased the guy but lost him, we think we have his car though. I'll let you know what develops." She said.

"Alright." Jackson said, ending the call.

"What's that all about?" Owens asked in his classic southern accent.

"We got our assignment." Jackson said, handing his partner his notebook.

"Regal Arms huh? Cherry pickens, I thought they were gonna give us something good."

"What the hell does cherry pickens mean?" Jackson asked.

"You wouldn't understand. It's a southern thing."

"Right, just drive rebel boy." Jackson said to his partner, who smiled at the remark.

Jason Brewer's home phone rang four times before his family's answering machine turned on giving the usual message that the family recorded together. The machine beeped and a scared, crying voice began speaking quickly, leaving one final message to whoever would eventually hear it.

"I couldn't do it." The sobbing voice said. "I couldn't do it, and now they're dead, I'm so sorry, I couldn't do it. I wasn't strong enough and I've killed them. Please don't think badly of me, I just couldn't do it. I'm so very sorry. I loved them so much, I couldn't do it. Tell Mom and Dad that I love them, and that I loved Shelly and Matt with all my heart but I couldn't do it. I'm so..." The recording ended abruptly because the answering machine reached its time limit, beeped and cut off.

After pushing its way through midday traffic, the taxicab pulled up in front of Bellevue Square, which was next to the Regal Arms Hotel. Rent leaned forward to look at the meter then exited the cab, taking the fare out of his wallet after he closed the door. He handed the money to the cab driver and told him to keep the change. The driver thanked him, and then started writing down the transaction in his log. Rent looked up and down the busy street before starting towards the hotel. When he was out of earshot, the cab driver opened his cellular phone, dialed a number and began to speak.

"He's here." Kicham Bradley said to Qudamah. "He didn't say anything during the trip, I believe he will not be a problem."

"Good," Qudamah told him, "I will inform Nasir." Qudamah ended the call and stepped over to one of the laptop computers. "Is it up?" Qudamah asked.

"Yes." The man working the computer replied before hitting a button. "Nasir? Can you hear me?"

"I hear you brother." The twenty-something with short hair and a mustache whispered into the bluetooth headset connected to his ear.

"Thank you Nasir, Rent will be there soon." The man turned to look at Qudamah. "The streaming is working perfectly. The radio message cannot be intercepted, and no one will think to look for a cell transmission on a wireless internet signal. We are ready." Qudamah nodded his head and the man turned back to look at his computer.

"He just came in." Nasir said a few minutes later.

"Good, watch him from a distance." Qudamah ordered, he wanted to let Rent sweat for a few minutes before he called, the excess wait making Rent more malleable to commands. Rent stood for a minute just inside the lobby doors waiting for his next order, when it didn't come immediately he took out the cell to make sure he was still getting a signal, he was. He scanned the room slowly, looking for anything out of place but seeing nothing. He decided he couldn't stand there all day so he began walking through the lobby, the sign for the hotel lounge catching his eye. He judged that a drink might ease his nerves and stepped the way that the sign suggested. After strolling down a short hallway he reached the entrance to the lounge.

"Tequila. Shots." He said, sitting down at the bar. The lounge was almost empty for an afternoon, most who still lingered were finishing their lunches. "You'd better make that a double." The bartender poured his drink. He swallowed his alcohol whole, without a chaser and ordered up another.

"That's pretty heavy for this early in the day pal." The bartender commented, pouring another shot and watching Rent down it.

"That's a matter of opinion." Rent tapped the glass on the counter.

"You having a bad day or something?" The bartender poured another.

"Not yet." Rent said looking into the man's eyes. "But I'm gonna." He downed the shot again, putting the glass on the bar and letting out a gasp of air as the hot alcohol warmed his throat. The bartender picked up the bottle to refill but Rent lifted his hand when he heard the phone ring. "Yeah." Rent said into the phone. He took a bill out of his wallet and laid it on the bar.

"You shouldn't drink Carey, it's against Allah's word." Qudamah said to him almost lightheartedly, but really telling him that he was being watched.

"Yeah." Rent replied, looking around.

"Leave the bar so we can talk." Qudamah ordered. Rent told

the bartender to keep the change, then stepped outside the entranceway to the lounge and into the hallway.

"Okay, talk." Rent said into the phone.

"You are doing very good Carey. I will make you a deal. I offer you four lives in exchange for one. Do you think that is fair?"

"Who is he?" Rent asked.

"That is of no concern to you, what is of concern to you is that if you don't kill him, I will send four heads to you, so that you can entertain the notion that you could have saved them for the rest of your life. Make no mistake Carey, if you do not kill this man, I have someone else that will, and Liz Austin and her children will die for nothing. Do you understand?"

"Yeah, I got it." Rent capitulated.

"Good, your target is in room 1404, he has security, two in fact."

"What about them?"

"I don't care what you do with them, you can kill them or not. Kill the man in the room and the Austin's will live. This is simple Carey, one life for four."

"Alright. What happens when it's done?" Rent asked.

"Once you are done, escape, and when I have confirmation that this man is dead, I will call you and tell you where to find the Austins, agreed?"

"Let me speak to Liz." Rent told him. Qudamah agreed, and

stepped outside the door into the hallway, putting the phone to Liz's ear.

"Liz?" Rent said after he heard her sniffle.

"Carey? Carey please help us." Liz managed to stammer out.

"I will Liz, I'm going to get you out, I swear." Rent told her, realizing how real this situation was. Ever since he had gotten the first call he'd been operating on auto-pilot and now it was hitting him how dangerous a situation he was in. "Liz, you will get out of this." He reassured her.

"Please help us." Was all she could say over and over. Qudamah took the phone from her ear and put it to his own.

"Are you satisfied?" He asked.

"Yeah, I'll do it."

"Good, I will call you when I have confirmation, the sooner it is done, the sooner this will be over for this family."

"Why?" Rent said but Qudamah had already hung up. He looked at the phone and put it back into his pocket. "Why me?" He asked himself. "Why them?" Rent didn't have the answers he was looking for, but he knew that if he was going to keep Liz alive, he had to act. He walked over to the elevator and pushed the button, all the while planning things out in his head. When the door opened he stepped in and pushed the button for the fourteenth floor. Two more people got in behind him one pushing a button for the tenth floor and another pushing the button for the eighth. After letting the two other passengers off at their respective floors, the elevator finally arrived at the fourteenth floor. When the doors opened, Rent saw that he was in a very short corridor, about ten feet in front of him was the main hallway with the rooms.

He stepped out of the elevator and reached for the pistol on his belt, but decided against it. He started walking differently, making his feet heavier than they were before, staggering as though he couldn't keep his balance, and changing the expression on his face every few seconds. When he reached the corner of the small corridor that housed the elevator, he leaned against the wall, using the moment to scan both directions of the hallway. He immediately saw a large man standing outside a door to his right. The man was tall and stood straight up, he had on khakis and a blue pullover shirt that hugged his large muscular chest and thick arms. Rent turned and waddled down the left side of the hallway away from the man. He curiously looked at the numbers on every door, even though he already knew which room was 1404. When he reached the end of the hallway he turned around clumsily, and started down the other direction, mumbling to himself the entire way. The man standing outside the door watched Rent with nothing more than idle curiosity until Rent got closer to him.

"Can I help you sir?" The man asked. Rent turned to the man and closed the gap with his exaggerated walk.

"I can't seem to find my damn room." Rent said, lightening his voice slightly and tilting his head, but being careful not to appear to over act while he let his breath ease over to the man's nostrils.

"Well it's not on this floor." The man told him.

"Oh, ok, thanks buddy." Rent nodded, gazing past the man at the number on the door behind him. "Wait." Rent nodded and smiled. "That's it." He said pointing to the room.

"No it's not. What room are you looking for?" The man said sternly.

"Mine." Rent replied sarcastically.

"What number?"

"Oh, um," Rent said feigning trying to remember. "Um," Rent stalled for time. "Oh, yeah, 1204, that's it." He said pointing.

"That's 1404." The man informed, becoming slightly annoyed.

"Nope, buddy can't you read, that's 1204." Rent said loudly. "I'm going in." Rent said, trying to push past the bodyguard who wouldn't bulge.

"Sir, you're not going in there." The bodyguard said loudly. "Now you need to leave sir. Go back to your room!"

"No sir, we think it's best if you stay here for now." The second bodyguard inside the room said to his employer.

"I have a schedule to keep, I don't care how many attacks there have been, I will not be terrorized." The employer said to his bodyguard.

"Sir, I understand, but you can call the television studio and they can talk to you over the phone, we've already discussed it with them."

"No," the man said earnestly, "the public needs to see my face, it reassures them."

"I understand sir, I'll get your car, but I want you to know that this is over my objec..." The second bodyguard stopped when he heard the voices in the hallway. "Excuse me sir, I'll be right back." He said. He left the bedroom of the suite, crossed the living room to the door and stepped outside, closing the door behind him. "What's going on out here?"

"He says this is his room." The first bodyguard answered in annoyance.

"Hey, what the hell were you doing in my room?" Rent said, purposely slurring his speech. "I wanna know what you're doing in there!"

"Sir, you need to leave sir, if you don't we'll be forced to call the authorities!" The second bodyguard said, pointing his finger in Rent's face.

"I just wanna get in my room." Rent reiterated, not showing hostility.

"Get him out of here." The second bodyguard ordered. Pleased with his instructions the first bodyguard grabbed Rent's shoulder.

"Ok, let's go." The first bodyguard said, his grip mutating Rent into sobriety. Rent quickly jabbed two fingers into the first bodyguard's neck, just below his throat, slamming the man back against the wall next to the door, and forcing him to release his grip to cover his throat. The second bodyguard lunged at Rent who quickly sidestepped and smacked him in the face with the instep of his hand, following it up with a punch to the man's jaw. The second bodyguard shook off Rent's punch and grabbed him, tossing him like a rag doll against the wall and enveloping him in a bear hug. Rent used his legs to push off from the wall and when the second bodyguard turned him toward his partner, Rent reached his leg up and performed a crescent kick to the first bodyguard's face.

Before the first bodyguard could recoup, Rent grabbed the second bodyguard's bottom two fingers and yanked then unnaturally away from the others, breaking them at the knuckles. Rent twisted out of the arms and landed a devastating elbow to his face. Rent next used the bottom of his fist to attack his groin and immediately followed up by crashing the back of the same fist into his nose, breaking it. Switching hands, he jabbed the area between his thumb and index finger into the second bodyguard's throat while simultaneously sweeping his legs out from under him with the back of his calf. The second bodyguard hit the floor with the sound of thunder just before Rent grabbed his hair and smashed his head into the floor to make sure he was unconscious.

Rent jumped for the first bodyguard who was also moving towards him. The bodyguard threw a wide punch which Rent blocked with his left forearm and sent his right elbow in an upward direction into the man's face while using his left arm to lock the bodyguard's punching arm. Once the arm was locked, Rent slammed his free hand into the bodyguard's throat flinging him against the wall where Rent slammed his elbow into the man's face several times, each time sending the man's head rocketing against the wall. The moment he fell limp, Rent lowered him to the floor and started searching both bodyguards for the card key that would unlock the door to the suite.

"Wow, you know I've never been in here before." Owens said, his southern accent noticeably sticking out. "This is nice." He said with a grin just before is phone beeped. "Oh look, I have messages."

"Come on," Jackson said. "We have work to do." He said with seriousness.

"Hold on, there's nothing going on here." Owens pressed the

button on his phone to retrieve his message. "Besides, I might not get reception in there."

"How would you know that if you've never been in here?" Jackson asked, falling for the trick.

"You never get it in these places." Owens responded while reading his text message. "That girl's a freak." He said with a laugh.

"Now!" Jackson pointed downward. Owens looked at him, nodded and started walking. "You and your damn hoes." Jackson commented on their way to the elevator.

"You're just mad cause your wife don't never get you strawberries and a bag of ice." Owens told him.

"A bag of ice?" Jackson stopped and looked at his partner.

"Well you only need a few pieces, but I use the whole bag." Owens joked. They reached the small group of people waiting for the elevator.

"With the women you date you probably have to. They are a little thick." Jackson returned quietly, waiting.

"What can I say, I know a good girl when I see one." The elevator doors opened.

"Is it that one you were seeing?" Jackson asked. The crowd of half a dozen or so entered the elevator and the one closest to the door started pushing the numbers.

"Floor fourteen." Owens told him when asked. "No," he

turned back to Jackson and whispered, "she dumped me, weird too, since we weren't dating."

"She dumped you?" Jackson whispered back in surprise, careful not to disturb any of the others in the elevator. "The short fat brunette that works dispatch?"

"Yep, that's the one."

"The one who walks like a duck?" Jackson asked again.

"Well she does have kind of a wobble, but I wouldn't..." Owens replied.

"She dumped you?" Jackson asked.

"Yep, but we weren't even dating, we were hanging out a bit. Just friends, didn't even tell me why, just stopped talking to me." Owens emphasized. Jackson scoffed at the remark. "What?" Owens asked.

"You're the only guy I know that can get dumped by somebody he's not even dating." Jackson laughed.

The card key opened the door and Rent pushed his pistol out in front of him with both hands. He slowly entered the room with bent knees so that he would have a better shooting platform as he walked, this method of walking also caused the weapon to stabilize in his hands instead of moving up and down with each step. He slowly turned the corner to the living room by "cutting the pie" a technique in which he limited the exposure of his body while he rounded the corner. Since he was cutting to his left he leaned his body to the right and slowly covered each inch of ground theoretically only exposing his pistol and his right eye. When he had rounded the corner enough to see the door to the bedroom he saw a bewildered Senator Bob Cale standing in the doorway. Rent immediately righted himself. He recognized the government official having just seen him on the television that very morning.

"Who are you? What do you want?" The Senator asked with authority. Rent approached his prey quickly, scanning around the room with his weapon to see if anyone else was present, before training the weapon back on the Senator.

"Hands up!" Rent ordered. "Get out here!" The Senator slowly moved towards Rent raising his hands.

"Who are you?" The Senator demanded. Rent quickly checked the bedroom from the doorway, then turned back to the Senator.

"Put your hands on your head, interlock your fingers." Rent ordered in an equally authoritative voice.

"The United States does not negotiate with terrorists." The Senator proclaimed as he complied with Rent's order.

"Turn around." Rent said before patting him down for weapons. "Get on your knees." The Senator again complied.

"Whatever it is you hope to accomplish, you won't." The Senator said. The realization that he was about to die hit him. The Senator looked straight ahead, almost resigned to his fate, he had always known that this could happen, but could not prepare mentally for it.

"Cross your ankles." Rent ordered, positioning himself behind the Senator and putting his pistol to the back of the old man's head.

"God, forgive me my sins." Cale said in prayer just before he heard Rent cock his pistol.

"I'm sorry about this Senator." Rent told him.

Chapter 4:

Rent ordered his finger to close on the trigger of his weapon. To Rent's astonishment, his trigger finger did not obey the command. Cale, not knowing why he was not yet dead, closed his eyes and waited for the inevitable. Rent extended his arm fully, locking his elbow and looking away and again ordering his finger to pull the trigger. Again, nothing happened. Rent couldn't get the thought out of his mind that something was wrong with this entire scenario. He pulled his gun hand back a few inches before trying again. He simply couldn't do it. Some unknown thought seemed to be stopping him. After his third attempt he realized that there was no way that he was going to let himself kill this man, and yanked the old politician onto his feet, spinning the senator around to face him. Rent punched the weapon an inch from the Senator's face, he tried one last time to overcome his restraint. When he couldn't, he took a step back and removed the weapon from the Senator's face. Senator Cale stood staring at the man in front of him in awe, he couldn't believe that he was still alive, perhaps he wouldn't die today after all.

Rent began cursing loudly and started pacing while running his free hand through his hair. A moment later, Rent had calmed slightly and began to think out what his subconscious was telling him. "Why me?" He asked himself, "why her?" Rent had almost become oblivious that Cale was even in the room at this point, nevertheless out of habit he kept glancing back at the bewildered Senator to see if he was moving. "How could he know?" Rent said, trying to work out what was happening.

"Know what?" Cale asked, hoping that he could perhaps talk Rent down.

"Why them?" Rent said, ignoring the old man's comment.

"Why who?" Cale asked beginning to think that Rent wasn't a terrorist at all, but a crazy lone gunman.

"What?" Rent finally acknowledged Cale.

"Who are you talking about?" Cale asked, seeing some hope in the situation.

"Shut up Bob." Rent ordered, now at an even voice. "He said I have to escape, why would he do that?" Rent thought a moment longer. "Unless he has something else for me to do." Rent paused again, "but what, and why?"

"I won't be some sort of bargaining chip!" The Senator demanded.

"That's it, that's gotta be it, he's got to have a plan." Rent said, the Senator's latest question producing an idea in his mind.

"He's gone to too much trouble." With that thought Rent also realized that he was also in a great deal of trouble, and that he had to formulate his own plan and move fast.

"Whatever your problem is, we can talk about it." The Senator said in an erroneously calming voice just before Rent pounced on him. Rent grabbed the Senator and violently threw him onto the sofa of the room, then jumped on top of him, grabbing him by the chin and putting his gun to his left temple.

"Listen buddy, I'm not crazy so quit trying to talk to me like I am! I got a problem and I need you. Somebody has kidnaped a family, a mother and her three children. They told me they're gonna kill them unless I assassinate you. That's why I'm here, but if I do that, I think they're gonna kill them anyway, so you're gonna help me get them back." Rent spat the words into the Senator's face with anger.

"The only thing you can do for them is turn yourself in. If you're telling the truth then the police will help you." The Senator informed Rent.

"No, I can't do that. If they know you're safe, they'll kill them for sure." Rent returned in a logical tone. "You need to understand something." Rent's tone turned angry again. "I don't care about your politics. I don't care about the cops. I don't care about right and wrong. The only thing I care about is getting that family back alive, that's all that matters in the world today, and you're gonna help me do it!" Rent proclaimed. "Congratulations Senator, you just became a good person!" Rent looked around the room. "We gotta get out of here." He said, taking his knee off the old man's stomach and helping him off the couch. "Take off your tie." Rent ordered, Cale stood staring at Rent for a moment but complied. Rent looked around the room, grabbed Cale's suit jacket and threw it to him. "Put this on." He ordered and the Senator obeyed.

"What do you hope to accomplish with this?" Cale asked.

"I don't know yet." Rent hastily replied. Then realizing that he was moving from one difficult situation to another, he approached Cale, lifted his gun next to the Senator's head but didn't point it at him. "Let's get something straight Bob." Rent said with a seriousness no man should ever have. "Through circumstances beyond my control I have become the only person who has a snowball's chance in hell of helping these people. To do that I need you. You need to understand that the only reason you're alive is because I am not one hundred percent certain that this guy will release them.

"We are going out in public now Bob and if you make a move; if you alert anybody to either who you are, or what is happening then I'm going to get cornered very quickly. Keep in mind that if the cops get you, then game over, Liz and the kids are dead. So if we get cornered, I will have no choice but to kill you and take my chances with this guy's word." Rent stopped and got very close to Cale's face. "Trust me Bob, you don't want me to get cornered." Cale swallowed and nodded.

"Of all the inconsiderate rudeness." Owens said the moment the elevator doors closed and the lift started moving again. "Can you believe that?" He asked his partner.

"You didn't say anything." Jackson returned dryly.

"I was being polite, and besides, isn't it your job to do that?" Owens prodded.

"Didn't matter to me." Jackson said purposefully stirring his partner some more.

"She stood there in the doorway talking to that guy for ten minutes and it didn't matter to you?"

"I agree it was rude, but that's how people are and it was more like five minutes." Jackson told him. "Besides if it bothered you so much why didn't you say something?"

"What was I supposed to say? Hey manner-less moron, get out of the elevator doors so the rest of us can get on with life?" Owens responded.

"Well I would hope you would have more tact than that." Jackson told him. "'Excuse me, we need to go now.' That might work."

"You know, this is what I hate about living up here, nobody cares about the other guy. You northwesterners are just plain rude."

"And you chose to move up here and show us the error of our ways. I'll be grateful in a minute." Jackson said dryly.

"I'm just saying that we don't act like that to each other, where I come from. We got respect for our neighbors." Owens said, the elevator doors opened to the fourteenth floor.

"That's because you're all related." Jackson stepped out into the short corridor.

"It's because we know how to be considerate of others." Owens followed his superior. "Besides which, we aint all related, just some of..." Owens stopped when he saw Jackson who was a step ahead of him draw his weapon. Owens did exactly the same thing and looked down the hallway to see two men unconscious on the floor. The two cops quickly approached the downed men and the door they were next to. Both cops trained their weapons on the door to the room which was closed, while Owens checked the pulses of each of the bloodied bodyguards with his free hand. "They're alive." He whispered and took up position on the opposite side of the door as his partner.

Jackson nodded to Owens who quickly spun in front of the door and kicked it open, the door slamming against the inside of the wall before they entered the room, their weapons at the ready. Each man scanned his section of the room, Jackson buttonhooked to his right and Owens moved to the center, training his weapon on the door to the bedroom, which was open. Jackson checked behind the bar. When his side of the room was clear he trained his weapon on the door to the bedroom also. Jackson approached the door from an angle and Owens entered it, moving through the doorway. Owens quickly checked the closet and then the bathroom before yelling "clear" to inform his partner that the suite was empty. Jackson holstered his weapon and raised his hand for the radio which Owens tossed to him and they both moved into the living room.

"Dispatch, N.S.1, we need backup at the Regal Arms Hotel in Bellevue. We have two private security down and Senator Cale has been kidnaped, suspect unknown at this time. Say again: need backup, Regal Arms Hotel in Bellevue, need ambulance, two security down, Senator Cale is missing!" He bellowed into the radio before tossing it back to his partner who began answering the dispatcher's questions. Jackson picked up the room's telephone and dialed 0 for the hotel operator. "Give me security," he said when the operator began her greeting, she connected him to the security office and soon a man began to speak but Jackson interrupted him. "Sergeant Dave Jackson Seattle PD, Senator Cale in room 1404 has been kidnaped, lock down the hotel, every exit, do it now!" Jackson hung up the phone and turned to look at his partner.

"Doesn't look like much of a struggle, there's a tie on the

floor over there, those guys in the hall are still out so this was recent." Owens told him. "Elevator?" They stepped into the hallway.

"Would you get caught in that box?" Jackson returned.

"Two sets of stairs, each at opposite ends of the hall." Owens pointed.

"You take left, I'll take right, we'll flush him out, get me on my cell." Jackson ordered.

"Yeah, let's go with this." Bethany Knox said to an officer, handing him back a piece of paper. "What about the others?"

"We're still calling, sometimes they go fishing or hiking and you know how the reception is out there." The officer told her.

"Well we need to get every officer in here, keep trying." She ordered.

"One more thing ma'am." The officer informed.

"What is it?"

"Lieutenant Austin hasn't reported in yet, he was supposed to be here at nine. He's taking over the personal crimes unit." The officer told her.

"That's odd, do we have a patrol that can swing by his house?" She asked.

"Doubtful, it's like Mardi Gras out there, between the regular stuff and the Fremont Festival downtown, we're swamped."

"It's not like him, and I hate to let this go." Knox told the officer. "Ok, when you get a free patrol, see if you can't get them to..." She saw an officer run into the hallway in front of her.

"Sergeant Jackson just called in, he's reporting that Senator Cale has been kidnaped!" The officer yelled to the Assistant Chief, who dropped the paper she was holding and started moving with the officer to the dispatch center.

"Get every car you can over there!" She ordered the officer that was leading her, then she pointed at the officers she was passing and started giving orders. "Get Terry Bannister from the FBI down here now! And inform the Chief! Call up forensics and get them started down there, go now!"

"Nasir? What is happening?" Qudamah asked anxiously to his man stationed in the lobby of the hotel. Nasir didn't look up from his newspaper or make any indication that he was receiving a message through his earpiece.

"I don't know, nothing is happening here." Nasir whispered.

"The police radio is saying that the Senator has been kidnaped." Qudamah told him.

"I don't know, I haven't seen anyone yet." Nasir informed.

"Keep looking." Qudamah ordered.

"Rent has failed." Aziz said, standing next to Qudamah.

"We don't know that yet." Qudamah insisted.

"He was a poor choice." Aziz argued, causing Qudamah to turn to face him.

"You do not decide that. I am in command here and you will not challenge me." Qudamah reprimanded. "Rent will complete his task."

Owens slammed the stairway door open while training his Smith and Wesson .45 caliber automatic down the turning staircase. The stairwell was brightly lit, the light shining off the white bricked walls. Since the fourteenth floor was the top floor of the hotel, another staircase intermingled with the main staircase, this new staircase led to the roof. Since Owens knew his suspect would want to go down instead of up, and because there was no entrance to it on the fourteenth floor, the young detective decided not to cover it.

Owens moved rapidly down the stairs, training his weapon on each new threat area. When he passed the thirteenth floor door, he didn't see Rent laying face down on the adjacent staircase with Senator Cale next to him. Rent's gun to the back of the Senator's head. The two did not move, instead they listened and saw only glimpses of the young officer moving down the stairs. Rent was easing the pressure of his pistol against the back of the Senator's head the further Owens got down the staircase.

"Christ that was quick." Rent whispered more to himself than to the Senator.

"What did you expect?" Cale asked, proud that the police were moving so fast.

"I was hoping to have more time." Rent said, waiting a minute before continuing. "Ok, let's go."

When Owen's reached the bottom of the staircase, he holstered his weapon and opened the door to the lobby. He found himself in a back area of the lobby floor of the massive hotel with conference rooms and banquet halls surrounding him. Owens hit a speed-dial button on his phone.

"Jackson." The voice on the other end responded.

"I'm clear." Owens told his boss.

"I got nothing too, meet me by the front door." Jackson ordered before the line went dead. Owens moved quickly through the corridors to the main lobby where Jackson was talking to two patrolmen who just arrived.

"We got a problem." Jackson told his partner. "On the East side of the hotel, there's an entrance to Bellevue Square Mall."

"Damn." Owens said under his breath.

"Yeah," Jackson agreed and pointed to one of the other officers. "Take the entrance to the mall." He pointed to the another officer. "Take the front door, any backup that arrives send the first to secure the room on the fourteenth floor and send the rest to cover other exits." He pointed to Owens. "Get to the security office. I need eyes on the cameras. Get their guys to cover any exits we don't have manned and call mall security and get them to do the same."

"I'm on it." Owens started to walk away. A thought suddenly occurred to Owens. "Hey, that guy at the mall downtown, is it possible he came here, is that our suspect?"

"I don't know yet, downtown's a good distance from here, I don't know if he'd have time. I'm going to get the manager and map this place, give me your radio and get the other one out of the car."

"Got it." Owens said before stepping outside toward his car.

"What's happening?" Bannister asked, walking up to the dispatch desk.

"We're trying to cordon off the building but it's connected to a mall. We have every patrol in that sector responding but with traffic it'll take a few minutes." Knox reported.

"You two get down there." Bannister told the two FBI agents that had come downstairs with him. "Do we have a suspect yet?"

"No, but we think it may be related to the man who tried to shoot up a mall downtown earlier. We have the suspect's car, his name is Jason Brewer. We've sent units to his house, they should report back in the next few minutes." Knox told him.

"What about the Senator?" Bannister asked.

"We don't know, my guys arrived at the hotel and found his two bodyguards on the ground, they're still alive but we don't know about their condition. The Senator wasn't in his room and we don't know where he is or what his condition is."

"Is there anything we do know?" Bannister quizzed in frustration. "Somebody hasn't tossed him out a window yet? We know that right?"

"Cops are arriving, one is stationed at the front door." Nasir whispered from the hotel lobby.

"How many?" Qudamah asked.

"At least four, wait, I see another one pulling up, now it's five." Nasir told him.

"Rent is changing the plan." Aziz commented.

"Why would he do that, he knows we'd kill the children." Qudamah countered.

"The cops must not be allowed to get the Senator." Aziz reminded.

In the hotel manager's office, Jackson laid out a large map of the hotel and adjoining mall on the manager's desk. The three men in the room, Jackson, the hotel manager and the security supervisor looked at the map. Jackson took a black marker and immediately began circling all the exits to the buildings.

"There are twenty-three exits between the hotel and the mall. We need all of them covered." Jackson ordered.

"I have three door officers already stationed here, here and here." The security supervisor said, marking the exits with a red marker. "I have one roving patrol that I can put here." He said, making another mark. "The mall has six roving officer's, they can put them at the four main entrances and the two secondary entrances."

"That leaves thirteen ways out, assuming that the Senator is still in the building." Jackson commented. "Get this map to Detective Owens in the security office. Tell him to place our guys accordingly." He ordered the security supervisor who immediately took the map and left the room.

"Do you think they're still here?" The manager asked Jackson. Jackson didn't respond because his cell phone rang, he put his finger up to signify that he'd be a second and walked out, answering it.

"It's Knox, what's happening?" The voice on the other side of the line asked.

"I'm sticking my fingers in the dam, where's the backup?"

"They'll be there in five minutes." Knox told him.

"In five minutes they'll be gone, if they aren't already." Jackson told her. "Could this be the shooter from the mall downtown?" He asked.

"We don't know, hold on." Knox said, an officer approaching her.

"Ma'am, we're at the house, there was a definite sign of a struggle there, but this guy and his family are gone. There was a message left on his answering machine." The officer told her reading from his notes. "It's a male voice, crying, saying something to the effect of he's sorry he couldn't do it, whatever that means."

"Call the phone company, I wanna know where that call came from." Knox ordered.

"I already did." The officer handed the Assistant Chief a piece of paper. Knox read it with Bannister looking over her shoulder.

"What does that mean?" Bannister asked, confused.

"Dave?" Knox said into her cell phone. "You won't believe this."

Rent emerged in the same spot Owens had earlier. He looked around before moving out of the doorway and pulled the Senator out with him, holding the gun to the government official's side to conceal it. They had just began down the corridor when they heard a voice coming straight for them. Rent checked the door to the banquet hall next to him, it was locked, so he moved backwards a few feet and across the hall to a door that led to a large conference room, this door was unlocked. He and the Senator stepped inside. Leaving the door open just a crack, he placed the Senator behind it, and put his gun back beside the man's head. Rent watched David Jackson rounded the corner, speaking into his cell phone.

"Ok, then we've got a new mystery man. I'll lock this place down, but there's a good chance the Senator's already gone." He said to Knox before closing his phone and then reopening it and pressing a number on his speed dial. "Jesse, send all the incoming officers to cover the hotel entrances first, then the mall, and don't forget the parking garage." Rent listened to Jackson who paused, probably listening to the person he was talking to. "Yeah, that's fine, tell them we need to set up a five block radius, but only after we get enough officers to cover the hotel and the mall. Oh, one more thing, we have units at the house of that guy who almost shot up the mall downtown, his name is Jason Brewer and we think he left a message on his answering machine." Jackson paused again. "No, they tracked the call to a pay phone at the corner of Harvard Avenue and Denny Way." Jackson paused one more time. "Yeah, nobody can get from Pill Hill to here that fast so he isn't our guy, keep an eye out." Jackson hung up his phone and started back towards the manager's office.

Jackson rounded the corner and Rent opened the door, taking another look to see if the coast was clear. He and Cale moved out into the hallway with caution. They slid to the end of the corridor where Rent gazed at a fire exit map for a few seconds.

"You can't escape, they've got every exit covered by now." The Senator told his captor.

"That would be very bad for you Bob." Rent said, forming a plan from the map. "Let's go, and remember, you don't want me to get cornered." They reentered the conference room and headed to a door in the back of the room.

"If the cops get the Senator, then we have failed." Aziz told Qudamah, who had just listened to Nasir report the arrival of more police.

"You are right my friend, we must not allow that." Qudamah admitted. "Nasir?"

"Yes." Nasir whispered.

"The police must not get the Senator alive, it is important that Rent have the opportunity to kill him. You know what to do."

"Yes." Nasir whispered.

"Allah be with you." Qudamah blessed him.

"I need all the elevator video for the past half hour." Owens ordered in the camera room, the camera operator hit a few buttons on his computer and put the cameras on the three monitors in front of Owens. "Thanks" Owens pressed a button and started winding back the digital files.

"What's that?" The camera operator looked at his monitor which was looking at a back hallway in the bowels of the first floor. He saw two men moving away from the camera, one a tall stocky man in a short sleeved button up shirt and another in a suit jacket, the latter man, appearing older and losing his hair slightly. "Hey, Detective!" The camera operator shouted when he realized what he was looking at. Owens turned around and his stare immediately fixed on the large monitor.

"Where is that?" Owens demanded.

"It's the back hallway, they're heading for the kitchen." The camera operator informed.

"We don't have anybody there yet!" Owens pulled his radio off his belt. "Suspect and hostage spotted on the first floor, heading to the kitchen!" Owens yelled into his radio. He grabbed a security radio and slipped it on his belt. "Keep me informed on this!" He directed the camera operator before he dashed out.

Jackson heard the radio call and shot out of the manager's office like a bullet. Sprinting through the hotel, he took his radio from his belt.

"All officers stay on your post, get me any arriving units to the back of the kitchen. Owens with me, and send the officer's covering the entrances of the mall to the kitchen!" Jackson ordered.

"We think we have them!" The dispatcher said to the Assistant Chief and the Assistant Director of the FBI standing right behind him. Both leaned over to listen to the radio and watch the dispatcher's computer.

"Something's happening, I'm going." Nasir said after he watched Jackson run through the lobby. He picked up the medium sized leather satchel sitting next to his chair and followed the policeman.

"Hey, you can't come in here!" A waiter in the kitchen said to Rent just before he was pistol whipped and sent to the floor. It was at that point that one of the female cooks in the kitchen screamed, catching the attention of everyone in the large room.

"Everybody out now!" Rent pointed his pistol at them. While Rent and Cale crossed between the many counters in the kitchen toward the back door that led out to the dumpsters, the kitchen staff exited the room from the two other entrances on the opposite side. Rent could almost smell the success of his escape now that he was so close to the outside. He was holding the Senator in a tight grasp by the top of his suit jacket. Certain he'd succeeded, Rent reached for the handle of the door.

"Police! Drop your weapon and put your hands in the air!" Jackson yelled, leveling his Smith and Wesson at his suspect. Rent didn't comply, instead he threw his arm around the Senator, spinning around in the process and putting his pistol to the Senator's head. As he spun around, Jackson saw his face and stopped his approach, more in astonishment than anything else. "Carey?" Jackson stuttered.

"Dave." Rent said, his eyes fixed firmly on the pistol threatening him. "This isn't what it looks like." Rent told him.

"Really," Jackson managed to regain his composure "It looks like you've got a gun to a United States Senator's head."

"Ok, it is what it looks like, but it's not what you think." Rent said, searching his mind for what to do next.

"Really," Jackson argued, "because I think you've got a gun to a United States Senator's head."

"Look Dave I can't explain right now, but trust me, I haven't lost it." Rent told him.

"That's a hard sell right now Carey." Jackson returned.

Nasir stood in the entranceway behind Jackson, hiding himself against the wall so that Rent couldn't see him. He took a fully loaded Mac-10 machine pistol with two additional extended clips from the satchel and readied his aim at Jackson.

"Yeah, I suppose so." Rent said, formulating a plan. "Seattle Police Department's policy on hostage situations specifically states that if the suspect is coherent and if there is a chance that a reasonable person would believe that the suspect can be talked down, then deadly force is to be used as a last resort only."

"I remember reading that, thanks." Jackson told him sarcastically.

"Yeah, well I don't wanna kill the Senator, I just need to borrow him for a while, and I am a huge Wayne Newton fan. So as soon as I get a contract promising that Mr. Las Vegas will come and sing for me in prison, I'll surrender without incident." Rent told the cop with a smirk.

"Carey, that truly is the most ridiculous thing I've ever heard!" Jackson responded in annoyance.

"Yeah, but it's coherent because I know I'm going to jail, it's rational because everybody loves Wayne Newton, and it presents a possible end to the this scenario without violence, and that means that you can't shoot me right now."

"Wanna bet?" Jackson returned. "That policy also states that deadly force may be used to prevent a suspect who has a hostage from escaping, and since I doubt you came in here to order room service..."

"Dave behind you!" Owens emerged from the other hallway and saw Nasir about to shoot. Gunfire suddenly erupted all over the kitchen.

Chapter 5:

Owens fired first, but his aim was hasty and in the excitement he yanked the trigger instead of squeezing it like he'd been taught. His rounds went left and high, hitting the wall next to Nasir. Nasir fired second, he attempted to spray Jackson but he changed his aim to Owens at the last second. He fired a barrage of bullets that sprayed the room, hitting no one. Rent didn't fire at all, when he heard Owens yell, he threw Senator Cale to the ground, then fell on top of him to protect him from any stray rounds or ricochets. Jackson fired, but late, he had instinctively turned toward Owens voice. Seeing his partner take aim and fire, Jackson dove to the kitchen floor, between two large ovens. Once on the ground he turned toward the automatic weapon and released three rounds, also hitting the wall next to Nasir.

Nasir wasn't put off by the two cops firing at him, he took cover for a second then turned and leveled his aim at the only target still visible, Owens, and fired four rounds consecutively. Owens saw Nasir move from behind the wall, and spun behind his own, just narrowly escaping Nasir's fire.

"Oh screw this." Owens said aloud and took off back down the corridor from which he came. Nasir fired several more rounds, changed magazines, then noticed a stream of daylight permeating through the windowless kitchen. A moment later it was gone. When the daylight dissipated, Nasir took aim at Jackson and unleashed a spray in his direction. Jackson was taking shelter between two counters now, and felt the contents of the counters explode in a frenzy of vegetables, fruit and olive oil. Jackson stayed close to the floor until the bullets stopped dousing him with their contents. He raised his weapon to Nasir and unloaded his magazine. Nasir took cover back behind his wall and waited until he heard Jackson's slide lock back before he finished off his own magazine.

Jackson dove back to the floor, making his silhouette the smallest possible and was doused with more culinary additives. He crawled between two freezers where he turned over, dropped the magazine from his weapon and reloaded a fresh one. Once that was done he fired several rounds in Nasir's direction, hitting the wall again because Nasir had taken cover to change magazines. Reloaded, Nasir reached his weapon around the wall and fired at Jackson without aiming.

"We have shots fired! Officers reporting shots fired at the hotel!" The dispatcher told Bethany Knox.

"What the hell is going on there?" Bannister asked.

"Where's the backup?" Knox asked, not really sure how to handle listening to her officers conduct a gun battle and knowing that there wasn't much she could immediately do.

"We have two cars that will be there in three minutes."

"Christ!" Bannister exclaimed. "They won't make it in time."

Owens sprinted through the maze of corridors that led to and from the hotel kitchen. He kept his weapon at the ready in front of him when he turned down the hallway that led to Nasir. He moved around the corner and found Nasir still firing at Jackson, unaware that Owens was behind him. He leveled his aim at Nasir, this time carefully holding the trigger and closing his left eye.

"Drop it!" Owens yelled. Nasir heard the order through his Mac-10 discharging and instantly turned to face Owens, his weapon turning with him. Owens fired one round and saw a plumb of blood and brains instantly hit the wall behind Nasir. He fell to the floor, lifeless. Owens kicked Nasir's weapon away from him. "Clear!" He yelled.

Jackson responded to Owens words by jumping to his feet, his weapon pointing to where Rent and Senator Cale went down. He moved so fast he slipped in the oily mix that was covering the floor.

Soon he was up and seeing his suspect and hostage were now gone, he flew out the door just in time to see that about fifty yards away in the street, Rent was yanking an elderly man out of a sedan. Jackson raised his weapon and moved toward them but Rent threw the Senator in and took off. Jackson ran at a sprint after them but by the time Jackson reached the old man, Rent had turned a corner and was gone. Jackson holstered his weapon and grabbed for his radio. He looked back and saw Owens running for him.

"Get the car!" Jackson yelled to his subordinate who turned around and started running back to the hotel. "One suspect is down, another suspect is at large and has left the hotel with hostage," Jackson said into his radio, "Suspect is in a light blue eighties model Chevrolet four door sedan heading North on Bellevue Way Northeast, looks like he's going for Eighth Street. Say again, suspect has escaped, heading North on Bellevue Way Northeast. Suspect is Carey Rent! Standby." Jackson looked at the old man, "What's your license plate number?" The old man simply shook his head and raised his shoulders. Jackson cursed out loud and turned back to his radio. "Dispatch we have unknown 27 on that."

"Roger that N.S.1. All units pursue." The dispatcher ordered with Bethany Knox standing over him.

"What did he say about the suspect?" She asked frantically.

"He said one suspect down ma'am." The officer working the dispatch computer told her.

"No the other one."

"He said it was Carey Rent, wasn't he..."

"Order Jackson to disengage pursuit!" Knox interrupted. Bannister did a double take.

"I copy you want to abort the pursuit?" The dispatcher asked, puzzled.

"No, I want Jackson to disengage *his* pursuit. Order patrol to maintain theirs."

"But ma'am Jackson's the only one who's seen the vehicle?"

"Order it now!" Knox said sternly. "Tell him to report back here for de-brief."

"Yes ma'am" The dispatcher gave the order to Jackson.

"What the hell are you doing?" Bannister asked, visibly angry.

"Jackson can't go after Rent." Knox informed.

"Who is Carey Rent?" Bannister asked sharply.

"What?" Jackson screamed into his radio. The patrol cars sped by him followed by Owens driving their unmarked car. "We can get him!"

"N.S.1 you are to return to Police Plaza immediately for de-brief." The voice on the other end of the radio reiterated. Owens stopped the car and Jackson got in.

"Negative dispatch we are in pursuit." Jackson argued with the device he was holding in his hand

"Sergeant Jackson!" Bethany Knox's voice came through. "Get back here right now!" She ordered with the voice she used with her children.

"On our way dispatch." Jackson said angrily into the radio. Jackson threw his radio on the floor of the car and punched the dashboard. One of the uniformed officer's approached his window. "She's gone too far!" Jackson yelled.

"When doesn't she?" The officer at Jackson's window commented. "What do you want us to do about this mess Sarge?"

"Yeah," Jackson said, regaining a little composure. "Look, get forensics in there, get that guy's prints and fax them to the office at the plaza, I need it run through AFIS ASAP, and get that old timer's license and find out what car we're looking for, coordinate that with the pursuit."

"Will, do." The officer affirmed.

"Where to?" Owens said looking at Jackson curiously.

"Police Plaza like she said. She stepped over the line this time." Jackson muttered.

Almost the moment he turned onto Bellevue Way, Rent turned off of it. He took a series of turns intended to get him the farthest away from the hotel while at the same time avoiding the cops. He turned down several alleys and into a residential area before he reached highway 520 where he got on and headed for downtown Seattle.

"That went well." The Senator said after several minutes to break the silence and reassess what was happening.

"We got out didn't we." Rent returned, concentrating on his driving.

"Who was shooting at us?"

"The bad guys I suspect."

"What happened to those cops back there?" The Senator kept quizzing.

"Beats the hell out of me, but I hope they're alright."

"That cop knew you?"

"Yes he did."

"What is going on?" The Senator demanded, now allowing his frustration to overflow.

"I told you, somebody kidnaped a cop's family and is trying to use me to kill you."

"Yeah that explains a lot thanks." Cale said, sarcasm in hand.

"Look Bob, I don't like this anymore than you do."

"Then stop the car and turn yourself in."

"That's not gonna happen." Rent returned casually

"Why not, why wouldn't they believe you?"

"Cause they don't exactly trust me, I'm kind of a felon."

"You're kind of a felon?" Cale stammered in surprise and confusion.

"Gives ya confidence don't it?" Rent answered with a smirk.

"Qudamah," Aziz said to his commander. "The police radio says that a man is dead and that Rent has escaped."

"Nasir has done Allah's will. We shall not mourn him, he is in paradise." Qudamah answered.

"Yes, but what about Rent, he has altered the plan. Shall I kill the family?" Aziz returned.

"No, we don't know what happened and Rent may still kill the Senator." Qudamah answered.

"What if he doesn't? Why didn't he do it before?" Aziz asked.

"He will." Qudamah said while dialing a number on his cell phone.

"You're full of it." Cale told Rent while they sped along the interstate.

"That's not nice Bob, you saw that guy shoot at us, did he look like an all-American to you?" Rent answered calmly just before his cell started ringing. "You want proof, listen up." He pressed the button to answer the phone.

"Rent you have condemned that fam..." Qudamah started but was interrupted by Rent.

"I have the Senator now, here talk to him." Rent gave the phone to the Senator who put it to his ear.

"Who is this?" The Senator asked.

"That is none of your concern, give me Rent!"

"What do you want?" Cale said recognizing that the accent was Middle Eastern.

"I want you to give the phone back to Rent before I kill a mother and three children!" Qudamah screamed, his anger boiling over. Cale handed the phone back to Rent who spoke with gusto.

"The Senator is now in my hands, I decide his fate! If you want me to kill him, you're going to have to release the Austins first."

"You have just sealed the deaths of an entire family!" Qudamah screamed at him.

"Nah, I don't think so cupcake. You see I don't know how you know about me and Liz but I'll tell you that wasn't on CNN.

You see you went to way too much trouble to set this whole thing up just to kill them that fast." Qudamah didn't respond to Rent because he knew that Rent had a point. Rent took his silence for agreement and continued. "Now how am I supposed to believe that if I kill the Senator you'll really let them go? I mean after all, it's gonna be kinda difficult for you to prove that you're trustworthy."

"You'll know when you receive their bodies!" Qudamah returned, flustered.

"In that case, Senator Cale here will become the safest person on earth and your pedestrian little plot won't have much teeth." Rent returned. "So here's the deal, even trade, one life for four. You give me the Austins and I'll cough up one Senator. Otherwise he stays safe and sound. You see, if you can't find him, you can't kill him, and both of us know that if I don't wanna be found, I won't be!" Rent allowed Qudamah to take a second to let the proposal sink in.

"You will ki..." Qudamah started but was once again interrupted by Rent.

"Tell you what porkchop, I'll give you an hour to think it over, call me back in sixty minutes." Rent hung up the cell. Cale sat in the passenger side of the vehicle staring at Rent, not knowing what to do or say. "Relax Bob, I've got no intention of handing you over." Rent said to comfort the old man.

"Then what's your plan?" Cale asked, skeptical.

"Well, maybe they'll agree to the trade, in which case I'll meet them, and then I'm going to kill them all."

"You can't be serious?"

"I'm kinda winging it here, but I'm sure I can work out the details." Rent told him.

First Hill was always very busy during the afternoon hours, the only time it was busier was in the late evening. First Hill was just east of Seattle's downtown area, and thus named because if one headed east from downtown it was the first hill that they came across. Historically, Seattle's first courthouse was placed atop the hill, however in the late eighteen hundreds most people had to walk to get to the courthouse, thus nicknaming it "profanity hill" for the curses that were made by Seattle's citizenry while they had to walk up the steep slope.

In later times, the hill became home to three of Seattle's massive medical centers, Harborview Medical Center, Swedish Medical Center, and Virginia Mason Medical Center. It got its new nickname of Pill Hill largely from a combination of the medical centers and the amount of "medicine" that could be found on the streets. Starting in the early nineteen sixties, as downtown Seattle grew outward, the wealthy that had stabled in First Hill began to move out, leaving mostly the unemployed to reside in the rundown area. Practically overnight First Hill became a playground for drugs and crime.

Surrounded by Seattle's downtown area, and the crime ridden areas of the Central District, the International District, and Capital Hill, First Hill became more or less junky central, attracting all kinds of underground elements. Since the Seattle Police Department's main objectives had largely been to battle crime in the surrounding districts, First Hill had been largely ignored by the police. Except of course for the immediate areas around the hospitals in the district, which were given very good attention. The police edict on the matter was that as long as the population could easily get to the medical centers, then the rest of First Hill wasn't very important. Because of the police coverage in the neighboring districts, many of the criminal element took sanctuary in the highly populated, yet heavily overlooked area. It had been described more than once as a place that the cops often drove through but never stopped. It was truly a place where someone could disappear.

That's one of the reasons that Jason Brewer fled there after his aborted attempt to shoot up one of the larger malls downtown. The other reason was that as a youth living in the International district, it was easier for him to go to Pill Hill to meet with his friends and spend his evenings than in his own neighborhood. Brewer had never exactly been a criminal, but he had been a wild youth. Brewer felt safe in Pill Hill, he knew the area and he believed that he knew the people. However, he had recently discovered that Pill Hill had changed drastically since he was a teenager. The people there were now much angrier than he remembered them, and they looked a lot meaner also. He didn't realize that the hill had been subject to an influx of nefarious types in the last few years because of the police's attempts to clean up the surrounding districts. It appalled him that drug deals that used to go on in dark alleyways were now being largely conducted in early afternoon on just about every street corner.

Having served in the Army, Brewer was not scared by the differences he saw in his old stomping ground, though he should have been. He also didn't notice that his dress was decidedly different than the residents of the neighborhood. When he walked down the sidewalk in one of the busier areas, people tended to notice his new shoes, his clean pants and his nice shirt, though Brewer was oblivious to this.

The people of Pill Hill at one time were of the wealthiest sort in Seattle, that had faded around the time that the downtown area expanded. With the crime setting in, the middle class left. The poor would soon go too, looking for better opportunities and government assistance. All that was left now was below poor. The mostly young and completely penniless had moved into the area. Teenage runaways, drug users, and youthful victim's of such crimes as molestation, rape, parental abuse whether it be physical, mental or sexual now bent on self-destruction were all that populated the inner sanctums of Pill Hill. Their clothes were uniformly ratty, jeans were of the dirtiest, and holy kind, shirts were mostly T's and most had not been washed in weeks, shoes were any kind that would cover the feet, in part or whole, it didn't matter. Hair was also very different, Brewer's short military style cut stood out like a sore thumb amongst the lice ridden, overgrown styles that flavored the area.

It could be said that one didn't have to be rich to be thought to have money in Pill Hill, even the poor were thought to have wealth there. In Pill Hill, if a single person was thought to have enough money to buy a fix, then that person was considered to have more wealth than most, and Brewer's decidedly middle class features made him the topic of everyone's jealous gaze whenever he walked down the avenue.

His demeanor didn't help. Typically, like most who had been schooled in the fine art of soldiering, Brewer usually held his head high, and strolled as though he were ready to take on Godzilla himself. However, Brewer had picked a bad mental state in which to go to one of the worst places in Seattle. Earlier in the day, he had witnessed his family kidnaped and been ordered to shoot up a crowded shopping mall in order to facilitate their release. His failure to complete this task served only as a factory of guilt for the young medically discharged soldier. Thus his thoughts were of his family, his wife and son, and how they were most likely dead now. He pondered his parents and in-laws and how grieved they were going to be when they found out. Some of his thoughts, though very few centered around himself, and what would happen to him. He couldn't very well show his face to his or his wife's parents, he didn't even think he could show it to himself because he was the man who willingly let the people he loved the most in the world be murdered. He had truly failed everyone, society, his wife, his son, even himself and the prospects for such a person were limited at best. His life, at least in his mind, was effectively over. Unfortunately for Brewer, his demeanor now reflected that.

Jackson burst through the doors with enough anger to topple a government. Owens was right behind him, though not as angry, he was more distraught, having shot a man dead less than a half hour before. They had parked in the large parking garage behind Police Plaza and had entered through the double glass doors that led into the back hallways that held offices. Jackson moved at a quicker pace than usual, first going straight to Bethany Knox's office in the back of the building. After finding her absent from her desk, he briskly marched to the dispatch room on the east side of the building.

Owens didn't particularly wish to be a part of Jackson's soon-to-be outburst so he conveniently stopped and started talking to one of his friends in patrol who was on a desk assignment because of an injury to his back.

"What happened man?" The patrolman asked, the news of the kidnaping and shooting had flowed through the headquarters quickly in the last few minutes.

"I wish I knew man, that guy just came out of nowhere and started shooting." Owens told his friend, his nerves still a little shot.

"You get him?"

"Yeah it was me." Owens said without pride, he'd never killed anyone before.

"Rumor has it they're not going to put you on administrative leave until this is resolved, they've called everybody in." The officer told him. The Police Department's policy on officer involved shootings was that the officer go on administrative leave until the shooting could be cleared, however this day was obviously shaping up to be different. "You look like hell dude, you want a cigarette?" The officer asked.

"No, I quit about a year ago." Owens responded, a little nervous.

"Let's head out back and smoke one." The officer again suggested, taking out his pack of Camels.

"Ok." Owens capitulated.

Knox and Bannister were still standing over the dispatcher giving orders when Jackson burst into the large room that was filled with computers and operators. Knox looked up and saw the door swing open and an angry Jackson trample in.

"Sergeant, this is Terry Bannister, Assistant Director of the FBI, he has some que..." She said pointing at the man next to her before she was interrupted.

"What the hell are you doing?" Jackson spouted in such a loud, angry tone that everyone in the room stopped what they were working on and turned around. Knox was taken aback, she was used to Jackson voicing his opinion with passion, but he had never been insubordinate with her.

"In my office Sergeant!" She ordered.

"What is he doing?" Aziz asked. Qudamah didn't respond immediately, he had to think out Rent's behavior. When he had thought for few moments he sat on a table and responded to his trusted Lieutenant.

"He wants me to think he actually is losing it. He is smarter than I thought, but he doesn't know us."

"What should we do?" Aziz asked.

"He's not losing it, his demands are too coherent, but why

does he want an hour?"

"Contact the police maybe?" Aziz speculated.

"No, after what they did to him, he wouldn't do that."

"We should kill the family and take our losses." Aziz suggested, which caused Qudamah to look him in the eye.

"That would be premature." He commented. "There is little he can do in an hour, we should give him the time."

"My friend, I fear that is a mistake, you yourself said not to underestimate the Americans."

"I am not." Qudamah countered. "Rent is playing a mind game, but he does not know that he can't beat me. We will let him play his game, but in the end he will have no choice but to kill the Senator." Qudamah thought a second longer before continuing. "This will fit into our plan nicely, America will be on edge waiting for the news of their hero's death."

"What about the police? If they find Rent before he kills the Senator?" Aziz asked. "They are looking for him. It is a possibility."

"Have we released the families in Atlanta, Chicago and Utah?" Qudamah asked.

"Yes, they have been released, I think it will hit the news very soon." Aziz informed.

"Good, prepare to take the little girl to the church. I think it's time we throw this city into chaos." Qudamah told him.

"Of course, Allah be with us." Aziz said before leaving the room. Once gone, Qudamah picked up a different cell phone than before and dialed a number.

"Yes." The scared voice on the other end of the line answered.

"Lynn, it is time, after it is done, your daughter will be delivered."

"Tha...thank you." Lynn said softly.

"Lynn, we have prayed with your daughter for you. We have done so to your God. She knows that you will not let her down, and she loves you very much." Qudamah told her in a comforting tone.

"I love her too, tell her that." Lynn replied.

"I already have." Qudamah responded. "Now it is time. Your daughter loves you."

"Thank you." Lynn said before Qudamah's line went dead. She sat in a car, parked on the side of the street and looked at the playground next to the elementary school in front of her, wondering how many parents would be forced to save their children today. She noticed a little girl that looked like her daughter playing on the slide and cried some more before shutting off the car and stepping out. She zipped her heavy jacket all the way up over the suicide vest, and started walking down the sidewalk in front of an elementary school. In front of the school, she turned, watching her target with a deadly hopeless stare that tunneled through the doors of the target. She crossed the street but her stare never wavered and completely drowned out everything else in the world. It was called the million mile stare by some, because in many aspects she wasn't just looking at her target, she was looking through it. She thought only of her daughter's life and the video that Qudamah had shown her. Her stare never shifted.

Every person in the building watched the two men and one woman walk through the halls of Police Plaza to Bethany Knox's makeshift office in the back of the building. Inside, Knox slammed the door shut and draped the large window behind her desk so that the other officers couldn't see through it. Jackson stood next to the window peeking outside at the stone wall of the parking garage. Bannister stayed closer to the door, he wasn't exactly sure if he should jump into an interdepartmental matter such as this, but he wanted to know what had transpired at the hotel. Plus, since Knox had already slammed the door shut, making a discreet exit in order to let the Assistant Chief clean her own backyard was out of the question.

"Let's get something straight. You don't talk to me like that, especially not in front of the other men!" Knox opened the bout.

"Where the hell do you get off pulling us out of there?"

Jackson verbally parried and returned, all the while pacing the office. "We could've had him. This could be over right now."

"Patrol didn't have any luck with it and I doubt you'd have been able to assist them. Especially in your current state of mind." Knox returned equally loudly. "And let's get back to the matter of respect. You don't yell at me." She countered.

"That's your problem Bethany! You're more concerned with how people talk to you, than getting Senator Cale back alive." Jackson parried again.

"Oh yeah, you did knockout job! How many men did you have there? And didn't Rent slip right through your net?" Knox threw back.

"See that's what I'm talkin about. You've got no clue how things go in the field." Jackson yelled, knowing he had something to hurt her with.

"I know exac..." Knox started.

"You know shit Bethany! You're a desk jockey, you always have been." Jackson moved in closer to his superior, which caused Bannister some slight alarm. "You're a bureaucrat, more concerned with policy and numbers than getting the job done!"

"I did my time on the streets, you know you can't go after..." Knox started again.

"When was that?" Jackson interrupted. "You did five years of patrol, in the financial district of all places. The biggest crime you ever investigated was some mutt who threw himself out a window cause his stock crashed. You've had your butt in that chair ever since."

"My time on the street is well documented and I'll point out that it was fifteen years before you even got a badge, so you should probably show some respect, because I just might know what I'm doing!"

"It's been twenty years since you documented anything but a coffee requisition!" Jackson yelled.

"Well maybe you should get me some because that's all you're going to be doing for the rest of your career!" Knox yelled back.

"Maybe we should all calm down." Bannister interjected.

"Why don't you tell him why your so mad Dave?" She pointed to Bannister.

"That has nothing to do with it and you know it!" Jackson returned.

"Oh yes, it has everything to do with it, you've always hated what I did to Rent!" She waited a split second before continuing. "What? You don't think I know what you tell other officers? Why do you think I pulled you? You've taken his side in that thing since the beginning."

"What thing?" Bannister asked.

"That is such B.S.!" Jackson retorted. "You pulled me for

that? That has nothing to do with how I do my job Bethany and it's insulting that you would think otherwise. No, you pulled me because you didn't want your mess mopped up by somebody who knew that you stabbed that man in the back!"

"I pulled you because you know that there is no way anybody would let you go after your former partner! Furthermore you know I was right to do it so you can shove it straight up your righteous ass!"

At that moment, Lynn pressed the button on her suicide vest, the resulting explosion sent nails, ball-bearings and Lynn hurtling in a thousand directions throughout the lobby of Police Plaza. The ensuing shockwave sent desks through walls, staplers through heads, and glass through everything, and everyone. It blew the cars in front of the building into the air and sent debris in every direction. A huge smoke cloud flew out of every window on the first floor. Due to Lynn's proximity to one of the pillars supporting the second story, and the decimation of that particular pillar, the entire forward foundation of the building gave way sending the front portion of the second floor crashing down onto the first, with the third right behind it.

Out on the street, the children playing on the elementary

school playground just across the five lane road felt a concussion unlike any of them had ever felt before. They watched the entire front part of the building collapse in a whirlwind of smoke, shrapnel and debris which enveloped them a few moments later.

Chapter 6:

Rent and Senator Cale remained silent while Rent drove the stolen car off the interstate just northeast of Seattle's downtown area. Cale assumed Rent took the exit because traffic suddenly become gridlocked. Rent on the other hand, had other intentions. He took several turns until he turned into a vacant lot where several ramshackle cars had been abandoned. He negotiated the stolen vehicle to the back of the lot, which was overshadowed by the nearby buildings and out of sight of the street. Rent parked the car, and lowered his head to the steering wheel. Cale watched him with curiosity but didn't speak. He was letting Rent think things through for a moment.

"I can't keep you like this." Rent said in a low tone from his head's position on the steering wheel.

"I was wondering when you were going to figure that out." Cale responded, Rent lifted his head from the wheel and turned to the Senator.

"How do you figure into this? Why do they want you dead?" Rent asked.

"I'm a Senator, it could be any one of a thousand reasons, or it could simply be because I'm a Senator. I don't know." Cale told his captor.

"You were in Vietnam?" Rent asked.

"Seven years, the last five as a POW." Cale responded. Rent thought for a moment.

"Liz is very important to me, so are her kids." Rent confided. He couldn't help but show his pain at the situation. "If you go to the cops, then they'll know you're safe and they'll kill the Austins. If I kill you and your body is found, then they'll kill the Austins. So this is the gamble, if you stay with me, then they won't know if you're safe, and they won't know if you're dead. I have to keep you in a middle ground, not dead, but not safe. As long as you're in danger, I think I can hold them off. If they don't know, then there's a chance they won't kill the Austins. That's why I took you."

"But you can't find the Austins if you've got to babysit me, right?" Cale finished the plan.

"Yeah, that's right." Rent admitted. "So I'm giving you a choice. You can leave now. I've bought myself an hour, I'll do everything I can. Or you can stay with me, give that mother and her three children a chance, and we do this together."

"So you're letting me go?" Cale asked. Rent paused a moment to think.

"Yeah, I'm letting you go. But you need to know that if you walk, you're condemning that family to death." Rent told him. "Senator," Rent told him. "I can't find them in an hour, they've got no chance without you. Give them a chance, please."

"I believe you, I really do." Cale told him. "But I'm not going on any crusade with you, you're a crazy man, help the cops find this family. That's all you can do."

"I told you, if we go to the cops they'll kill them, the only chance they've got is in that middle ground." Rent reiterated, Cale sat back and thought for a minute. After he thought the situation out, he opened the car door. Before he got out he turned back to Rent.

"You took me at gunpoint, I believe you, but I can't trust you, I'm sorry." Cale got out of the car.

"Don't give me a chance, give them one." Rent said so that the Senator could hear him just before the door slammed shut. Rent sat back in his seat. Was it over so quickly? Without the Senator, Rent had no hope of helping Liz and her kids. Rent knew he shouldn't have let Cale go, but didn't figure he had much choice. He ran his fingers through his hair before he collected his cell phone in the center console and the gun that was under his leg. Getting out of the car, he slipped the gun back into the holster on his belt and the cell phone into his pocket. He didn't look around, instead he looked at the ground. He sensed someone behind him and turned around to see Senator Cale standing there.

"Four years into my imprisonment in Vietnam," Cale stopped a moment, still trying to decide if he was going to tell Rent, "the Vietnamese warden in the prison camp I was being held at brought this little girl into my cell. She was about six years old. An American, Vietnamese, probably the daughter of a serviceman. She had blonde hair." Cale stopped, trying to dam up his own emotion. "You see they'd asked me questions, I tried to resist but when they break your legs and wait for them to heal just so they can break them again, well eventually they break you." Cale couldn't look Rent in the eye any longer. "I didn't know anything important anyway, they just did it to break me." The Senator looked down. "And they did." He looked back at Rent. "They didn't ask me anymore questions because I was already broken. They simply said 'You can't defeat us' and then they shot her." Cale looked down again. "She never had a chance, and for over thirty years, there hasn't been a day where I haven't thought about that." He looked at Rent. "If it gives these people a chance, then I'll go with you."

"Thanks." Rent said softly, and the two began walking through the junked cars toward the street.

Police Plaza shuddered violently, indicating the rest of the building wanted to collapse. It didn't, but in making its decision, it scared the hell out of everyone that was still alive within the building. The smoke was now dissipating enough to see the extent of the damage, the unforgivable carnage and destruction brought forth by one mother trying to save the life of her daughter. The entire forward section of the building, all three floors now lay in rubble on the street. Its victims buried beneath tons of broken concrete and steel. The cars on the street, the ones not blown over by the explosion had exploded and were on fire, some of their occupants still inside. One car had been blown sideways through the wall of the elementary school across the street and into one of the full classrooms. An officer inside the station had been blown out one of the windows and his remains were now decorating the side of a neighboring building, unrecognizable as even once being a human, the corpse was now splattered on the side of the building like fresh paint.

Jesse Owens limped around what used to be Police Plaza, another officer adorned with shrapnel and glass from head to toe being carried in his arms. The officer had been between Owens and the building when the explosion occurred and had inadvertently shielded him from most of the debris. Though Owens did have a piece of glass just above his right eye. An inch lower and he'd have been blinded in that eye. Owens walked stiff and zombie-like, carrying his friend. He took small steps, swaggering to the street.

Fire trucks were now arriving and soon the ambulances and more police would arrive. Owens continued to carry his friend toward the salvation of the gigantic red trucks. Within seconds of stopping, the trucks gave birth to a virtual army of firefighters who spread out like light enveloping a dark room. Two of the firemen saw Owens and ran to him. He didn't say anything when they took the dying man from his arms. The one who took him turned and began running with him toward a newly arrived ambulance, the other firefighter stood in front of Owens asking if he needed help in a yell which Owens did not appear to hear.

Owens turned in place, listening to the sounds of devastation. He watched firemen emerge from one of their trucks with a large hose and begin spraying one of the burning vehicles. He watched the wounded begin spurting from the building, some carrying other wounded, others carrying the dead. Everyone was bleeding, everyone was covered in soot, everyone's clothes were torn and tattered, everyone was crying. Circling in place he saw paramedics and firefighters running to the injured people, wrapping them in bandages, and walking them to safety. He saw several of the children on the elementary school playground had been downed from flying shrapnel. He saw the teachers out on the playground trying to tend to the wounded or dead students. One teacher in particular crying like he'd never seen over the body of one of the first graders who'd been decapitated by a large piece of debris. He heard the cries of the people coming out of the building. Two officers were dragging another out by his arms because each of the officers had shrapnel up and down one side of their bodies, and the officer being dragged was screaming in agony because his legs had been amputated in the explosion.

Owens saw about ten feet in front of him, the body of a civilian who'd simply been on the street when the explosion had occurred, the man didn't appear to have any wounds, his lifeless body just laying silently on the sidewalk. The first responders running around him to get to the wounded in the building. Owens wondered if the man had a family, children, or a job. He wondered who the man was that was dead simply because he was in the wrong place at the wrong time. He wondered what this man had done to deserve such a fate. He wondered what kind of God would allow such a tragedy to occur. He stopped circling, glowering at the dead man whom he'd never met and wondering what the man was like in life. Was the man nice? Was he mean? Was he fair? Why did he deserve this end? The thoughts in Owens mind circled like a hawk over this man whose only crime was being an American to people who hated Americans. Why? Was soon the only thought in Owens head.

Just outside the building, several firefighters debated whether or not to enter the building that could collapse at any time. The debate lasted only a second before the men decided to accept the danger in the hope that more people could be found and saved. Other firefighters bravely followed the first group inside, the regard for their own lives placed significantly further down the list than possibly saving others.

Inside Bethany Knox's office in the back of the building, Dave Jackson pushed himself up off the floor. Soot, debris, concrete and water was everywhere. The explosion had set off the sprinkler system, which had broken down because of the collapse of the front section. The open pipes sprayed water through the building, filling it like it a bathtub. The only light in the room was provided by the window in the back of the room which supplied a steady stream of sunlight. Jackson yelled to Knox who confirmed that she was alive and could move. She sat up slowly, leaving the glass in her right arm. Jackson yelled to Bannister who did not respond. The door had blown off its hinges and landed on the FBI Assistant Director. Once on his feet, Jackson helped Knox to hers and removed the door from Bannister, checking his pulse thereafter. He was alive, however unconscious. Jackson picked the man up and slid him into his arms. He looked out the bare door frame to see the familiar gleams of artificial light emanating from the firefighter's flashlights coming down the hallway by the office.

"Welcome to First Hill Senator." Rent told his companion when they reached the top of the long hill. Senator Cale was still panting from the walk, but took a look around nonetheless. People adorned the sidewalks of the street they were on, most loitering, others walking.

"What is this place?" Cale asked.

"It's drug heaven, called Pill Hill because you can find just about anything you're looking for here." Rent waited for the Senator to catch his breath.

"You're looking for that guy?" Cale determined.

"I am." Rent said, the two began walking. "He said the guy used a pay phone at the corner of Harvard and Denny, this is Harvard, Denny's just up there." Rent pointed.

"But you don't even know what he looks like?" Cale observed.

"Yeah, I'm banking that he doesn't look like these people so he'll stand out."

"That's an awful big assumption." Cale told his new friend.

"Not really, this guy chose me for a reason, he chose this guy for the same reasons." Rent elaborated. "I'm figuring that this guy is somebody like me. All that are down here are junkies, and you can't get a junkie to do something like this because junkies don't care about anything but junk. No, this guy's gonna stand out."

"I hate to pop your bubble or anything, but we don't even

know if this guy is connected." Cale told him.

"It's too much to be a coincidence. I think this guy is connected, and I'm willing to bet he knows something that could help us." Rent returned.

"What if we don't find him." Cale asked.

"I don't know." Rent said. They came up on Denny Way. "But this is a good lead for two reasons. First the cops aren't going to look for us down here, only narcotics ever comes down here, and even then they do it in force. Second, it's the only lead we've got, so if it doesn't pan out, we're screwed." He observed the payphone for a moment, then the people around it. "I think this guy is gonna stand out like a sore thumb, I just hope nothing happens to him before we find him."

"What do you mean?" Cale asked.

"Well, Pill Hill isn't exactly known for its hospitality, and I gotta tell you, if this guy is the petite little white boy that I think he is, these people are gonna eat him alive." Rent informed.

"Great, and we're walking right into the middle of it." Cale thought aloud.

"Don't worry." Rent reassured. He turned and looked at a twenty-something who was standing on the street corner selling drugs. The man looked at Rent, glared for a minute, recognized the former cop and bolted down the street. "I think we'll be ok." Rent said with a smirk. "Keep your eyes peeled for anything out of the ordinary here, it's needle in a haystack time."

Qudamah watched the police and firemen scurrying about on television with a gleeful smile. Apparently there had been news people near to Police Plaza when Lynn detonated her bomb, and they were on the scene very soon after the explosion. That footage was on the television. Qudamah sat back in his chair and sipped on his cup of tea. His plan was going masterfully, with the exception of Rent of course, but masterfully none the less, and Qudamah was confident that because Rent still had the Senator, he could persuade him to kill him.

"We have achieved a victory in this." Kicham Bradley said in Arabic, entering the room through the door. "They will not be able to regroup in time."

"Yes my friend, I am pleased." Qudamah approached Kicham. The two embraced in a hug and released each other.

"I am told that Rent is not cooperating." The large muscular Moroccan told his friend.

"Aziz is worried, I am not, I did not choose Rent at random, he will do what he is told." Qudamah returned. "Chi?"

"Yes please." Kicham said. Qudamah reached for the pitcher and served his friend some tea. "Even if Cale isn't killed, this is still a great victory. We have attacked four American cities, our method is sound, we have done what the others could not."

"Of course," Qudamah agreed, "and the Americans will react exactly as we have predicted, but it's Senator Cale that is..." Qudamah paused, thought for a moment and started again, "the icing on the cake. Americans are too self-absorbed to appreciate the danger they are in, but if we show them that someone like Senator Cale can be our victim. That is when they will truly fear us."

"Do you think Rent will go through with it?" Kicham asked.

"Yes, he will be easily manipulated like the others. All that is needed is to press the right buttons."

"I have no doubt that you will succeed my friend." Kicham professed his loyalty and confidence, two things he'd always kept for Qudamah. "What about Brewer?"

"There has been little on the police radio about him, I called our contact on the inside, but he has heard nothing. It appears that Brewer has dropped off the face of the earth." Qudamah informed.

"We still have the wife and son, we should dump them in the Sound." Kicham suggested.

"Not just yet my friend, I think I will need you here in a little while. I have something for Rent. Afterwards we will do away with Brewer's family. How are your men?"

"They are good, I left them on the boat, they were nervous at first, but they have acted wonderfully." Kicham answered.

"That is good, I worry about them all, none of these men have ever taken on a mission, much less one of this size, and they have not been trained." Qudamah confided.

"I wouldn't bother myself with it." Kicham responded. "They believe, experience and training be damned, they believe, that is all they need. I would put one believer against ten trained, experienced Americans any day. And I would know, I am a trained, experienced American." Kicham said with confidence.

"Of course you are right again, come, let's watch our work on television." Qudamah said.

"Jesse!" Jackson yelled from a short distance, Owens jerked his head in his direction. "They've set up a triage in the school gym," Jackson pointed to the elementary school, "go find FBI Director Bannister and report back his condition."

"Right." Owens got up and looked at the paramedic who was dressing the wound on his forehead. "Thanks." He told her before heading to the school. Jackson went to see Knox who was surrounded by people attempting to report to her. Jackson strolled up to the gathering and waited his turn.

"Even if we could get in, the water would have destroyed all the hard drives." One of the computer technicians told the Assistant

Chief.

"You can't get in." A fire department official chimed in. "That building is still very unstable, I'm surprised there's even part of it still standing."

"What about survivors?" Knox asked the fireman.

"We're still looking, but chances are, anybody in the collapsed section is dead. Sometimes there are pockets, so we're bringing in search dogs, they should be here in half an hour or so."

"Ok, how's our infrastructure?" Knox asked the group.

"Non-existent right now." The technician took his turn. "Like I said, we have no computers, and the entire department runs on computers."

"What about the other precincts?" Knox asked.

"Their hard drives are fine, but the intranet servers were in this building so the entire system is down. None of the computers can talk to each other, and we can't communicate with any of the national databases. AFIS, NCIC, UCR, they're all down, we can't even run a driver's license at this point."

"Damn it." Knox said in frustration. "What about the backups?"

"There are no backups. This hasn't ever happened before, this building was supposed to be safe." The technician told her.

"You're telling me that we put every crucial system we run in this one building?"

"Basically." Was the technician's response. Knox didn't really acknowledge his answer because she knew what it would be, instead she turned to another officer.

"What about dispatch capabilities?"

"They were all here too." An officer with a large bandage on his face told her. "Right now we don't have any way to dispatch our units anywhere."

"What about North precinct? They handled it before we built this building, why can't we transfer there?" Knox asked.

"The antenna is still up, but we don't have any computers."

"What about just grabbing a computer from a store?"

"Software." The technician responded. "We wouldn't have the software to put in. It's all inside there, where we can't get at it. That's also why we just can't take one off a detective's desk and plug it in. The dispatch center uses specialized software to communicate with the laptops in the patrol cars. We also need software for the repeaters the radios use. Even if we could get that portion of the intranet back up, we don't have the software."

"Wait," Jackson interrupted, "the fire department runs their own dispatch, it has to be compatible with ours, why not use their computers?"

"Except that because we got hit, they're getting every call. We can't pull enough of their computers to make it work." The technician responded.

"They have backups don't they?" Knox joined in.

"Yeah, I think so."

"How many?"

"Half a dozen at the most, at the least two." The technician responded.

"Can we run dispatch off two computers?" Knox asked. The technician thought very hard for a moment before answering.

"It'll be unreliable but I think we can make do." He said.

"Get them, and send them to the North precinct, we're going to be moving everything over there." Knox ordered.

"Yes ma'am." The technician said before leaving.

"Ok, what's the status of the precincts?" Knox next asked a Captain who was covered in cuts and bruises.

"We're doing it the old fashioned way, with phones. I got five guys on cell phones with every precinct, they're reporting huge spikes in all areas. Traffic is screwed royally. Calls are coming in on assaults, robberies, vandalisms, everything by the truckload. Since the radios are down we've got to contact the patrols through cell phones. Which means that there isn't any backup available for our guys. We need the radios."

"That's the first on the list." Knox said. "Ok, lets concentrate on damage control now, I want all patrols reactive, no investigations, only handle calls where things are in progress, we'll handle the rest later. Everybody else, get whatever you can, and whoever you can, we're leaving for the North precinct in ten minutes!" Knox told them. The group broke up, leaving only Jackson and Knox standing face to face. "We need to put our personal issues aside." Knox told her subordinate.

"I couldn't agree more." Jackson responded. "The Chief is dead."

"I heard." Knox said in sadness. "What about the others?"

"I don't have any numbers yet on casualties, they're still finding people, but we think Deputy Chief Milchan was in his office on the second floor, since its collapsed, we have to presume he's dead too. Deputy Chief Roberts is in L.A. for a convention, and of the four other Assistant Chiefs, two are dead, one is missing and Stein is in critical condition, they don't know if he'll make it." Almost on cue, when Jackson was finished, Owens arrived. "What's Bannister's status?" Jackson asked.

"He's ok, they think he may have some nerve damage in his left arm, but he said when they finish stitching it up, he's gonna make them release him." Owens informed.

"He can do that?" Jackson asked.

"He's the Assistant Director of the FBI, I guess he can." Knox told them. "We'll leave a car for him when we leave. He needs to get to the North precinct ASAP." Realizing the complexity of her newfound responsibilities, Knox remained silent for a long time. When she spoke again, she used her authoritative tone.

"Dave, get me the Mayor on the phone."

After lunch, Pill Hill's various underworld element typically came onto the street to gather and affirm their predicaments to each other for the evening. Most of Pill Hill's residents didn't have jobs anyway, or if they did they only attended them every other day because they didn't particularly take to flipping burgers at the local fast food joint. So at midday they started gathering on the streets in small groups. Socializing in the summer heat, they pondered the meanings of life, money, sex, drugs, crime and sometimes even religion. Mostly they sat around, got drunk and griped about being unemployable.

The most notorious of these street lizards was a young man in his late twenties commonly referred to as Johnny Carson. Johnny Carson wasn't his real name of course. When he was a teen, he and a few of his friends had been caught shoplifting by a small grocer. When the grocer asked his name, he'd replied that it was Johnny Carson and then he'd beaten the grocer to the verge of death with the drawer of the cash register. Ever since, the nickname and a brutal reputation had stuck. Both the nickname and the reputation had been even more cemented because of Johnny Carson's talent for crime, propensity for violence, and inability to be caught by the police, who had seven outstanding warrants for his arrest.

Johnny Carson was one of those bad seeds that everyone hears about on the news. He was born to a career drug addict and prostitute, who wasn't even sure she'd had a child until he was arrested at the age of eleven for stabbing a teacher in the leg with a pen. She'd let him rot in juvenile for several days. Possibly because the choice between bailing her son out or buying drugs with her money was a no-brainer for her, but the teacher felt sorry for the boy and decided not to press charges. After his mother was arrested for accessory to murder when one of her dealer boyfriends killed one of his own clients, Johnny Carson was sent into the foster care system at the age of thirteen. That particular system didn't agree with him, so after eight families, sixty beatings, four arrests, and the fact that he beat one of his foster mothers to within an inch of her life, he ran away, right back to Pill Hill.

Johnny Carson earned his money through muggings, robberies and drugs. He frequently spent his days out on the street at Pill Hill, socializing with the other economically challenged miscreants of the area. Today, he was sitting on the steps of an abandoned building with several of his friends. The three other men he was talking to ranged in age from fifteen to twenty. All three were in awe of Johnny Carson's friendly demeanor in light of his particularly mean reputation. Johnny Carson didn't pay these boys much attention though, he was concentrated on the only female in the group. Crystal was a drug addict who supported her habit with associations with "bad boys" similar to Johnny Carson who demanded occasion favors. She was dressed rather provocatively, in a tight form fitting light blue top which accentuated her c-cup breasts and tight, torn, blue jeans. Today's topic was fellatio and Johnny Carson was determined to have received some before his conversation was over.

"So tell me, how many have you done at one time?" Johnny Carson asked the girl.

"Five, but that was only once." Crystal replied, proud of the accomplishment.

"Damn ho, what do they call that?" Jas, a large Samoan former highschool football player, and besides Johnny Carson the oldest of the group pondered. "I got it, multi-tasking, that shit's called multi-tasking."

"That's cause I got talent." Crystal proclaimed.

"That don't take no talent." Johnny Carson commented.

"Can you do it then?" Crystal asked Johnny Carson. Everyone laughed at her question.

"Hell, I bet even Benny over there could do that." Johnny Carson replied not at all put aback by Crystal's insult. Benny, a fifteen year old looked down and didn't say anything, he'd gotten used to being the punching bag of the group and was incredibly scared of Johnny Carson.

"I bet Benny did it this mornin'." Jas commented, pretending to stroke the baseball bat he'd stolen from a convenience store that he and Johnny Carson robbed the night before.

"Look," Johnny Carson said, gazing at Crystals breasts. "If anybody can stick their dick in your mouth then anybody can get a dick stuck in their mouth, that aint no big thing. What's talent is if you can make a guy holla as you suck on his balls."

"And they all did." Crystal replied, laying down on the steps in-between Johnny Carson's legs, facing away from him, and putting the back of her head in his lap so she could look up into his eyes.

"Like I said before, I think you're full of it." Johnny Carson replied.

"Really," Crystal rubbed her hand up and down his leg, "I'll make you scream right here, right now."

"Hey, Johnny, I think she wants to show ya her talent." Jas said. "C'mon do it, hell I'll even pay ya for that."

"How much?" Crystal asked.

"Nah, I don't think so." Johnny Carson told her. "What about back there?" He said pointing to the alley behind the building. Crystal didn't say anything, she just smiled. Johnny Carson got up and took her by the hand. "Boys, if you hear me scream, you'll know she's worth it." He told the three others before he led her into the alley. He found a nice spot that obstructed the view from the street behind a dumpster and unzipped his pants. "Well get to it."

"Maybe I'm shy?" Crystal reached into his pants. "Nah, I don't think so." She said just before she began her work. A few minutes into her work, Johnny Carson realized that it wasn't nearly what she'd advertised, though he had no intention of telling her to stop, he was enjoying it. When he heard something further down the alleyway, he began to look around. He let Crystal continue until he heard it again, he couldn't be sure what it was, but it had sounded like someone was crying.

"Wait, hold up a min." He jerked his penis out of her mouth. "You hear that?"

"Hear what, I's just gettin started." She said, a bit annoyed.

"Yeah, right, you suck like your grandmother," Johnny Carson said just before he heard the sound again. "Go get the guys." He zipped his pants up. Crystal got off her knees and ran to the street. Johnny Carson walked a little further down the alley until he saw Jason Brewer sitting against the brick wall of a building, weeping with his face in his hands. "What is this?" Johnny Carson asked. Brewer saw him and got to his feet.

The other three men and Crystal approached them. "Hey Johnny what's up?" Jas asked.

"This guy's sitting here crying. I can't get a good blow job listening to that." Johnny Carson told his friends.

"Look guys, I'm sorry to get in..." Brewer started to say when Johnny Carson yelled at him.

"Shut up. Aint nobody talking to you!"

"This is strange Johnny." Jas commented.

"Tell me about it." Johnny Carson reaffirmed.

"Look guys I'm from..." Brewer started, but was stopped short because Johnny Carson punched him in the face. Brewer fell back against the wall, and once he regained his balance he lunged at Johnny Carson but was caught in the back of the head by Jas' baseball bat. Brewer fell to the ground clutching his head.

"I told you to shut up!" Johnny Carson yelled. "Give me that bat." He ordered Jas who complied. "When I tell you to do something pretty boy, you do it!" Johnny Carson yelled and began hitting Brewer in the back with the bat. Soon everyone but Crystal joined in by kicking and hitting Brewer. Within a minute, Brewer was beaten and bloodied. "Who is this pansy?" Johnny Carson asked when the group got tired of assaulting the man. Benny bent over and picked his wallet out of his pants. He quickly went through it and took out some money.

"He's got about forty bucks." Benny said before Johnny Carson yanked the money from his hands and put it in his pocket.

"He's broke now." Johnny Carson commented with a laugh.

"What are we gonna do with him now?" Jas asked.

"Well, we can't leave him like this," Johnny Carson said to his friends, "we gotta do the right thing boys." The boys smiled. "Hey Crystal come here." Johnny Carson ordered.

"What you gonna do Johnny." Crystal asked nervously.

"You ever see a man die?" Johnny Carson asked her. Crystal didn't respond, she was getting very scared. "C'mon Crys," Johnny Carson put his arm around her. "It's a natural part of life." He told her. "I killed three men in my days, and I gotta tell you, there aint nothin on earth like it, not even screwing." Crystal's eyes were beginning to tear up, and Johnny Carson could tell that she was about to freak out so he decided not to push her any further. "Hey, Benny. You aint done this have you?"

"N..No man, I don't wanna kill nobody." Benny said faintly.

"Benny," Johnny Carson squeezed the back of Benny's neck tightly and handed him the baseball bat. "Look bro, I know you're kind of weak and all, but you gotta run with the big dogs here. You hear the cops got bombed today? The cops got nothing, they couldn't pop anybody for anything today. Aint nobody gonna know. I'm telling you, this is a freebee."

"I don't know man," Benny started.

"C'mon, just do it." Jas interrupted.

"It's ok Benny, you aint got the balls, that's ok." Johnny Carson said into Benny's ear.

"I got the balls." Benny retorted. Johnny Carson didn't say anything; he held his hand out to show Benny the way to Brewer. Benny went.

Chapter 7:

Benny looked at the bloodied pulp of a man in front of him. Brewer could hardly move and what movements he did make were caused by pain. Benny didn't want to kill him but for years he'd looked up to Johnny Carson's reputation. He desperately wanted to run with Johnny Carson's crew and this seemed to be the only way he was going to get in; by killing a defenseless man for forty dollars and crying when Johnny Carson was trying to get oral sex. It didn't seem right, in fact it seemed downright wrong to kill someone like this. Benny wasn't averse to killing but doing it simply because he could was never something he'd contemplated.

"Do it!" Jas yelled. Everyone's eyes were now on Benny. Would he do it? Would he cross that line, take that plunge?

"Don't listen to him Benny, just raise that thing and swing. That's all you gotta do buddy." Johnny Carson said in an encouraging tone. Benny took his words to heart and decided against his conscience. He raised the bat above his head and prepared to strike.

Much like the rug being pulled out from beneath someone's feet, the bat was suddenly yanked right out of Benny's young hands. Benny hadn't expected such force to be enacted on him, and thus went flying backwards, landing on his butt about a foot from where he'd been standing.

"Damn, this is a nice piece of wood." Carey Rent tapped the bat against his hand. "Where'd you boys get this?" He said in a teasing tone. "Better yet, why are you carrying it around with you?"

"Who is this?" Johnny Carson pointed to Rent.

Senator Cale stood leaning against one of the buildings up the alleyway, a safe distance away.

"Oh, I'm sorry guys." Rent said with his usual commanding style. "I'm jumping in the middle of your business. Sorry about that."

"I think we oughta jump in the middle o'his business." Jas told Johnny Carson.

"Look guys, I don't wanna be rude, but I just need to know who this rather..." Rent trailed off and surveyed the bloodied Brewer, "this rather bruised fellow is. That's all." Rent raised both his hands up, including the one holding the bat, as a peace gesture before leaning down to Brewer. "Are you Jason Brewer?" He asked loudly so that Brewer could hear him, Brewer didn't immediately respond but after a moment he nodded. Rent stood back up and looked at the four men and one woman whose attention he now commanded completely. "I just wanted to know that, you guys can go back to work now." He took a few steps away from Brewer.

"Maybe we oughta see how much money this weirdo's got?" Johnny Carson recommended.

"You know, one last thing." Rent continued to ignore their comments. "I just need to see some I.D.." Rent looked around and focused on Benny who had hidden Brewer's wallet behind his back when Rent said his name. "That Brewer?" Rent asked Benny. Benny shook his head no, but Rent saw right through the lie. "Ok, guys, I'm sorry, but by order of the United States Senate, you guys are going to have to cease and desist your pummeling of this fine young American." He casually leaned on the baseball bat. Johnny Carson turned and looked at Senator Cale because he heard him chuckle at Rent's remark.

"That so?" Johnny Carson asked, Rent nodded and Johnny Carson used his hand to signal the other three men to surround Rent. Crystal slid backwards a safe distance, she no longer wanted to be a part of this but seemed to be stuck. "Guys, Jimmy Stewart here wants to teach us about government."

"You know who Jimmy Stewart is. You get points for that." Rent replied.

"Yeah, I also know that we live in...what's that called...a democracy." Johnny Carson retorted, holding his hands out to his side to show Rent that he was outnumbered and surrounded. "And I believe that we are four to your one are in favor of you getting beat down."

"Democracy huh?" Rent looked around, he was now in the middle of the alley, Johnny Carson was about five feet in front of him, just out of striking distance. To his right was one of Johnny Carson's cohorts, a medium sized Latino named Manny, behind him was Benny. To his left, about two feet away was Jas, the very large Samoan who had obviously done this before because his lack of distance indicated that he knew Johnny Carson was going to have him pounce first and secondly because Johnny Carson's eyes kept looking over at him expectantly. Rent switched the bat from his right to his left hand. "Ok, let's vote." He swung the bat fiercely into Jas' left knee, breaking his leg and causing one of the splintered bones to pop out of his skin. Jas dropped like a sack of potatoes, a sack of potatoes that was screaming like a little girl.

The man on Rent's right moved in next, but Rent's strike on Jas had put him in a good position, he simply swung the bat in an upward arc, catching the man in the face and sending him flying backwards to the ground. Johnny Carson, not put off by Rent's success, moved in with a wide punch meant to knock the fight out of Rent. Rent used the bat to block the punch, which broke Johnny Carson's right hand, Rent then moved in and used the bottom of the handle of the bat on Johnny Carson's stomach before twisting his wrist which sent the shaft of the bat into Johnny Carson's groin. As

Rent anticipated, Benny didn't attack at all.

"My balls, my balls!" Johnny Carson moaned, writhing around on the ground. Rent motioned for the Senator to come over and help Brewer. While the Senator was walking over, Rent squatted down next to Johnny Carson.

"You don't live in a democracy. You live in a republic. Do you know why?" Rent asked rhetorically. Rent started accentuating each syllable of his words, smacking Johnny Carson on the head with the bat with each one. "You-elect-your-rep-resent-atives-to-vote-for-you. Go back to school." Rent stood up, tossed the bat away and helped Senator Cale with Brewer.

"You like that?" Rent asked Cale.

"I should put it in my next education bill." Cale responded. Rent and Senator Cale got Brewer to his feet and started carrying him further into the alley.

Johnny Carson and crew slowly picked themselves up. Before they could regroup, their prey were out of sight, not that there was any real fight left in them.

"He needs a doctor." Cale told Rent.

"Not yet, we've got to get him to talk first." Rent told the Senator.

"Where are we taking him?" Cale asked.

"I know a place." Rent did know a place, it was an abandoned building, there were quite a few in Pill Hill. This one was special because Rent knew that he could patch Brewer up there. It only took a few minutes to reach it, even carrying Brewer like they were. They entered the building through a back door, which was found with the lock smashed and partially open. It had at one time been an apartment building, but when Pill Hill degenerated into the hell hole that it was, it had been abandoned. Cale became alarmed when he heard people moving around and talking inside the building.

"Carey, this place is supposed to be abandoned." Cale whispered to Rent.

"I know." Rent said in a normal tone. "It's become a little bit hovel, a little bit pharmacy over the years, but it's cool, trust me."

"You brought us to a crack house? What about the people?" Cale stammered in surprise.

"Yeah, they only occupy half the rooms at most."

"Carey, we can't do this here?" Cale asked, with more of a question than a statement.

"Sure we can, everything we need is here." Rent shifted all of Brewer's weight to Cale and peered down the hallway.

"What about the people?" Cale asked.

"Oh, that." Rent said, faking surprise at the question. He closed his hand into a fist and banged it very loudly on the wall several times, the last time so hard it burst through the drywall. "This is the police!" Rent yelled at the top of his lungs and took out his gun. "We're conducting a search warrant, nobody move!"

The instant he finished his command, the entire building went nuts. Druggies were running out of every door in the place, down fire escapes, through the hallway past Rent, who simply stepped aside and let them pass. One even jumped out a plate glass bathroom window. Within seconds, the building was vacated of all living things, even the rats had run off.

"Done." Rent said again.

The police motorcade slithered through the city streets like a worm through a maze. The long line of police cars and SUV's moved with their red and blue lights on, occasionally activating their sirens when they went through intersections. Inside the cars were the last remnants of the Seattle Police Department's command and control structure. There weren't many left, and of those that had lived through the explosion and building's collapse only a few had escaped critical injuries. It was these people that Bethany Knox mustered, the gear they retrieved from areas of the building that the Fire Department would let them enter riding with them in their vehicles. The motorcade stopped directly in front of the Seattle Police Department's North Precinct. When the vehicles came to a stop, all their doors opened almost simultaneously.

"Captain Carrasco?" Knox stepped out of one of the middle cars. She soon saw a large Latino man running to her. He was older, in his forties, but appeared to be in very good shape. His clothes were black BDU's or Battle Dress Uniform, consisting of black boots, black cargo pants, a black t-shirt, and a black blouse that came down past his waist and was filled with pockets.

"You're on security Captain." Knox informed the SWAT commander. "I want all civilians out of the building, and no civilian will enter the building without expressed permission from the command staff, understood?"

"Yes ma'am." The Captain told her. She nodded to him and proceeded inside with the other Police officers from the Police Plaza site.

The civilians and officers inside the lobby of the North precinct hadn't expected the command staff to arrive with such fervor, they entered the precinct quickly and immediately began ushering everyone who was not a police officer or technician out the doors. Officers who were a moment before taking reports from victims and witnesses had to stop. All suspects that were being interrogated or processed were immediately put back in holding cells. All the civilian employees were quickly gathered up and told that they needed to go home until this emergency was over and then watched until they exited the precinct. Bethany Knox stood in the center of the lobby, watching the chaos with David Jackson and

Jesse Owens standing right behind her.

"We're clear of civilians ma'am." Carrasco informed Knox a few minutes later.

"Good, Terry Bannister with the FBI is going to be arriving soon, make sure he gets in." Knox ordered.

"Yes ma'am, we're going to be cordoning off the area around the building for about a block. In case of car bombs." Carrasco informed.

"Very good." Knox told him before she turned a chair around and stepped up on it with her high heeled shoes, of which the heels no longer remained. "Everybody?" She said very loudly, "everybody, can I have your attention?" She waited a few moments for everyone in the room to turn to face her. When she was sure she had their complete attention she began speaking. "Everybody, I know we've already had a long and horrible day. Many of our friends, our partners, and our brothers and sisters have been killed today in an act of terrorism. I know that we are all concerned for our families and the people in Police Plaza, but right now we have a job to do, the city of Seattle needs us." She paused for a moment before continuing. "It is my sad duty to tell you that Chief Bill Rodgers was killed in the bombing, as was several of the other Deputy and Assistant Chiefs. I know that all of our prayers are with them and their families." She gave a moment for the information to sink in.

"We were hit hard today, and a senseless and brutal tragedy

has taken from us some of the most brave and giving men and women this city has ever known. I feel the loss as much as all of you. But we must carry on. By order of the Mayor, I am taking command of the Metropolitan Police Department. We are now upgrading to Terror Alert Level One. The Mayor has full confidence in our ability to function as Seattle's peacekeepers, even in light of this crisis. That is why I recommended to the Mayor, and he agreed with me that while even though a state of emergency does exist within Seattle, it does not warrant the implementation of martial law, and the National Guard will not be needed.

"What does this mean for us? It means that our job just got harder. It means that we are Seattle's last line of defense, that we are the people charged with protecting Seattle's citizens, and it means that that is exactly what we are going to do! Terrorists are in Seattle right now, and we must assume that they are planning another attack. It's crunch time. Lets show'em what we're made of!" She finished, hoping to inspire the men, which she succeeded at for the most part.

Rent entered one of the apartments on the ground floor first, he had his pistol out in front of him and cleared the apartment before he yelled for Cale and Brewer to come in. Cale entered the room with Brewer's his arm around his shoulder. He sat Brewer down on the sofa before looking around the room himself. For the most part it was exactly how Cale anticipated it would look. The walls had no paint left on them, the room was cluttered with plates of half eaten food, junk, wrappers, and garbage adorned the floor, on the tables were needles, razors and bags of pills and powders. There was a small television inside the room, an older set, with rabbit ears atop. Cale couldn't see inside the bedroom but judging from the living room and kitchen, it would be equally messy. The Bathroom door was hanging open, it was off it's bottom hinge, and Cale could see that the window was broken, probably the glass breaking he had heard when Rent had announced the police were there.

Brewer lay on the couch, falling in and out of consciousness, the pain he was experiencing from his wounds visible on his face. Rent holstered his pistol and was rooting around in the kitchen picking up bottles of pills and reading their labels before quickly dropping them and searching for more. When he found a bottle that suited him, he picked up a dirty glass that was sitting in the sink and turned the tap water on. A sludgy brown mix spurted out of the tap and Rent almost jumped back. The tap continued to spurt out the mix of water and whatever it was mingled with until it started flowing regularly, and the water only had a slight brown tint. Rent filled the cup and took both it and the bottle of pills to Brewer, where he sat them on the short table in front of the sofa. He picked at Brewer to sit him up.

"Ok, buddy, go ahead and down this." Rent told Brewer, picking two pills out of the bottle and stuffing them in Brewer's mouth followed by some of the water, most of which dribbled down his chin.

"What is that?" Cale asked.

"It's Codeine." Rent replied.

"You're giving him Codeine that you found in a drug house?" Cale asked with repugnancy. "You can't do that Carey! He needs a doctor!" Cale demanded.

"We can't get him to a doctor, not until he talks to me." Rent replied, placing the cup down on the table.

"Only a doctor can prescribe that! You don't even know how much you're giving him, or if it's homemade or not. You could kill him!"

"Relax Senator, I was a narcotics cop for five years, I know where this stuff comes from and I know how much I can give him." Rent said, hoping he was right.

"Right Dr. Narcotics Cop!" Cale spouted. Rent ignored him and slapped Brewer's face lightly.

"Jason, you there buddy?" Rent tried to wrest Brewer from unconsciousness. "Jason, come back to me buddy?" Rent gave a few minutes for the medication to take effect. Finally, after what seemed like an eternity, Brewer began to come around.

"I killed them, I killed them." Brewer announced, coming back to cognition. Rent grabbed his head and shook it slightly.

"Listen to me, no you didn't, you didn't kill anybody. You have to help me." Rent told the distraught man.

"No, I did, I killed them." Brewer said in a daze, out of his delirium, he looked at Rent. "Who are you?"

"Jason, listen to me, my name is Carey Rent. You are here with Senator Bob Cale. Do you understand?"

"A Senator? What?" Brewer said, still in a stupor.

"I don't have time to explain. Listen, we need to know what you know." Rent told him.

"They came in last night with guns, they took Shelley and Matt, my wife and son." Brewer announced.

"What did they tell you to do?" Cale asked.

"They said I had to kill people at a mall downtown or they would kill my family." Brewer said, slurring his speech, wanting to lay back down into unconsciousness.

"Look, you don't know that they've killed your family, you don't know. We might still be able to help them. They've taken others, we need to find them." Rent held Brewer upright.

"I don't know anything, I had a bag over my head." Brewer told them in his daze.

"Yes you do, we just have to find it inside your head." Rent said.

"We've got the radios back up." The technician told Knox and Jackson. "But we're having problems connecting the computers to the databases, the lines here are old and out of date. I've got a couple of guys working with the network boys, but I don't know when we'll be up."

"Ok, keep working. We need those databases." Knox replied, and turned to Jackson who was on his cell phone with one of the men that was still at the hotel.

"The feds took the fingerprints off the guy that Owens killed at the hotel. Until they let us know, we're in the dark." Jackson said after hanging up.

"Great. What about Rent and Senator Cale, anything on them?" Knox asked.

"Nothing, they've dropped off the face of the earth." Jackson told her.

"Damn it."

"You know full well that Rent knows every nook and cranny of this city. We won't find him, he's too good." Jackson informed.

"I'd rather not surrender to Carey Rent because we think that he can outsmart us Dave. Give a list of possible hiding places to patrol and let them check them out. Anywhere you think he might go."

"Right." Jackson said, a minute later Owens entered the room.

"What is it?" Knox asked.

"Bannister just arrived, and he's got like thirty guys with him." Owens told them. Knox led them out of the office they were in and out into the lobby where the FBI was entering with various boxes and electronic equipment. Bannister made a beeline for Knox.

"How are you Director?" Knox saw Bannister's left arm taped to his torn and stained white suit shirt.

"It hurts like hell, but they doped me up." Bannister told her. "I hear you're in charge?"

"The Chief was killed." She told him. "Who are all these people, I thought all your guys were on the third floor of Police Plaza?"

"Agents from the Tacoma office who just helicoptered in. We'll be taking over your investigation and running the cleanup."

"Ok, I assume you'll be using our guys?" Knox asked, knowing that Bannister didn't yet have enough people to completely run things.

"I will, we've got some new information, do you have a briefing room here?"

"Second floor." Knox responded. Bannister nodded to the agent next to him who began issuing orders to other agents.

"We'll have a briefing in fifteen minutes, get your staff together, I want them there." Bannister ordered, and walked off to confer with some of his other agents.

"Did he just punk us?" Owens asked, knowingly out of place.

"That's how it works. A terrorist act gets the FBI, we knew that." Jackson told his partner.

"He's in charge now, let everyone know, they take orders from the FBI, but local business still goes through me." Knox told her two subordinates. "Dave I want you in that briefing."

"I thought you didn't want me involved?" Jackson asked, patronizing.

"Rent is a big part of this, and you know more about him than anyone alive."

When Aziz returned from his mission to drop off Lynn's daughter Jamie at the church, he found Qudamah and Kicham in their makeshift control room sipping tea and watching the carnage they had created through Lynn on the local news. Aziz entered the room quietly and although the two knew he was there, they did not immediately acknowledge him. They were discussing Rent, Qudamah was telling Kicham that he had made a mistake when he predicted Rent's mental state, but that all was not lost. Rent would still undoubtedly complete the first half of his mission, although they would have to change their plans for Rent. Qudamah no longer thought Rent capable of doing what he originally planned for him. Kicham comforted his friend by reminding him, that these missions never go exactly as planned. He brought up the 9/11 hijackings and how flight 93 had gone down over Pennsylvania instead of crashing into the White House per their plan.

"But we have not even accomplished the killing of Senator Cale?" Aziz chimed in, which brought dirty looks from both his leaders.

"The operation is not over." Kicham said patiently. "Sit down."

"Forgive me, but I worry about this. It is very important that we succeed. If we do not, the others will hunt us down." Aziz took a seat.

"You are correct, they will not tolerate us if we fail, but success will be worth that risk." Qudamah assured him. "Besides, most of the operation is complete, they will have to accept us now."

"That's if we can make it back to them." Aziz wondered.

"Do not fear that, the Americans are hurt, they will not notice us." Kicham told him.

"But why did you allow Rent to not kill the Senator?" Aziz asked.

"Because I wanted to give Rent time to go wherever he was going to be hiding." Qudamah answered him.

"Why?"

"It is simple my friend, I wanted it to take them time to find the Senator. It benefits us even more than if Rent had killed him in the hotel. The longer it takes them to find him, the more on edge the American public will be. The worse the fear when they find him dead."

"Yes, you are right." Aziz told his leader.

"Do not doubt us Aziz, we know what we are doing." Kicham said with the tone of a mentor.

"Kicham is correct, I have mastered this plan, and all contingencies. Now it is time for the Senator to be killed. Get the children and the mother and bring them here." Qudamah ordered.

"No!" Brewer shot back to full consciousness with the realization of what was happening to his family. "I killed them! They're gone! They're gone!" Brewer unsuccessfully tried to push Rent off of himself. Rent responded by putting more of his weight on Brewer and grabbing both sides of Brewer's head with his hands. Rent got very close to his face.

"Stop freaking out!" Rent yelled at him.

"But I didn't do it! I didn't do it!" Brewer returned.

"Stop it!" Rent yelled back. He waited until Brewer had calmed down, then released him, shifting his weight to the adjacent seat on the sofa. He began his questioning again. "Where did they take you?"

"It was a boat I think. I don't know." Brewer replied without thinking.

"A boat? What kind of boat?"

"I don't know, they put a bag on my head. I saw a little from underneath the bag when I stepped on the boat, it was big."

"Like a yacht, or cruise ship?"

"No, more like a large fishing boat, and it was blue, it was painted blue." Brewer told the men.

"What did the inside look like, did it have many rooms?" Rent asked.

"Only one, no it had two, you could walk down some steps to a bathroom, they let Matt go to the bathroom."

"Tell me what you remember about it." Rent ordered. Brewer strained to remember, it was fuzzy, but he tried.

"It was like wood all around...um...there was a wood floor, and the walls were covered with wood. It was big, but narrow, only about eight feet across I think, but in the front," Brewer remembered.

"Towards the bow?" Cale asked.

"Yeah, towards the bow, you could go down steps, there was a bathroom and maybe a bed too, I don't know I didn't go down there. There were two doors, one in the back, the other in the front, but on the side, I think my right. The sofa was white, and was the length of the room, they sat Shelly and Matt on it."

"Go on, tell me everything you remember about it." Rent urged. At this point he was just letting Brewer ramble until he said something he could use.

"It was like the inside of a Winnibego, it had a sink and fridge and it was old like used, that's all I remember, I swear, when we left they put the bag over my head again."

"What did they tell you when you were there?" Rent asked.

"They tied me to a folding chair, like a movie chair. They showed me a video, it was of a girl getting her head cut off."

"Who showed you a video?" Cale asked.

"This black guy, he was...he said his name was Kilam, Kenam, Kehan..."

"Kicham?" Rent asked, surprised.

"Yeah that's it Kicham, he wasn't from here, I could tell but he didn't have that much of an accent. He was in charge and the other guys were Arabs, they did what he said."

"You know him?" Cale asked Rent.

"A black guy named Kicham drove my cab this morning. Damn it. I had him right there and didn't even know it." Rent cursed himself for not suspecting the cab driver. "Listen, Jason, do you know which docks you were at?"

"No," Brewer strained to think again. "I couldn't tell but, it was all the way down the peer, we walked on the peer for a long time."

"Did the boat have any windows?" Cale asked.

"Yeah, but they had blinds down, wait, there was a light that came through them."

"Like flood lights?" Rent questioned.

"No, it was there then it was gone, then there again, it filled the cabin." Brewer answered.

"Like a lighthouse light?" Cale asked.

"Yeah, yeah, that's what it was."

"Jason, did you see the lighthouse, what was around it?" Rent asked, thinking this might be just what he needed.

"I saw between the blinds that there were buildings but I couldn't see the lighthouse. It was dark."

"What kind of buildings? Like a sewage treatment plant?" Rent asked as he now paced the room.

"Maybe I don't know...yeah...before they put the bag over my head I could see a little, the sun was coming up."

"It was coming up, which side of the lighthouse did it come up on?" Rent thought he might finally be making progress.

"The left side I think."

"You know where he's talking about?" Cale asked Rent.

"Yeah, Ballard. I think he was at Ballard docks. It's the only view of Discovery Park, there's a lighthouse and sewage treatment plant there." Rent told him. "But there's only like two hundred boats there." Rent switched back to Jason "When you left, did they keep your family on the boat?"

"I think so, they didn't go with us."

"Then they may still be there." Rent speculated. His phone began to ring. Fishing the phone from his pocket, he looked at his watch. "I said an hour shit for brains, it's only been fifty-five minutes, learn to count!" He said into the phone.

"Really. Dylan Austin will be disappointed, he would've liked those extra minutes." Qudamah shot back, his tone ruthless. His words caught Rent off guard and he didn't reply. "What? No witty comeback, I was looking forward to being called more names." Qudamah stood in the middle of the room with the three children sitting in chairs, lined up in front of him. The tape gone from their mouths, Qudamah wanted Rent to hear the children. Liz was standing next to her children, being held tightly around each arm by Kicham's large hands.

"Are you ready to meet and make the trade?" Rent pushed.

"We shall make the trade now." Qudamah told him. "But first there is the matter of the hotel."

"What about it?" Rent asked. "You said to escape, I did."

Both Brewer and Cale watched and listened to Rent anxiously. They could hear Qudamah's voice emanating from the speaker of the phone but couldn't make out all of his words.

"You were ordered to kill the Senator, and then escape. I lost a good man getting you out. There must be punishment for not obeying your orders." Qudamah told him, Rent's hand began to shake, and he suddenly felt his stomach drop.

"I got out, let's make the trade." Rent tried to bargain.

"Before you kill the Senator, I want you to know that Dylan Austin's blood is on your hands." Qudamah told Rent.

"If you harm one hair on that boy's head, I swear to God, not only will the Senator stay safe and sound, but there won't be anywhere on Earth you can hide from me!" Rent proclaimed defiantly into the phone, causing both Brewer and Cale to step back from where he was standing.

"Really?" Qudamah leveled his pistol at Dylan Austin and fired two shots into his chest. Calleigh was sprayed with her brother's blood and screamed for her life. Becca sat and watched like she were watching a program on television.

"No!" Liz screamed and tried to lunge for Dylan, but was held in place by Kicham's grip. She continued screaming and Rent pulled the phone away from his hear. All three men in the apartment heard the devastation in the room. Dylan's chair had fallen backward and the dying boy was writhing in pain. Qudamah took a few steps and stood over him, pointing his pistol at the boy's head.

"Oh No. No. No." Brewer muttered to himself after he heard the shots.

"This is the price of disobedience!" Qudamah shouted into the phone before firing his weapon and splattering Dylan's brains over the floor. Liz's knees gave way and she fell to the floor weeping in a manner few people have ever seen. Kicham knelt down to keep hold of her.

"You motherfucker!" Rent spat into the phone with such great anger his words were almost incomprehensible. "I'm gonna to rip your fucking skin off!"

"You dare to defy me again!" Qudamah screamed at Rent. "The oldest girl dies next!"

"No!" Rent replied leveling his own gun at Senator Cale.

"Kill the Senator!" Qudamah pressed. Rent stared at the Senator with the phone to his ear in one hand and his pistol pointed at the Senator in the other. His mind raced, his throat was choking, his stomach was pushing it's acid up his esophagus. Both his hands shook.

"How do I know you'll release them?" Rent questioned, trying to buy time.

"You don't, but unless the Senator dies right now, this family will die one at a time!" Qudamah grabbed the back of Calleigh's hair, pulling her head back.

"Mommy!" Calleigh yelled out in a long shriek. "Mommy help me!" The little girl cried out.

"Goddamn it, Carey just do it!" Liz screamed at the top of her lungs.

"Wait, give me a minute!" Rent yelped into the phone. Cale felt his knees shaking, and he raised his chin into the air in a gesture of acceptance.

"Enough talk, the girl dies now!" Qudamah released Calleigh's hair, took the gun from his belt and put it to her head.

"No!" Rent fired his weapon, then threw the phone against the wall, shattering it into pieces before dropping to his knees, his face in his hands, screaming through his tears.

172

Chapter 8:

Kicham let go of Liz, and she ran to her daughters. She untied them from their chairs, first Calleigh, who grabbed her mother in a tight embrace, then Becca who continued to sit peacefully in the chair. Liz nevertheless scooped her youngest daughter into her arms. Becca didn't resist but didn't comply either. Liz took the two little girls away from their murdered brother's body and sat with them in a chair on the other side of the room. Holding her daughters, quite possibly for the last time, she tried to comfort Calleigh who was crying uncontrollably, and she held onto Becca who didn't make a sound or shed a tear.

Qudamah walked over to one of the tables and was fumbling with his cell phone. The line had suddenly gone dead after the gunshot. Qudamah tried to call the number again but all he received was a message saying that the phone was off. Kicham looked outside the door and saw that all the other men were there, he stepped over to Qudamah and got his attention. Qudamah put his phone back into the slot on his belt and then stepped out to see his men with Kicham.

"We can move forward now." Qudamah told the seven men standing in front of him. "Rent will no longer be dependable enough to complete the rest of his assignment, so the mother will have to do it. I will go to the house for one last attack against the Americans." He gave a moment for that to sink in. Kicham knew that it was a bold faced lie, but didn't say anything because he knew what his comrade was doing.

"My friend," one of the men spoke up, "we can not allow you to do this, you are too important." Kicham smiled at how easily Qudamah controlled his men.

"Mustafa, this is also too important. I am the leader, this is my plan. I should be the one chosen to complete it." Qudamah told the man.

"Allow me to have that honor in your place." Mustafa said, wanting the glory for himself.

"I can not." Qudamah said after a moment's reflection, though he'd needed no time to reflect on it.

"Please my friend, we need you to continue fighting. We need you to lead us. I am but a soldier, it is my duty." Mustafa argued.

"We do need you brother. Mustafa is right." Kicham played to Qudamah.

"Alright, Allah be with you my friend. Take Ratib and the girls to the house, the mother will stay here with me." Qudamah ordered.

"I haven't finished the last vest yet." Ratib announced.

"Is the one for the house completed?" Kicham asked.

"Yes, but the other one you wanted is not." Ratib told them.

"How long?" Qudamah asked.

"An hour, maybe less."

"Alright, Mustafa take the children..." Qudamah looked in the door to see Liz holding her children, her youngest shying away slightly. "Mustafa, take the oldest one to the house, when Ratib finishes the vest he will take the youngest one." Qudamah didn't want anyone else to know, but he had begun to feel bad for Becca. He'd seen Becca's reactions, he'd even studied them, and though he didn't know why, they were disturbing him on a personal level. "Aziz, Sajid, Esam, and Fida will stay here. We must prepare this building for our departure. Start with the boy's body." Qudamah ordered and the men broke up, each to their respective assignments. Two went to get Dylan's body. Aziz and another man took Liz and Becca back to the room that the children had been kept in. Mustafa and Ratib went about their tasks, Mustafa taking Calleigh from her mother. All that remained outside the door was Qudamah and his faithful friend Kicham.

"What would you like me to do?" Kicham asked.

"We'll take Aziz with us, he will be useful. We'll send the others to the house. Kill Brewer's family, leave them in the Puget

Sound where they will be found like the other two. Then prepare the boat for its journey." Qudamah told him.

"Are you sure you want that many to go to the house?" Kicham asked.

"We cannot escape with all of them, besides the more there are, the bigger the fight they will put up. We already have men there, the FBI will not want an all out battle, and when it does happen, the confusion will allow us to escape up the coast." Qudamah answered.

"Allah be with you my friend." Kicham took his leave.

"Alaikum Salaam." Qudamah replied.

Brewer watched Rent cower on the floor. Brewer's state of mind wasn't any better than Rent's now. He was more sure than ever that his family was dead, the preceding minute or so only served to confirm it that much more. He'd begun to look upon Rent with a slight hope that all was not lost, but clearly that hope had faded with Dylan Austin's life. He watched Rent continue to weep on his knees, his face in his hands.

Cale looked over at the bullet hole in the wall next to his head and for a few seconds he didn't know whether Rent had intended to miss or not. He stepped over to Rent and gently put his hand on his shoulder. He didn't say anything for a long time, waiting for Rent to get it out of his system before he spoke.

"Carey," Cale said gently, "Carey I know it's tough, but we have to worry about the ones that are still alive."

"It's my fault." Rent looked up at the old man. His words prodded at Brewer's mind. "It's my fault."

"You didn't do this thing, you're trying to stop it, don't forget that." Cale said in a gentle tone. Rent nodded and a moment later Cale helped him to his feet. Rent tried to gather himself. He looked down on the floor and saw his gun, which he picked up and placed back in the holster on his belt. He saw the remnants of the phone he had hurled across the room, and realized that there would be no more communication with the terrorists. He could only hope that what he'd done had kept the rest of the family alive, but alive or dead; Rent determined they would be avenged.

"Were you on the closest peer to the lighthouse, or the farthest?" Rent asked Brewer, switching his mind back to business.

"What?" Brewer asked, his concentration taken away from thoughts of his family.

"The boat!" Rent said loudly, showing that he was no longer treating Brewer with kid gloves. "Which peer were you on?"

"I don't know."

"Were there any other peers between you and the lighthouse?" Rent asked, his tone now becoming angry.

"Um, no, no I don't think there were." Brewer responded.

"Were there any other hostages on the boat?" Cale asked.

"No, just us." Brewer responded.

"What if they're not there?" Cale asked Rent.

"Then I'll get somebody to tell me where they are." Rent answered. "Ok Jason, would you know this boat if you saw it?" Brewer didn't respond for a moment, he couldn't think, thoughts of his family had invaded his mind again. "Jason!" Rent finally yelled to bring him back to reality. "Can you show me the boat?"

"I don't know." Brewer said truthfully.

"Well you're gonna." Rent told him. Brewer didn't reply, he went back to the family in his mind.

"How are we going to get there? We've got no transportation and we're hauling around a guy who doesn't exactly blend in now that he's high and beaten to a pulp." Cale looked out a window.

"We'll find transportation." Rent replied, he looked at Brewer who was still bloody and bruised. "Can you walk?" He asked.

"Yeah, I think so." Brewer said. "Whatever you gave me is kicking in now, feels better."

"Good," Rent said, throwing him a towel, "get in there and clean yourself up." Rent looked out the window with Cale. "We're in a bad spot."

"What?" Cale asked. Brewer slowly got off the couch and limped to the bathroom, shutting the door behind him.

"I was sure before, but now I don't know if we're going to be able to do this." Rent told him. Cale frowned at the statement. Rent heard the bathroom door shut. "He's losing it, I don't know if he's going to make it."

"His family is probably dead Carey, I don't know if I'd make it either."

"We have to keep him going long enough to find that boat, it's all we've got left." Rent told the Senator.

The conference room was large and rectangular shaped, in the center was a table that spanned the length of the room and accommodated eight people on each side. The walls of the room were bare and had no windows. On one of the shorter walls was a large screen for presentations, and its opposite side contained the main door to the room. Several FBI agents were already in the room setting up two laptops and two projectors, one projector would allow Bannister to give his presentation. The other projector would be to project an image on one of the longer walls. Outside the room, several more FBI agents and high ranking police officials were gathering.

"Dave, this is Dr. Michael Seacrest." Acting Chief of Police Knox announced. "He's our psychiatrist."

"Yes, we've met." Jackson shook the man's hand. Seacrest was a tall man of thin build, his jet black dyed hair poorly disguised his age. His suit was clean and proper, unlike everyone else's in the hallway. He wore a blue suit, with a red tie, his shoes were shined, and his white shirt blended with the walls of the police station. Seacrest hadn't been in Police Plaza during the bombing, he had been at his office in the North Precinct building, and therefore hadn't seen the carnage.

"It's nice to see you again. How are you holding up today?" Seacrest asked Jackson.

"Good, thanks."

"Doctor, do you know Carey Rent?" Knox asked, the idea hitting her when she found out that Jackson and Seacrest knew each other.

"Not really, as you know, I have to evaluate the mental state of all officers. The last time I saw Rent was after a shooting two years ago." Seacrest told her.

"Do you still have his file Doctor?" Knox asked.

"No, I sent it to the parole board when he went to jail." Seacrest informed.

"I have to ask before we go in here, but did Rent ever see you about any personal issues while he was on the force?" Knox asked.

"No. You know I couldn't discuss it even if he had. Doctor client privilege still applies, even today."

"Is there anything you can tell us about Rent Doctor?" Knox was grasping at straws.

"No, I got the impression that he was one of those guys that doesn't like talking to shrinks." Seacrest told her.

"Thanks Doctor, we're going to need your input in here." She said before an FBI agent opened the door and told them all to come in. Entering, they saw Bannister at the front of the room, conversing with another agent. They sat, Knox next to the head of the table, with Jackson next to her and Seacrest further down the table on the opposite side. All the other chairs soon filled also. Various police Captains, Lieutenants, and FBI agents sat in, along with a representative from the Mayor's office, the Fire Chief, Captain Carrasco the SWAT team commander, and some others.

"Thank you for getting here so quickly everyone. We have a lot to go over and not a lot of time to do it in. Jonathon Pewitt, the President's National Security Advisor will be sitting in on this briefing, we'll put him and his staff on that wall right there." Bannister pointed to the wall where the image of the National Security Advisor was up. "Can you hear me sir?" Bannister asked him.

"Yes Assistant Director, I hear you fine." Pewitt said over the linkup. "Let me just say that the President has been informed about the bombing and his thoughts and prayers are with you all."

"Thank you sir." Knox replied before nodding to Bannister to continue.

"Alright, can we dim the lights please." Bannister said, the lights went down and all that could be seen besides the National Security Advisor was the blank white screen made by Bannister's projector. "Ok, the first thing we need to show you is a video that aired on Al-Jazeera approximately seventy-two hours ago. Roll it please." An agent pressed a button on the laptop, and the image on the screen changed to a man with a turban wrapped around his face. The man began to speak.

"Too long our faithful have sacrificed themselves in Allah's name against the imperial west." The man began confidently in perfect English. "Too many of our brothers and sisters have become martyrs in our war for freedom from tyranny. American soldiers kill our people in our very own native lands, lands that belong not to America, Briton or even us, but lands that belong to Allah. Our soldiers have attacked New York and the Pentagon previously, sacrificing themselves in magnificent displays of loyalty to our cause and to Allah. Our soldiers fight the jihad in Iraq, Palestine, and even in this country. They fight with courage, respect, and impunity. Throughout this America has retaliated with atrocities committed against Islam and its people's. On the surface, America is a strong and courageous empire, they are to be feared by those without

Allah's spirit on their heels, but America cannot win against Allah's soldiers. America's strength shall be rendered useless by their own laws which they claim to hold in such esteem. America's courage will be used against them in a way never before conceived. Today we will use America's courage to bring our jihad to the people of this country. A country that is fighting a war against Allah that it can never win. America's sacrifice will show that no one is safe from Allah's wrath, and that all infidels everywhere will tremble at Allah's reach." When the video finished, the screen changed back to a white screen.

"Immediately after this video aired on Al-Jaseera, it was picked up by all of the American broadcasters and aired here." Bannister briefed. The moment it aired, the National Security Agency began picking up intercepts from Al-Qaeda operatives that had previously refrained from using normal communications modes. Intelligence concludes that this video has caused a stir among Islamic extremists. Al-Qaeda operatives all over the world are now communicating with each other with little or no regard that they're being monitored. We have henceforth gained a lot of information in the last few days.

"The video itself peeked our interest as well. We have long known that in light of our electronic surveillance capabilities, Al-Qaeda has taken to using these televised messages to give orders to it's sleeper agents in the United States and elsewhere. This message is very different from previous messages from Al-Qaeda because we know that Al-Qaeda did not make or send it. The first notable aspect of this video is that it is in English. We think that this is very important because we have speculated that Al-Qaeda would use an English language message to activate their sleeper agents."

"Let me interrupt you one second Mr. Director." The National Security Advisor said. "How many sleeper agents do you believe that this message was supposed to activate?"

"Mr. Secretary We believe that a message originally spoken in English would activate every sleeper agent within the United States. As far as numbers go, we simply don't know how many sleepers there are." Bannister answered before continuing. "Also of significance is this line, 'On the surface, America is a strong and courageous empire'. We believe that this line is the mission code that tells the sleeper agents which assignment to carry out. Before I continue, it's necessary to give you a little more background on this.

"A few years ago, angry over the lack of attacks made in the United States, a small group of Al-Qaeda operatives broke away from the main organization. Because Al-Qaeda concentrates its intelligence gathering capabilities on committing terrorist strikes, we believe that its top leadership has only limited awareness of this splinter sect. Since we monitor as many terrorists as possible, we've gained several pieces of intelligence on this splinter group. First, they work within the Al-Qaeda organization in order to recruit new operatives from within. Second, they are very upset with Al-Qaeda's emphasis on political maneuvering and that it's not waging the war they would like to see. Since these operatives have to lay underground so that they don't get caught by either us or Al-Qaeda, they are notoriously hard to find and monitor, but recent intercepts tell us that they have concentrated on recruiting Al-Qaeda's sleepers within the United States.

"The man that was killed at the Regal Arms Hotel this morning was one Nasir Nidal, a college student at the University of Notre Dame. He doesn't show up on any watch list or in any database. He has no criminal record, and no record of social activism, so I think I can say pretty assuredly that he was a sleeper agent.

"When I arrived in Seattle earlier this week, the FBI was watching a person of interest. Do we have Baday's picture?" A moment later, the picture came on the screen. "This is that person of interest. His name is Kicham Baday, though he generally goes by the alias Kicham Bradley. Intercepts that we have received tell us that Baday is an Al-Qaeda operative whose main job is recruitment of sleeper agents here in the United States.

"To give you a little history on Baday, he is the son of a Moroccan immigrant, he was born in the United States, so he's a citizen, but has traveled to Morocco on many occasions. He also served in the Army, he served as an infantryman in the 82nd Airborne in both Afghanistan and Iraq. We think that it was in one of those two countries that he was recruited to work for Al-Qaeda. Though we don't know how he became involved with this splinter group, recent intercepts indicate that he is a high ranking member. We were going to pick him up yesterday, but he shook his tail, and has been missing ever since. Baday has never been connected with radical Islam before, but we expect that from placed operatives, it's now part of their instructions not to draw attention.

"From the intercepts, and a background check into Baday, we have discovered that the man speaking in the video is one Qudamah Al-Khalifa. Al-Khalifa also has no records of activism, no association with radical Islam and no connection with Al-Qaeda. In fact he's a professor of Psychology at UCLA. We've concluded that he's one of the sleeper agents that the message is directed to. We knew something was strange from the beginning because a message of this type would have been spoken by a member of Al-Qaeda's top command. Possibly Al-Qaeda's leader himself."

"Wait a minute," Pewitt interrupted again, "you're saying that an Al-Qaeda sleeper agent sent orders to all the other Al-Qaeda sleeper agents to begin their mission. Why would he do that?"

"Because we believe that he intends a coup d'etat." Bannister replied.

"Of the United States?" Knox asked.

"Of Al-Qaeda. This splinter group has been positioning their men all over the country. We think that Al-Khalifa is using it to stage a takeover of the organization." Bannister answered.

"So this is a power play?" Pewitt asked.

"Essentially, Al-Khalifa needs to do two things to take command of the organization, first he needs a major terrorist strike inside the United States to show that he's powerful. He also needs the United States to strike back very hard and very violently against the leadership of Al-Qaeda to show that they're weak. Once that is done, we think enough Al-Qaeda operatives and supporters will turn to his side that he can effectively take control. That's where Al-Khalifa's plan comes into play.

"Our recent intercepts have given us great insight into his plan. The sleeper agents are to kidnap the families of how should I say...malleable Americans, and use them to extort terrorist acts out of them. The bombing at Chicago's O'Hare International Airport was committed by a guy named Joe Stinson. Basically he's the son of a lawyer but he himself ended up a bus driver. After he blew himself up at the airport, a briefcase was found with information on him and his family. His family was found alive and well, they were dropped off at a church in south Chicago. We have them sequestered now. The Atlanta underground mall shootings, and the suicide bomber in Utah both had similar circumstances, and their families were also released. We're questioning them now but they aren't able to give us much information. We have determined from documents in a nearby vehicle that the woman who blew up Police Plaza earlier today was a single mother. Her daughter was just dropped off at a church downtown, my agents have her.

"Mr. Director, on the video, Khalifa says that our courage will be used against us, is that what we're seeing?" Pewitt asked.

"Very possibly sir. These strikes are meant to shatter the American spirit."

"I can't believe that someone would even consider something like that, it's lunacy." One of the police Captains said.

"Maybe to you, a successful career cop, but not to somebody who's lost a great deal." Seacrest stopped him.

"Mr. Pewitt, this is Dr. Michael Seacrest, he's the police psychiatrist here in Seattle." Bannister told the National Security Advisor. "Go on Doctor."

"I was just saying that to most people, blowing themselves up or shooting up a mall might seem ridiculous, even to save their family, but there are people out there that will do it. All you need to do is find them, and from what I just heard, this terrorist has a Ph.D. in Psychology, he knows exactly what to look for."

"What is that Doctor?" Knox asked.

"I would look for somebody who has placed hope for the future on their families, someone who has maybe become a failure, or not as successful as they should be, someone who hasn't lived up to their potential. These people tend to place more and more emphasis on their families because they see them as one of the great successes of their lives. That's why it would be risky to use a successful business man, or anybody else who has power and control in their career. While they may love their families, they don't place all of their hopes on them like these others. If you find these people and threaten their families, chances are, they'll do whatever you want."

"What about Rent?" Bannister asked.

"Rent doesn't have any family that I know of. I'll let Sergeant David Jackson take it from here. He was Rent's partner and friend." Knox replied.

"Simply put," Jackson began, "Carey Rent is one of the best cops to have ever put on a badge. He was raised in the Police Department, his father was Chief of Police for five years until he retired, his grandfather was a cop, so was his father, and on down the line. When I say Carey grew up here, I wasn't kidding, he was at the academy practicing self-defense moves as soon as he could walk, he learned his multiplication tables on the firing range. Carey Rent was a cop's cop. He always did whatever it took to get the job done. He still holds the record for most felony arrests by a single detective and he was only on the force for ten years.

"After his parents died, I always thought his hardcore style was because he wanted to get out of his father's shadow, everywhere he went people asked if he was Chief Rent's son. I always felt bad for him like that. He was always trying to prove himself. I think that's what finally did him in. We were working a narcotics related homicide. We liked a local drug kingpin for it but he'd already weaseled out of three indictments, two of them put down by Rent and myself. We had a fingerprint linking him to the crime but it was only a partial and smudged, we weren't sure if it would hold up. When the forensics guys started analyzing it, they discovered that it wasn't the same partial that was originally logged. Internal Affairs came in and got Rent on video surveillance switching the prints in the evidence room.

"Chief Knox used a loophole in the union bylaws to have Rent's delegate pulled during the IAB interview. Apparently that wasn't enough though and she eventually got his union paid lawyer yanked also." If looks could kill, Jackson's stare would have murdered her twice over. "In the end Rent had to settle with a public defender who only managed to get him eighteen months for a rap that he should've been able to plea down to a misdemeanor. Before this afternoon, I hadn't seen him since he went up."

"Do you know of anyone that Al-Khalifa could use as leverage against him?" Bannister asked.

"His parents are dead, he's an only child, he's never been married, no kids." Jackson replied.

"Well I doubt that he's lost it, not today, it's too much to be a coincidence." Bannister said.

"I agree, what Rent said to me in the hotel leads me to think something more is going on." Jackson told them.

"Then we have to find out what kind of leverage they've got on Rent."

"But why Senator Cale?" Knox asked.

"I think I can answer that." Pewitt chimed in. "About a year ago, the NSA intercepted a list of high profile targets, politicians, high profile businessmen in the United States, etcetera. Al-Qaeda sent the list to several of their operatives, presumably so that they could integrate it into an attack such as this. Senator Cale's name was at the top of the list. You see the Middle East sees the President as the great evil, but whenever the American people waiver in the war on terror, it's Senator Cale that pumps them back up. He's seen as America's hero over there. The voice to the President's muscle in the war on terror."

"That's most likely a large part of their plans then, killing Senator Cale would be a great victory for them." Bannister continued.

"There's more to it than that, Senator Cale is the voice of reason in politics. With extremists on both sides of the aisle, the moderate Senator Cale always calms both parties down, that's why his own party chastises him so much." Pewitt said.

"You're talking about when we retaliate?" Bannister asked.

"I don't think he's talking about that." Knox interrupted. "I mean, before we start thinking about retaliation, we need to talk about damage control.

"She's right." Pewitt said.

"Think about it, this is going to hit and hit hard." Knox said. "We have no idea how many of these sleepers are out there kidnaping people. Every wife, daughter and son in America is going to be at risk of either being a hostage or a casualty. Every parent is going to be at risk of becoming a terrorist. Once news of these families hit, the American public will go nuts and there'll be panic in the streets."

"She's right, there'll be fear beyond reason." Seacrest interjected.

"Then we have to contain these families, at least until this is over. Then we can spin it." Bannister determined.

"Can we do that?" Knox asked.

"We'll say we're holding them for questioning, and we'll have to pray that it doesn't leak." Bannister said.

"Very well, I'll brief the President, good luck to all of you." Pewitt concluded the meeting.

Johnny Carson sat in the passenger seat of the older model Ford while he taped his broken hand. The other two members of his

makeshift crew were with him, Manny, the Latino with a large
bruise covering the length of his face, drove and Benny was in the
back seat. The three were driving around Pill Hill looking for Rent,
Brewer and Cale. After Rent had beaten them up, Crystal decided to
take Jas to a hospital, which luckily for Jas, there were plenty of in
Pill Hill. Johnny Carson decided that he wouldn't let Rent's trespass
go unchallenged and thus gone to the hovel he called a home and
gotten his .357 Magnum Revolver, his preferred weapon to deal with
Rent.

"Hey man, I don't think they're here anymore." Manny told
Johnny Carson.

"They aint left yet. Keep drivin'" Was Johnny Carson's only
reply.

"Johnny, man, that guy, he's pretty bad, maybe we should let
this go." Benny said weakly from the back seat, which caused
Johnny Carson to spin around.

"Shut up you wimp! I didn't see your punk ass helping us!"
Johnny Carson yelled at Benny. "When we find that guy he's gonna
see what democracy is with a cap in his ass!"

The crack house smelled like it had been soaked in a mixture
of formaldehyde and month old milk. Rent was accustomed to the

smell, having worked narcotics for years, mostly in the Pill Hill area, but Cale was still having trouble with it. The old Senator wandered over to the window, which he opened. He took in the fresh Seattle air when it rushed inside the first floor apartment they were in. He looked up at the constant gray Seattle sky thinking that it always looked the same, no matter when he came to the city. It was like the sun never penetrated the thick clouds that constantly hung below it. Further outward, to the west, Cale surmised, a single ray of sunlight was barreling through the gray skies.

They had been waiting for Brewer for about ten minutes, during which time they discussed stealing a car to get them to the docks, and how they would search for the boat. First they would find a decent spot to look at the docks. There were plenty of such spots overlooking Ballard docks. Brewer would pick out which boats he thought most resembled the one he had been on, Rent would search the boats one at a time with Brewer and Cale a safe distance away. After the two agreed on this plan, they sat for several minutes in silence, with nothing but the sounds of water running inside the bathroom and the ambient noise of the street flowing past their ears.

"Do you think it will rain?" Cale asked, if for no other reason than to break the silence.

"It's Seattle Senator, it rains every day for at least fifteen minutes, so yeah, it'll probably rain."

"That's why this city is so depressing, the sky's never blue." Cale commented.

"We'd better go." Rent stood up, mostly because he didn't want to hear any more of Cale's musings. He stepped over some trash on the floor to the bathroom door that was off of it's bottom hinge and knocked loudly on it. "Jason let's go buddy, we gotta scoot." Cale turned from the window when there was no reply. Rent banged harder. "Jason, pinch it off, let's go!" Still no reply which irked Rent so he shoved the door open. "Christ!" He flew into the bathroom. Cale ran to the door, tripping over some trash on the way, when he got to the door he found Rent attempting to tourniquet Brewer's right arm.

The distraught young man had used a piece of the broken window to slice open the vein running the length of his leg. He'd also cut his right wrist, and up his right arm. Blood poured from the wounds onto the toilet that Brewer was sitting, from there it flowed to the floor.

Chapter 9:

Cale looked at Brewer's eyes, which had fallen to the back of his head, the once strong youthful man was now pale and weak looking. Rent was still attempting to tourniquet Brewer's arm. Cale stepped into the room and checked the pulse on his neck, there was nothing.

"Carey?" Cale said softly.

"No, damn it, no no no!" Rent yelled.

"Carey?" Cale said again, softly. Rent stopped this time and looked at the Senator. "He's gone." Cale told him.

"Goddamn it!" Rent yelled and threw the towel down on the bloodied floor before stepping out of the room. Cale silently stepped out behind him. After an awkward minute, Cale spoke.

"He must have thought he wouldn't get another opportunity." Cale said, almost whispering. "He knew he wouldn't feel it with the Codeine. After the phone call, he must have just lost it. I can't believe we didn't see it."

"Yeah, well he was just in the next room, how in the hell could we miss it!" Rent yelled at the Senator. "We should've known!" Cale didn't say anything, he stood watching Rent, who was determined to beat up the walls and furniture. Rent collapsed onto the sofa. He obviously didn't know what to do next, and the enormity of the situation was taking its toll on him.

Why wouldn't it? Cale thought. After all, in the course of just a few minutes the terrorists had killed one of their hostages, and Rent's only lead, who himself was a victim of the terrorists, had also died. Death seemed to be permeating Rent. The death of this day was winding its way deep down into Rent's soul, and Cale could tell.

Cale sat down in a chair across from Rent and watched him. Rent saw Cale's gaze and turned to look at Brewer's lifeless body still on the toilet in the bathroom. He stared very hard for several minutes, not deviating his eyes at all. Suddenly Rent stood, the purpose returned to his eyes.

"Let's go." He said forcefully, like a leader should. Cale stood and started out of the apartment with Rent.

"What are we going to do?" Cale asked when they got into the hallway.

"We're going to find that boat." Rent kept walking to the front door of the building.

"That's going to be a little difficult don't you think?" Cale asked.

"It's our only chance." Rent stepped out of the doorway.

Cale didn't say anything. Wherever Rent seemed to be going, Cale seemed to be following at this point. He knew he'd crossed the point of no return and he was in this until it was finished now.

Rent eyed an older model Toyota that was parked across the street, it seemed suitable for him to steal, or borrow as Rent would have said it. Rent looked up and down the street, seeing a few pedestrians and more than a few cars traversing the passageway. Rent decided he didn't have time to pick and choose his choices of transportation. He turned to Cale and pointed to the car they were going to take. Cale acknowledged Rent's objective, though he didn't agree with stealing a car. All he could think of is how it would be used against him on a pundit's news show one day. They would call him the Senator who stole cars because video games had corrupted him. The thought gave him a slight laugh, which he sorely needed at the moment. He thought of how he would spin it by saying that it was alright because the car was foreign made. He chuckled a little more, but his mood changed drastically when he saw the Ford break out of traffic and speed toward Rent when he started to cross the street.

Rent jumped back onto the sidewalk, using his arms to push Cale back with such force that Cale was almost knocked over. Cale was reclaiming his balance when the mysterious car stopped a few feet past Rent and the two front doors opened, with one back door opening a moment after the first two. Rent recognized the large

Latino who stepped out of the driver's seat. He saw Johnny Carson step out of the passenger front seat, walking toward him. Rent started to meet Johnny Carson half way, with Cale right behind him. Benny stepped out of the back seat and was following his leader.

No words were exchanged, no warnings issued, no declarations formed. Cale was astonished at how quickly the situation unfolded. Johnny Carson raised his weapon, it was a very large revolver with chrome plating. Cale didn't even see it until it had cleared Johnny Carson's chest. Cale thought it was odd that Johnny Carson was holding it sideways, but he'd seen in movies that was how they were doing it now. Rent most likely saw the weapon the moment it was produced because he instinctively drew his own. Apparently Rent was much quicker on the draw than Johnny Carson because by the time that Johnny Carson got his weapon to eye level, Rent had already drawn, aimed, and fired a round into Johnny Carson's head. Johnny Carson flew back into Benny and the two went down onto the street. Benny became hysterical, which Cale surmised was a natural reaction to the guy walking in front of him getting shot and his dead body knocking him to the ground. Benny rolled Johnny Carson off him and took off down the street. Rent didn't even break stride, the instant he fired the shot at Johnny Carson, he switched his aim to the Latino driver. He didn't even wait to see if he'd hit, he knew he had. Manny raised his hands and stepped over to the sidewalk. Rent followed him with the aim of his pistol while he approached the open driver's side door.

"Look Senator, fate has provided us transportation." Rent commented flatly.

"Great, it's American made, there goes that excuse." Cale said with sarcasm, getting into the car.

"Meanwhile at the Hall of Justice," Owens muttered to himself in a deep voice. He saw all of the people filing out of the conference room, "Superman breaks up yet another catfight between Wonder Woman and Batman." He saw Knox take Jackson aside in the hallway. Owens walked over to them and stood next to his partner.

"You're finished with this." Knox told Jackson.

"What?" Jackson returned.

"You've given your input, it was helpful. Now I want you to return to patrol." Knox ordered.

"Aren't you putting a team together to help Bannister?" Jackson asked her.

"I am, but you won't be on it." Knox answered.

"Nobody knows Carey Rent better than I do, we need to be there." Jackson argued.

"That might be true, but you've definitely got a conflict of interests with it. It's going to be like I told you before, you're out. I want you patrolling the Fremont district, we need more officers down there anyway."

"Tell me you're going to cancel that."

"That's up to the Mayor, and until he does, we secure the festival." Knox told him.

"Just like that?" Jackson asked rhetorically.

"Just like that." Knox returned. "Dave take the patrol, chill out, your partner shot somebody this afternoon. He should be on leave right now but I need every cop I can get, you both were in an explosion, all of our emotions are running high. Go down to the festival, get a hot dog or one of those pastry things with the powdered sugar and try to forget this okay? We're on it." She walked off. Jackson let slip a glare at Bannister who was talking to some of his agents, he looked up at Jackson, then looked away.

"Where to chief?" Owens asked Jackson.

"Patrolling Fremont." Jackson replied dryly.

"Ah man!" Owens blurted. "The hippy convention?"

After finishing his wiring, Ratib turned the vest over on the table, he flipped the switch on the small metal box that was located over the left breast of the vest. The volt meter jumped up, and he flipped the switch back before disconnecting the volt meter from the vest. Ratib sipped on a cup of tea and put his equipment away. He ran his fingers over the vest one last time and said a prayer for whoever would be wearing it.

"Is it finished?" Qudamah asked politely from the doorway.

"I'm just putting my things away." Ratib responded.

"Leave them, you will not need them." Qudamah told him. "Walk with me." Ratib set his things down and stepped out of the doorway into the long hallway with his leader. "Are you prepared for what is coming?" Qudamah asked.

"I am, I have been waiting for this for a very long time." Ratib told him.

"We are on the cusp of a new era my friend." Qudamah told him, they were walking down a set of stairs. "Soon our brothers will rise up with us and cast off the imperialists. Allah is going to be very proud of you."

"I am ready for this fight." Ratib assured Qudamah. "All of us are with you, the others were cowards for not using us. We are happy about what we will be doing."

"Kill as many as you can." Qudamah told him with a smile. He opened the door to the room where Liz and Becca huddled in a corner. Qudamah nodded to Ratib who entered the room and grabbed Becca from her mother's arms. Liz screamed and begged for him to stop but Ratib ignored her. He took the little girl, sat her on a table, and bound her hands and mouth with tape.

"Quiet." Qudamah ordered Liz. Ratib took the unresponsive Becca into his arms and walked out the door.

"Please don't take her, please don't." Liz cried, but the two men ignored her. They exchanged prayers with one another, hugged, and Ratib carried Liz's youngest daughter off. "Why are you doing this?" Liz asked with an angry tone. Qudamah almost closed the door, but stopped with her question. He opened the door wide and stepped into the small room.

"I do not believe you would understand." He told her.

"I'll give you anything you want." Liz looked up at him from the floor.

"I do not want that." Qudamah answered.

"Then what?"

"America is our enemy. We must strike our enemy." Qudamah answered.

"Those little girls are not your enemy! My Dylan was not your enemy!" Liz shouted at him angrily.

"Our children have perished also. Do not forget that." Qudamah said calmly.

"What are you going to do with them?" She asked, Qudamah didn't respond, he stared at his hostage and frowned, the look on his face conveying the meaning that he refused to speak aloud. "Please no, take me, I'll do whatever you want, take me."

Qudamah's gaze brought her to tears.

"That time may come also." Qudamah stepped into the hallway and grabbed the door. "You may pray for them." He slammed the door closed.

"Yes I understand that Mr. Mayor but we're under attack, and I can't guarantee safety at the concert." Knox said into the telephone. Bannister and Seacrest stood watching her attempt to talk the Mayor into cancelling the last night of the Fremont festival.

"I understand your concerns, I really do." The Mayor reiterated over the telephone. "But the fact is that we can't allow this city or our nation to be terrorized. If we cancel the concert it will show the terrorists that they've won and I can't in good conscience allow that."

"And what happens if they decide to attack the concert?" Knox asked.

"Then you'll have your people there, emergency services will be on hand."

"Mr. Mayor, Terry Bannister, the Assistant Director of the FBI in charge of this situation contends that the concert is a very real target. There is absolutely no way we can guarantee that it will be safe. Sir, I'm urging you, the FBI is urging you, and if necessary, the federal government will back us up on this, we must cancel the last day of the festival."

"Ms. Knox, my answer remains no." The Mayor stated emphatically. "To cancel the concert now will only encourage more terrorist attacks, it will show that we have been hurt by terrorism, and that we're terrorized. I will not do that. Now I've received the briefing you got and I am convinced that between the Seattle Police Department and the FBI, we can bring an end to this situation. However, unless something else happens or you bring me definitive proof of a direct threat against the concert tonight, it will go ahead. Do you have definitive proof?"

"No Mr. Mayor, we do not." Knox was forced to answer.

"Then I'll thank you to get back to work."

"Yes Mr. Mayor, thank you." Knox hung up the phone.

"How many officer's do you have scheduled to work that concert?" Bannister asked.

"I'm not sure yet, but I think we should double it. We'll also have the Seattle Center's private security there." Knox replied.

"It's a perfect target." Seacrest told them. "There's no way the Mayor will cancel it?"

"Not a chance, he says that it will only encourage more attacks."

"He could be right, the more damage they see done, the more it will inspire them." Seacrest told the two.

"It's a line of thought, Washington's going through the same thing now. When to reopen the airports, which events to cancel, that sort of thing. They are hard decisions." Bannister said. "We have to trust that good people are making them."

"Yeah well the Mayor's a politician, he always has been, and now he's gotta be seeing this as the opportunity of his political career."

"The Rudy Giuliani syndrome?" Seacrest asked.

"Yeah, he probably sees himself leading Seattle confidently out of this crisis just like Rudy led New York after September 11th." Bannister answered.

"That's great, but he's doing exactly nil to help us find our missing Senator, or any of the terrorist sleeper agents." Knox added.

After taking a long route to the docks in an effort to avoid attention after Johnny Carson's shooting, Rent and Cale abandoned the old Ford in an area it wasn't likely to be found for quite some time. From there they walked the quarter mile to the docks. They stood on a hill overlooking the Ballard Marina. Looking down at the Puget Sound and the large number of boats anchored at the marina, Rent thought about which way was best to go about searching for his mystery ship. Cale gazed at the enormous view with a slight twinge of gratitude that he was still around to see it.

The hill they were on was slightly east of the marina, looking down, one could clearly see boats of various shapes and sizes. There were a dozen piers, each with at least two dozen boats, mostly fishing boats that were no longer in use because of a recent decline in Seattle's fishing industry. Beyond the docks lay the Puget Sound, a wide open body of water sandwiched between Seattle and Bainbridge Island, the barrier that led to the Pacific Ocean. The water was a beautiful shade of blue, sparkling in the late afternoon sun that was poking through the thick cloud cover on the horizon.

To the south sat the small peninsula that housed Discovery Park. Until a few years before, Discovery Park had been a National Guard training area. Long since abandoned, the only activity that ever occurred in Discovery Park was training conducted by various police departments and workers that drove through the park to get to the lighthouse and the sewage treatment plant whose buildings ran along the northern side of the peninsula. Around the lighthouse was a large bank of steep rocks which eventually transformed into the thick green grass that surrounded the lighthouse and the sewage treatment plant.

"Here it is Senator." Rent told the old man with him.

"Carey, how do we find this boat, we have only a color to go on?" Cale asked.

"We'll find it the same way we found Brewer." Rent began

to step down the dirt path leading down the steep hill. Cale followed, carefully watching his step.

Liz Austin stood alone in the small room in which her captor had left her. She wanted to cry for her children but she seemed to have run out of tears. Not knowing what else she could do, she stood with her back to the wall, hoping in vein for a miracle. Thus far this had been the most intense and frightening day of her life, and she searched her mind for options. Because she was a mother, she wanted to save her children, she wanted to grieve for the loss of her son, but she was also a human being and her terror had frozen her mind. She had to concentrate just to breathe. After a methodical search of her mind, she decided that she would make the only appeal left to her. Liz silently got onto her knees, she sat her rear back onto her calves, interlocked her fingers in front of her, closed her eyes and bowed her head.

Lord? Lord are you there? Please hear me Lord. I don't know who else to turn to. Please Lord, protect Dylan, I know that he's up there with you holding your hand right now. Lord, I know that you'll protect him, I know you love him. Please Lord take my husband Lewis, he loved you Lord, and I know he was a good man. I know you'll take care of them both. Lord I know you have a plan, and I know that I shouldn't doubt that plan, but I can't help but miss my little boy, I can't help but worry about my little girls. Lord, I know you do these things for a reason, I know that you love us, I know that no matter what happens, you'll be there for us. I know these things Lord, but I'm scared, I'm scared for my little girls, I'm scared that these evil men are going to kill us all, and I'm scared that there won't be anything I can do about it.

I know that anything is possible, I know that your will be done Lord, but my little girls, they're so precious, they're so innocent. I love them with all my heart, I love them as I love you Lord, and whatever I've done to deserve this Lord, they don't, they're so precious, they're so innocent. They don't deserve this fate, they don't deserve to become victims like this. Please Lord, I know that whatever happens is for the best Lord, I do trust in you and I do believe that you are our savior. They believe too Lord and I know I shouldn't ask, but please help them. Please deliver them from this evil. Lord please send them an angel of your mercy. If it's necessary that you take someone Lord, take me. I deserve that. I gladly offer myself up to you on their behalf. I praise your name for whatever you have already decided Lord, but please, if you have to take someone, take me instead. I beg you Lord, just spare my little girls. I know you'll look over them with your great wisdom and I know that you'll keep them in your heart as they keep you in theirs. Please protect them Lord, please show them your light. Amen.

When she finished, Liz slipped into unconsciousness and fell to the floor.

Ratib parked his car about a block away from the walled-in house that he was going to. He noticed that Becca sat through the ride in the back seat of the car in silence, he hadn't even seen her turn her head to look out the window at the passing scenery. She hadn't cried, she hadn't fought, Ratib didn't even believe he'd seen her blink, though he knew that blinking was an involuntary response and she would do such a thing whether or not she wanted to. Still, he hadn't seen it. He parked on the side of the street and got out of the vehicle first to make sure no one was around. Even though it was midday, he was on a rather secluded street just off the main road where many business were and didn't see any pedestrians in view, nor were there any cars traveling down this particular street.

When he was sure that the coast was clear, he opened the back door of the car and noticed that Becca had freed her hands from the tape that bound them. She also removed her seatbelt which had been carefully placed over her lap. Ratib wondered how the little girl freed her hands, but she turned her head to look at him and caught his attention with her innocent charm. When she looked into his eyes she smiled through the tape that was still over her mouth and held both her arms straight out in front of her signaling that she wished to be carried by the strange man that had been her chauffeur. Taken aback by the cuteness of her behavior, Ratib instinctively reached into the vehicle and picked her up. The little girl wrapped her hands around his neck with affection.

They walked up the street to the gate of the wall that surrounded the house. On the way, Becca removed one arm and pointed to the sky. Ratib took her cue and looked up to see the sun breaking strongly through an empty patch of cloud filled sky. Succumbing to his fatherly instinct, Ratib smiled at the little girl and tickled her nose with his finger. She responded by placing her arm back around Ratib's neck and holding it tightly.

The gate Ratib was to use to enter the large tree studded yard of the house was guarded by a control panel with a digital screen. The process to get past this was simple, Ratib would select from a menu on the display screen that he wanted to enter the gate. He would enter the key code followed by pressing the star button. After that the gate would open and he would enter.

When he got to the small square panel that was at eye level on the wall next to the gate, he noticed that the glare from the sun was making the light blue words on the display screen all but invisible. Ratib marveled at the fact that one single ray of light, peeking through the clouds, happened to be preventing him from seeing the screen. This problem didn't matter to him since he knew the process by heart. He pressed the menu button, hit the numeral 1, and entered the key code followed by the star button. He reached for the gate but it failed to open. He tried the process again, but again the lights on the screen blended with the sunlight and again the gate didn't open. He attempted to block the sun's rays with his free hand while using one of his fingers to press the appropriate buttons but when he couldn't reach the star key in time the gate failed to open.

Becoming frustrated he placed the little girl on her feet beside him and used his left hand to cover the screen while he entered the appropriate code. Again the gate failed to open. Again he tried to read the screen but again the gate didn't unlock. After two more tries he finally heard the low metallic buzzing he was looking for and the gate unlatched. Not wanting the gate to relock, he quickly shoved it open with his foot. Using his foot to keep the gate from closing, he turned to grab Becca but found that she was gone.

Chapter 10:

Knox stood, staring in awe at the piece of paper in front of her. What she was looking at was a casualty list from the bombing of Police Plaza. The number of dead was huge, the number of wounded was three times the number of dead, and the number of people still unaccounted for was almost equal to the number of dead.

"Search crews are still combing through the collapsed area, but almost half the building came down. I have to tell you that they don't hold much hope." The officer standing next to her informed.

"Do the press have these numbers yet?" Knox asked.

"Not yet, but they will. All they're doing now is speculating and with the other bombings, I'm afraid the press is going with the worst of that speculation." The officer replied.

"Far be it from the press to ever be on our side." Knox said sarcastically. "You can go ahead and give these numbers out to them but make sure they know that they're preliminary numbers and we won't have anything definite for quite some time. Maybe if we give them something, they'll calm down a bit."

"I doubt it." The officer responded.

"Chief?" Another officer said to get Knox's attention. "Director Bannister needs you in the conference room, something's happening." The officer told her. Knox left the large first floor office where the Seattle P.D. had set up a makeshift command center, and stepped up the flight of stairs to the conference room where the FBI had set up their own command center. When she entered the room she noticed that it was completely different than the room she had previously had her briefing in. Adorning the once clear walls were maps of every type, Seattle, Atlanta, New York, Los Angeles, and the United States were up on the walls. The once empty conference table was filled with laptop computers which spit wires in every direction. Lining the side of the long walls were several thirty-two inch televisions, each set to a different news channel, that wall's opposite was newly decorated with fax machines and copiers.

The room was awash with activity, FBI agents wearing white shirts and black ties moved about it in a sort of controlled mayhem, asking questions of their peers, taking freshly printed sheets off of copiers, typing on their laptops. The far end of the room remained silent while Bannister talked into the conference call box that was a permanent part of the table. Knox made her way over to Bannister and the three agents listening to the man on the box. She knew better than to interrupt what was going on. She stood and listened.

"We think they have AK-47's, maybe some explosives, we really aren't sure at this point." The voice on the box was saying when Knox came into earshot. "They appear to want to negotiate, so we think that there may be a chance to bring at least some of them out alive. They've said that they have a list of demands but that they'll only deliver them to a live person. We're preparing to send in the negotiator now."

"Who do you have down there?" Bannister asked the black box on the table.

"Brandon Brummett, he flew down with the task force this morning." The box responded.

"He's a good man but keep a safety on him, I don't want them doing anything stupid." Bannister ordered.

"We've got three sniper teams in good positions. If we think they're gonna go south we'll keep him protected, hold on, let me prep him." The box said, Bannister looked up at Knox.

"What's going on?" Knox asked, knowing that it was now an appropriate time.

"We got a lead on the cell that was responsible for the Atlanta attack. We tracked them to a farmhouse about thirty miles east of the city, now they're holed up with the family that lives there as hostages. We think there could be four kids plus the parents in that house." Bannister said, summing up the situation. "We have a Hostage Rescue Team about to go in but if we can talk them out that's what we're going to do."

"You think that what happens in Atlanta is a precursor to when we find the cell here?" Knox asked, summing up why she was summoned.

"Except we don't have a Hostage Rescue Team relatively close to here." Bannister confirmed.

"Our SWAT can do it. We have the best in the country behind Los Angeles."

"I'd prefer our guys." Bannister told her. The voice came back on the black box.

"Ok, he's approaching the house. We've got a micro-transmitter on him. We're going to pipe it through to you, give us a second." Bannister and Knox listened with anticipation. Static came through the box, followed by a new voice.

"Base, can you hear me?" The voice said.

"Loud and clear Brandon, you're good to go." The first voice replied.

"Ok, here goes." Brummett said, everyone listening heard the sound of feet stepping on wooden steps.

"Stop where you are?" A voice said. "Are you FBI?"

"Yes." Brummett replied. "I'm a negotiator for the FBI, I'm here to accept your demands and see what we can do about them."

"We have a prepared statement, we assume your people are listening." The voice said. Bannister felt a tingle edge up his spine, he hadn't expected this maneuver.

"Yes they are." Brummett replied, but got nothing back.

"Sir!" One of the FBI agents in the room yelled to Bannister. Bannister almost snapped his own neck he turned his head so fast. Almost all of the news channels on the televisions were now switching to a special report about the standoff in Atlanta.

"They're talking to the press." Knox observed.

"Dees, I thought you were jamming all wireless communication from that house." Bannister said into the box.

"We are!" Special Agent in Charge Paul Dees replied. "We don't know how they're transmitting."

"All the channels have them on now, and most have a visual on the house." Knox watched the televisions.

"We have attacked the United States with just cause for America's atrocities in Palestine, Saudi Arabia, Kuwait, Iraq and Afghanistan." The voice proclaimed over the linkup between Brummett and the black box and also the group of television sets.

"If they talk about the families we're screwed." Bannister said under his breath.

"The American people will curse us for what we are doing but by bringing the jihad to the American people we will expose the atrocities committed by the imperialists of the west. In the time to come America will bow to Allah's will. Now the American people will see the power of Allah." The message ended, Bannister noted that there were no demands contained within it.

"Something's going on inside the hou..." Brummett's line went dead.

"What was that?" Bannister asked, but got no reply.

"Holy God!" Knox watched a huge fireball rise from the now shattered house on the televisions.

"Oh my God, it's gone, the entire house is gone!" Special Agent Dees yelled over the link-up. "It just exploded!"

"On national television too." Bannister added. "Dees, get in there now, I wanna know if there are survivors!"

"No sir, I'm here, nobody could've survived that!" Dees told him.

"Then get in there and find out what the hell happened!" Bannister yelled into the box and shut it off. "This is getting completely out of hand!"

Ratib let the gate slam shut behind him and ran a few feet down the street. He knew that the little girl couldn't have gone far, but she was nowhere in sight. After a few seconds of scanning with his eyes, he began to check between the cars parked up and down the short street. With every second that passed without discovering Becca's whereabouts, Ratib grew more and more nervous. Finally, he spotted the girl at the top of the street, crossing over it to the other side and running as fast as her little legs would take her. She ran around a building and into the business section of the area. Ratib scrambled across the street with the speed of an Olympic athlete and rounded the building a few seconds later only to find that the girl had disappeared again.

"Here you go boss." Owens handed Jackson a hot dog. The pair were now on Fremont street where the annual Fremont Festival was in its last day. The Fremont Festival is an annual event whose official name is the Summer Solstice Pageant. Seattlites commonly refer to the event as the Fremont Festival because it occurs for one week during the summer on Fremont Street. Others, like Jesse Owens refer to it as "Hippy Fest" because the event celebrates pagan rituals for the summer solstice. The festival begins with a parade down Fremont Street that ends at a place called Gasworks Park, the park is special to the festival because of the huge sundial that was constructed there.

During the festival, vendors, entertainers, and various citizens contribute by setting up shops to sell tie-dyed clothing, cheap homemade jewelry, all kinds of food and other diversified cultural nicknacks. Some walk around naked and covered head to toe in extensive paint like the human tigress that Owens was currently staring at. Some wear makeup and costumes, such as the grim-reaper, or Native American garb. Others prefer to make-up their automobiles, one even had a large stone water fountain attached to its trunk. Most people attend the festival for the friendly atmosphere and intellectual conversations that often take place in the area.

Owens hated what he referred to each year as "Hippy Detail." He couldn't stand the people in the Fremont area, which he considered to be more communist than American. He did partake in the food though, he could never turn down a Fremont Festival hotdog, probably because it was three times the size of a normal hotdog and came with the option of being wrapped in bacon. Jackson, on the other hand, didn't care either way about being on "Hippy Detail" except that he didn't want to be on it today. He took a bite out of his super-sized dog–Owens had not had it wrapped in bacon–just before dumping the bulk of it into a trash container.

"Hey, that was five bucks!" Owens said.

"Then perhaps you should have asked me if I wanted one before you bought it." Jackson replied and started walking, Owens, as usual, had to work to keep up.

"Hey, can I ask you a question?" Owens said a few steps after finishing off his bacon wrapped dog.

"No." Was Jackson's flat reply.

"Well I got this itchy burning sensation in my johnson and well it started just after last week when I went to see your wife." Owens told him in his usual joking manner.

"Doesn't it bother you that this city is under attack and we're down here babysitting these loons?" Jackson asked, ignoring his partner's statement.

"Nah, I been shot at and blown up already today. I figure I done my part, stick a fork in me, I'm done." Owens replied. "Besides, back to my little problem, I had it once before, but I got some meds for it, even got your missus some. But now it's come back again..."

"Yeah well my friend is out there in this and I should be trying to find him and bring him in." Jackson said, his own words turning him angry.

"I was thinking," Owens simply continued, "maybe she got it from you, then gave it to me the first time."

"I can't believe Knox sent me out here to this, it's the most insulting thing I've ever done." Jackson kept telling his partner while completely ignoring him.

"I got her the meds, she got rid of it, but here we are all with it again? I think maybe you was the one giving it to us, and you gave it back to us after we got rid of it. That happened to that one guy working the desk, what's his name...Rivera." Owens concluded.

"She shipped me out because I'm not a 'yes' man. That aint

gonna cut it!" Jackson said angrily.

"Remember him? He was banging some rookie's wife, the rookie gave the wife the clap, the wife gave it to Rivera, Rivera got rodded, got the meds, shared them with the wife, then the rookie gave it back to the wife who gave it back to Rivera. That's messed up. Maybe you should get checked out, does it burn when you piss?" Owens asked but got no reply from his partner who kept walking. "Where are we going?"

"To the car, I'm not going to be her lapdog anymore." Jackson told him.

"Oh I get it, we're playing ring around the rosie with the STD's. That's cool, the wife likes it like that right?"

Ratib looked inside buildings, under and around parked cars, he even looked for anyone who noticed the little girl and might have stopped her, but she was gone again. Ratib wrenched his way down the street searching every area he thought she could hide. He knew her short legs couldn't take her far.

Ratib finally spotted her across the street. An automatic door opened for her, and Becca ran into a large mall which took up a whole city block. Ratib prayed that none of the people who passed Becca noticed the tape covering her mouth, and none did. Most didn't even see the short little girl, others ignored her, too self-absorbed by talking on their cell phones, or to their companions or working on their PDA's to notice one child running around. Ratib crossed the street without looking and narrowly missed a speeding car. When he reached the automatic door, he took the six or seven steps inside the doorway all at once and stopped to take a long look around to try to pick the little girl up again but again she had disappeared.

The cabin door flung open and Rent moved in, quickly scanning the interior of the boat he was on. He saw red carpet, a television, a sink, stove, some counters, a sofa and some chairs all packed into the tight little room on the boat. There was trash in the waste bucket and some dirty silverware in the sink but no terrorists and no sign of anyone at all. A look of disgust swept over Rent's face. He lowered the pistol he had pointed out in front of him. He took the few steps necessary to get back to the cabin door and exited the boat where he found Cale on the small patio deck that was just behind the door.

"I thought I told you to stay on the pier?" He asked the old Senator.

"I got bored." Cale responded sarcastically.

"That was thirty seconds ago." Rent replied.

"I have ADD."

"Alright, what's next?" Rent asked.

"There is no next. We've checked every boat that is even reasonably similar to the one Brewer described and nothing. Maybe we got the wrong place?" Cale told him.

"What about that one over there?" Rent said, pointing to a boat further down the pier.

"We checked it already, didn't you notice that the last three we checked weren't even blue?" Cale asked.

"This is useless." Rent sat down on the padded seat behind him. "What about that one?" Rent said pointing to a blue shape that was moving across the Puget Sound.

"It looks like it's coming this way, maybe." Cale strained his eyes to see the boat in the distance. "We've got a few minutes until it gets here."

"Yeah." Rent took out a pack of cigarettes. "Somebody left these things out. I thought I'd take'em off their hands." Rent said with a smirk, removing a cigarette from the pack and lighting it with the lighter he also liberated with the tobacco. He held the pack out for Cale who almost protested but decided to have one anyway. Once the cigarette was in Cale's mouth, Rent tossed him the lighter.

"The last time I had one of these, Reagan was in office." Cale said after coughing out some smoke. "What about you?"

"Only when I'm drinking." Rent replied.

"You said you were a cop earlier, but you also said you were a felon, which is it?" Cale prodded a little to start off the conversation. The sun was arching in the sky now, or would be if the clouds didn't obscure it and light was just barely beginning to fade, which made the breeze slightly stronger and the air a little colder.

"Both," Rent replied, "it's amazing how fast your friends can turn on you."

"You don't have to tell me, I'm a Republican." Cale said with a slight laugh. "If I don't tow the party line exactly the way they want, they turn like wild dogs. It would be funny if it weren't so sad. One day I'm one of their most respected Senators, the next they're telling people that I throw kittens into woodchippers for fun."

"You know, you don't strike me as a politician, you remind me more of a stand up comedian, what with that sense of humor and all." Rent observed.

"I wish I'd done that instead sometimes. Not all of us are the uptight pinheads we seem to be. I'll give you one thing though; all a politician consists of is a schmuck and an expensive suit. Sometimes I wonder why I even got into this business." Cale returned. "What's your story?"

"Nothing special." Rent said before taking a tote off his

cigarette. "I was trying to take down a drug dealer. I wasn't sure we were going to get a match from a partial we recovered off a weapon used to kill a cooperating witness, so I switched it with a better one. The courts took offense."

"They tend to with little things like that." Cale told him.

"Yeah, I know." Rent laid back and propped one of his legs up on the cushion. "My dad was Chief here you know...heh...he'd turn over in his grave if he knew what I'd done. I ruined everything in my life."

"That's not so uncommon, good thing is, your life isn't over yet." Cale said, understanding Rent's grief.

"All I ever knew how to be was a cop, kinda difficult to be anything else." Rent took a puff from his cigarette.

"So who are the Austins?" Cale asked, the thought just hitting him.

"You wouldn't believe me if I told you." Rent replied.

"Try me."

"I haven't seen Liz Austin in at least five years," Rent sat back up and took another puff, "ten years ago, Liz and I were engaged." Rent's speech slowed. His mind was flooded with memories. "God, how I loved her, we would sit up all night just holding each other and talking. We would finish each other's sentences. I'd never in a million years thought I'd find somebody that fit me like she did." He smiled at the thought. His smile quickly faded and he continued on. "But I was a rookie cop, everywhere I went people expected me to be my dad. I guess I wanted to just be me. So I worked a lot of overtime, I came home late, then left again early in the morning to get back to it. I thought I was doing everything right, but before I knew it, she'd fallen in love with somebody else." Rent stopped and let slip a sarcastic chuckle. "Another cop no less and to add insult to injury; he wasn't even a bad guy. You know, I don't even know the name of her youngest kid? I heard that she had a third one but I've never heard what the kid's name is."

"I know what you mean, my first wife left me while I was a POW in Nam'." Cale confided.

"The worst part of it was when that feeling set in, you know the feeling where you know you've screwed everything up and there's no way to salvage it. It hit me like a truck. Suddenly everything reminded me of Liz, everything was something else that I couldn't talk to her about, something I couldn't share with her. Nothing took that feeling away and believe me I tried it all, alcohol, other women, hobbies like building model airplanes, or hunting. I even tried therapy, but all those guys ever did was give me pills."

"Let me guess," Cale asked, "no pill can cure a broken heart?"

"Nope, but you know what did it for me? Work. Everyday I went back to work just a little more dedicated, just a little meaner.

Getting the bad guy was all I cared about, it was all I lived for. I used excessive force to apprehend suspects, I intimidated witnesses, I lied to get search warrants, I did it all. I guess when I decided to move up to planting evidence that was when all those sins hit me head on." Rent laid back down on the seat and flicked his cigarette out into the water. "I got so wrapped up in what I was doing that I forgot why I was supposed to be doing it."

"That happens to us all at one time or another." Cale told him.

"Then there's this." Rent continued, no longer responding to Cale. "These people, they didn't pick Liz because of Liz, they picked her because of me. Somehow they knew that I'd still die for her and that's why they picked her. They knew they could get to me and because I have that weakness, her husband and son are dead." Rent gazed out into the cloud filled sky. "Everything that's happening today is my fault. Either because I loved her, or because I screwed my career up, or maybe both, but she's in this mess because of me." Cale listened, he no longer felt the need to interject, instead he thought that it would be better if Rent got it off his chest. "I've let everyone down. I let Liz down all those years ago. I let my parents down by the type of cop I became. I let the force down by what I did. I even let the people who I swore my oath to down. You know, I thought that if I could only get Liz and her kids back, if I could only save them, then all the wrongs of my life might be made right. But now I've screwed that up too. If I hadn't done what I did, that little boy would still be alive."

"You didn't kill him." Cale finally responded. "You did everything you could to save him and you can still make things right. Now's not the time to talk like that. Now's the time to finish the job."

"Yeah." Rent wiped his eyes. "Hey, they're pulling in." Both men lowered themselves just in case the people on the new boat that was pulling into the last spot on the pier saw them. Once the boat was fully in and tied down, Rent and Cale saw a large black man emerge from inside of the vessel along with two Arabic looking men and one younger looking white man. The black man and Arabic men picked up very large gas containers and stepped off of the boat leaving only the white man onboard. Rent and Cale lowered themselves out of sight while the men walked down the pier with the gas cans.

"That's our boat." Rent said, after the men had passed.

"How can you be sure?" Cale asked.

"Cause that's the waste of oxygen who drove my cab this morning."

"But what are they carrying." Cale asked.

"Gas cans, they must be going to get fuel. I think they mean to escape in that boat."

"The fuel station is on the other side of the docks, why carry them so far?"

"Cameras." Rent speculated. "They had a real problem with people stealing gas a few years ago, so they monitor the pumps with cameras now. They must not want us to have a picture of the boat they mean to leave the country in."

"In that thing?" Cale asked.

"A boat's a boat, it's an easy jaunt up the coast to Canada, from there they could disappear." Rent whispered back. "We gotta get onboard. Go get his attention."

Becca used the mall for her very own playground. Like any other child playing hide-and-go-seek, she hid behind furniture, pillars, signs, sometimes even people to traverse one end of the mall to the other. Ratib continued to pursue her with the vigor of a true believer, though Becca didn't make this easy. Ratib would catch sight of her only for her to run off and disappear again a few seconds later. Ratib's luck with no one noticing the tape on her mouth didn't last long, several mall patrons observed it and contacted mall security. After a few minutes every security guard in the mall was looking for the phantom child that had been reported by stores and patrons all over the shopping center, yet was never really seen.

Becca had come to make it a game, gaining a little more

confidence each time she eluded another person who chased after her or tried to grab her. Once, two mall security guards ran right past her, within a mere foot or two when she hid behind a medium sized planter.

She was forced into several clothing stores by her pursuers, where she used long racks of clothing to hide herself until she could make an escape. She even hid from them underneath a bench where a blind woman was sitting. She marveled at how cute the German Shepherd seeing eye dog was so she petted him for a few seconds before disappearing again when she saw Ratib.

Ratib finally caught a long glimpse of the girl on the opposite side of the mall from which they entered. His problem was that she was now exiting another pair of sliding glass doors and running outdoors once again. Ratib took off at a sprint after her but by the time he cleared the doors, he found that the girl was once again no longer in sight. Ratib began searching the large parking lot that was only half full of cars.

"Three?" Knox asked in surprise. "What do you mean we're only sending three?"

"The festival committee was paying for the security at the concert themselves." The police Captain told her. "They had scheduled fifteen off duty officers to be there but since we've gone to terror alert level 1, there are no off duty officers."

"Well we can't leave it like that." Knox told the Captain. "Seattle center is huge, and we have to expect more terrorist strikes, since the mayor won't cancel the festival we're going to have to provide the officers ourselves." The Captain nodded at Knox's orders. "Pull them from different areas, that should keep our presence about the same."

"There is something else." The Captain told her. "Since the bombing, we've seen all sorts of crime shoot up, robberies mainly, but there are more serious things. A good example is that we just had a call about some guy in First Hill who shot somebody right on the street in front of God and everybody and took his car. That's not the only incident like that we're getting calls on. People out there are going nuts. I don't think that being reactive is helping us anymore, we need to start sending detectives down to investigate this stuff."

"Very well, but only the major crimes, robberies, rapes and homicides." Knox ordered.

"One last thing," the Captain told her, "Two bodies were just found in Salmon Bay near Ballard locks, we think they floated in from the Sound. I sent Allen and Trumball but the FBI is already there."

"Why would the FBI be so concerned with a body dump?"

Knox asked while reading.

"The bodies are female, one appears to be in her mid forties, the other looks young but we're not sure. They don't appear to have been in the water for long."

"Why aren't we sure?" Knox asked.

"Because the younger one has been decapitated, and the head is nowhere to be found." The Captain told her.

"That is odd, get us some I.D.'s on them and we'll go from there. Work with the FBI." Knox ordered. "Is that all?" The Captain nodded his head and took his leave, passing Captain Carassco on his way out. Carrasco stood out like a sore thumb in his black BDU's.

"You asked to see me ma'am?" Carrasco approached the Chief.

"Yes Captain." Knox put the papers she was reading on the table. "We may have to use your SWAT team, what's your status?"

"You know we keep our gear in our vans for easy access during call-ups, so we still have all of that, but we lost several people in the bombing, I'd say we're down at least one-third." The SWAT commander told his boss.

"Can you make that up with reserve members?" Knox asked.

"Absolutely, don't worry about us we'll be ready when you need us." Carrasco told her.

"Good, we don't have anything yet but I'm afraid we will need you at some point. You saw what happened in Atlanta? What do you think?"

"I think they're toying with us. I think that if we have to make an entry similar to that, then we're going to have to manipulate the situation beforehand to keep us from getting blown up." Carrasco told her.

"How do we do that?" Knox asked.

"It depends on the situation, keep me in the loop and we can probably do it. We're drawing up some scenarios now that should give us an idea of what tactics we could use."

"Very good, I hope we don't need you Captain, but be ready just in case."

Becca's game of hide and seek was playing thin with her. She rounded yet another corner, about a block from the mall, stopped running and starting walking. She was amazed by all of the tall buildings surrounding her. She looked around like she were a tourist taking in all the sights. Her curiosity for the world now overwhelming her, she stopped paying attention to where she was walking and narrowly missed being hit by a glass door that opened without warning directly in front of her.

Exiting the building she was next to was a man and a woman holding a white bag filled with thin square boxes. The couple was discussing something amongst themselves and didn't even notice the little girl who slipped into the building before the door closed behind them. Becca found herself in a large rectangular room filled with aisles of shelves that held thin square boxes similar to the ones that were in the bag the couple was holding.

Becca was in awe by all the images in the room. On each of the boxes there were pictures of various people and things, colorful pictures that immediately caught Becca's attention. The tiny girl wandered aimlessly through the maze of DVD's, looking at the pictures and forgetting the game she had been playing with her kidnaper. Fatigue was now setting in on the little girl and she decided she wanted to sit down but before she did she was caught by the very colorful images on the boxes in the children's section of the store. Like any good consumer, she browsed the all too familiar allotment of children's characters that were visible on the covers of the boxes. Finally, she chose one with a big yellow bird on the cover and picked it off the shelf. Smiling through her taped mouth, she traced the outline of the bird with her finger. Deciding that she would be better off sitting in a corner while looking at her selected video, she turned and took a step only to bump into the blue jean covered knee of a young man in his late teens. Startled, she looked up at the man and saw his distinct Arabic features, which caused her to step back quickly.

The young man said something that she didn't understand and put down the stack of DVD's he was holding so he could get on one knee to face the scared little girl. He said something else to her that she didn't understand but his voice seemed kind and caring so she decided not to run. The man looked her over very carefully, then ran his hand down her long blonde hair before yelling something else that she didn't comprehend.

"Father?" The man yelled in Arabic. "Father, come, you need to see this!"

"Not now son, I'm busy." The father yelled from a back room of the video store.

"Father please come quickly!" The boy yelled, which caused the father to stop pushing buttons on his calculator and get up from his chair, mildly angry at being disturbed.

"What is it?" The father said, approaching.

"It is a child, there is something strange." The son returned.

"Is she lost?" The father got down on one knee to examine the little girl. "There is tape on her mouth?" He stated, in almost a question.

"That is what is strange." The son told him. The father checked the girl carefully and noticed something at the bottom of the girl's pretty red and white dress. He took the cloth in his fingers and saw several small drops of blood staining the dress.

"Muhammad, call the police!" The father said nervously. "Call them right now!"

"Yes father." Muhammad ran to the back of the video store where he retrieved a cordless phone and dialed 911. When someone answered, he started telling his story.

"What is your name?" The father asked Becca after he removed the tape from her mouth. Becca remained silent, allowing the man to continue to check her for injuries. He didn't notice Ratib looking at the two through the front glass window of the video store. The father's concern raised when he couldn't even find any cuts or bruises on her. If the blood wasn't hers; who's was it?

Both Muhammad and his father heard the bell on the front door of the store ring when it opened then shut behind the man who had entered. Muhammad continued to talk to the 911 operator but watched Ratib round the corner of the aisle that Becca and the old man were in. When the father saw Ratib, he stood up to meet the man. Becca took shelter behind the old man's legs. A moment later, Ratib was standing face to face with the old man, looking him in the eye.

"Salam Alaikum." Ratib said in a polite tone.

Chapter 11:

Ali stood on the boat deck checking the lines that he'd tied to the dock. He was dressed in casual clothing, a t-shirt that had a brand name on it and blue jeans with white sneakers. However, his apparel was the only thing about him that did not stand out. The man was clearly Caucasian, his pale skin very different from Kicham's dark black complexion and the other two men's Arabic features. He had long black hair down to his shoulder blades and was trying to grow a beard, although not very successfully, possibly due to his young age.

After Kicham and the others left, Ali gathered some cleaning supplies and cleaned some blood from the back of the boat. Upon finishing that task, he took to rechecking the lines that anchored the boat to the pier. The boat wasn't entirely blue at all, the waterline and hull was of a dark blue paint but everything else on the boat was white. It was a trawler, primarily used for fishing. Coming in at just over 44 feet, it was a rather small vessel for its class. There was one cabin. Behind the white cabin was a small three or four foot section that was covered by a large white canopy and flybridge. The flybridge doubled as a driver's seat for the vessel.

The cabin had a white exterior, it was located in the center of the vessel with thin walkways on either side of its exterior. The sides of the cabin were lined with windows, though all the shades had been drawn. The bow of the vessel was covered in a thick black tarp that was used to secure much of the fishing equipment used by the vessel.

The cabin was small, only a few feet across but had great length in its front section, under the bow, small steps could take one down into a tiny bedroom, with an equally minute bathroom in its corner. In the topside portion of the cabin, the entire port side was covered by the galley, which was extensive. The starboard side of the room contained a large white sofa which spanned almost the length of the room stopping only at the forward door that led to the outside walkway on the starboard side. The sofa was a dirty shade of white, and in the middle of the cabin; a single pole propped up a thin square wooden table aft of which was a cheap wood and cloth director's chair. Next to the side door was a larger table propped up by four aluminum poles which held a television set, and VCR/DVD combo unit.

Ali looked up to see a rather short, slightly balding, pot bellied old man in dress pants and dirty white dress shirt standing on the pier staring at him. Recognizing Senator Cale, Ali jumped back in surprise. He turned hastily to the cabin door where he intended to obtain his gun but found Rent only a few inches from him. The next thing he saw was Rent's large fist slam into his eye.

Ali flew back, almost falling, but was caught by Rent who delivered several more punches to his face before tossing him to the deck. Cale took the opportunity to board the vessel. Rent grabbed Ali by the hair and flung him through the cabin door. Rent held his prisoner by the hair and quickly checked the cabin for other hostile parties. When the topside area of the cabin was cleared, he dragged Ali, again by the hair to the forward bedroom section and checked that. When finished, he returned to the main cabin, slammed Ali on the floor, kicked him a few times, opened up a counter door, put Ali's head in it, and slammed it shut twice. Thoroughly satisfied that he'd taken all the fight out of Ali, Rent propped him in the director's chair while Cale searched the cabin.

"They certainly have enough food." Cale looked through the cupboards. Rent replied with something that Cale didn't hear very well because of the noise he was making by beating Ali. "Look, quickties." Cale opened up another drawer and found a very charitable supply of the long plastic ties.

"I can use those, hand me a couple." Rent ordered. He stopped beating Ali, took the ties from the senator and tied Ali's arms to the chair. "No, no, no, don't you pass out on me." He told Ali, slapping his face lightly. Ali struggled to stay conscious. "What's your name?" Rent questioned, slapping his prisoner several more times. "What's your name?"

"Ali." The man replied weakly.

"Right." Rent replied. "I'm Saddam Hussein. Nice to meet you." Rent sarcastically added. "I doubt your parents named you Ali."

"I changed it when I converted." The man replied with slurred speech.

"Whatever. Look Ali, I'm going to ask you some questions ok? Tell me what I want to know, and we'll get along just fine, got it?" Rent informed.

"I'm serious, your kids look like me." Owens joked. Jackson pulled their car out of the parking space.

"Do you realize that those are my kids you're talking about?" Jackson asked, finally taking Owens facetious bait.

"Ok, one looks like Johnson, you can tell by that goofy look he gives you, it's just like Johnson's." Owens returned.

"Right, the only kids you ever had were with your sister and I don't think Johnson has ever even seen female genitalia." Jackson retorted, not quite with the anger he'd been previously exhibiting. Owens started his reply but stopped when he heard the dispatcher calling a patrolman in another sector. The patrolman answered, telling that he was backing up an officer who was at a domestic disturbance call in the area. The dispatcher told the patrolman that they'd received a report of a lost child and that both officers should leave the scene they were at and attend to the child. The patrolman argued with the dispatcher for a few seconds about the importance of the call they were on. Jackson and Owens listened, not sure what was happening. Jackson continued to drive down the road and turn onto a large four lane avenue. They were concerned because it was very unusual that a dispatcher would take someone off a call, especially to deal with something simple like a lost child.

"Hey," the patrolman's frustration with the dispatcher evident to everyone listening over the radio, "this guy beat his wife within an inch of her life. We can't leave now. What's so special about this kid anyway?"

"Her mouth is covered with tape. There is a possible terrorist link." The dispatcher returned. Jackson's mind went to work and he flung the steering wheel around which caused the car to spin 180 degrees into oncoming traffic. The driver of the car in the lane in which Jackson had intruded panicked, slammed on his breaks and attempted to switch lanes, but only slammed into the car next to him. Owens grabbed the dashboard and tried to keep his head from hitting his door window. Jackson gunned the gas; white smoke flew from the back tires and the car sped off down the road. After he regained himself, Owens flipped on the emergency lights of the vehicle.

"What the hell are you doing?" He yelled at Jackson.

"Is that child lost?" Ratib asked the old man in Arabic.

"No, she is with us." The old man whose name was Hakim
told him. Ratib stared at Becca for a moment then turned his eyes
back to Hakim's. Muhammad stopped talking into the phone. He
watched the interplay between his father and the stranger closely.

"I believe it will be better if I take the child brother." Ratib
told him. Hakim thought for a moment, his eyes not moving from
Ratib's.

"I will not allow that." Hakim said, making his decision to
protect Becca. "What is this about?"

"That does not concern you." Ratib told him. "Give me the
girl." He ordered.

"You are one of the people involved in today's attacks?"
Hakim asked, discerning why Ratib was so adamant about taking
Becca. Muhammad remained in the back room trying to listen to
what the two men were saying.

"I am trying to help you brother, give me the child now!"
Ratib replied to Hakim's accusation.

"What you are doing is wrong." Hakim proclaimed on

impulse. "I will protect this child, as it says to protect all children in the holy book of Islam."

"If that is so, you are traitors to Allah, traitors to your people!" Ratib remarked in anger.

"And you are a scourge upon Allah's great name!" Hakim replied loudly. Ratib had finished trying to talk to the man. He smacked Hakim and shoved him aside. The old man hit a set of shelves and knocked them over. Becca tried to run but this time Ratib was too quick for her and he grabbed her by the back of her dress. She didn't say a word when Ratib picked her up and put her in his arms.

"I will not allow this!" Hakim grabbed Ratib by the arm and tried to wrestle the child from his grip. Hakim however, was old and had never been in a fight in his life, his arms were weaker than the much younger Ratib's and he could not pull the girl away. Wanting to make a quick exit, Ratib drew his pistol and shot directly into Hakim's stomach. The old man fell to the ground clutching his bleeding wound. Ratib made his escape with Becca. Muhammad heard the shot and ducked under the counter, a moment later he raised his head and seeing that the danger had passed, ran to his father.

"Muhammad!" Hakim yelled through his pain. "Tell the police where they are going! Tell them Muhammad!" Muhammad nodded and put the phone to his ear, but something snapped in him.

He felt a sudden anger and an overwhelming urge to not allow this man get away with what he was doing. He made his decision. Instead of talking to the 911 operator, he tossed his father the phone, ran to the back, got a .38 caliber revolver that was under the cash register and started out the door. "Muhammad no, do not leave!"

"We cannot let him do this to our people!" Muhammad proclaimed to his father before running through the front door.

"I will not tell you anything!" Ali proclaimed just before spitting at Rent.

"Look bro, all I wanna know is where the Austins are, just tell me that." Rent said nicely, ignoring Ali's former statement.

"I will kill you." Ali announced in response.

"Ok, we'll do it your way." Rent said, standing up and looking around. "Find me a phone book will ya?" He asked Cale, who starting looking in the cupboards and drawers.

"No phone book." Cale said after a minute of search. Rent didn't like that answer so he looked himself. Opening one of the drawers, he found a large copy of the Qur'an, which he picked up and thumbed through quickly.

"This will do." Rent slapped the book against his hand.

"Do you know what that is?" Cale said, disgusted at Rent's

plan.

"The question you should ask yourself is, do I care?" Rent
stepped over to Ali. "Where are the Austins?" He asked in a casual
voice. Ali stared at the book and gave no answer. Rent took the
book in both hands and hit Ali very hard several times in the head
with it. "Where are the Austins?" He asked again.

"Praise Allah." Ali replied.

"Tell me when that starts to help." Rent said angrily before
pummeling Ali with the book several more times. Ali shook his
head to try to remove the pain that Rent was inflicting. He spit some
blood onto the floor and looked up at Rent with angry eyes.

"Do you even know what that book tells us?" He asked
Rent.

"I got the cliff notes." Rent replied. "Let me see if I
remember, oh yes." Rent started accentuating his syllables, like he
had with Johnny Carson earlier, only this time when he smacked Ali
with the book, it was with all the force he could put behind it. "It-
says-don't-hurt-people!"

"The terrorists are kidnaping families. It's no coincidence
that a kid turns up like this today!" Jackson moved from lane to
lane, narrowly avoiding hitting other cars. Owens was clutching the

handle just above his door, he'd been in plenty of chases, several in which Jackson drove, but never like this. Jackson was driving like a wild man, he wasn't even slowing down at intersections and had already caused several accidents.

"Ok, fine, but slow down!" Owens ordered, truly scared. Jackson didn't comply, then the report of gunfire at the location came across the radio and Jackson sped up. Running through a red light, one car had to ram straight into another car in the next lane to keep from hitting them. "Damn it, slow down, you're driving like a Tennessean!" Owens yelled.

Ratib walked confidently down the street, having taken the little girl, he felt that his error had now been undone. He held no remorse for shooting the old man, in fact he was proud of having shot someone he believed deserved to be shot. Ratib firmly believed that because Hakim was in league with the enemy, that he deserved to die even more than others because he was a Muslim. Becca sat silently in Ratib's arms, her head turned to watch the area behind them. She watched Muhammad sprint towards them with his gun in hand.

Unaware that he was being chased, Ratib continued to stroll down the street. He observed the pedestrians and motor vehicle operators like any other person who was carrying a child. That is until he heard the gunshot.

Muhammad had never fired a gun before and his first time did not prove to be a success. When he got close enough, he took aim and fired. Not only was his aim extremely poor but he jerked the trigger which caused the bullet to go into the windshield of a car traveling down the street, striking the driver in the throat and causing the car to slam into a parked car.

Ratib turned with his gun drawn. He saw Muhammad aiming for another shot. He hastily launched two bullets at Muhammad. Both rounds missed their intended target and ricocheted off the sidewalk about twenty feet behind Muhammad. After realizing he'd missed, Ratib turned and took off running down the sidewalk. Muhammad fired another shot at Ratib but like his first, it went wild, ricocheting off a car hood and into a second story window.

"Just tell me where they are!" Rent yelled at Ali, hitting him one more time with the sacred book. Blood was dripping from Ali's chin in regular intervals but the beaten man maintained his defiance. "Ok, then, onto phase two." Rent tossed the book onto the counter and picked up the pack of cigarettes. "You know I'm about sick of these games you people play." Rent lit the cigarette and took several long thick puffs on it. "I didn't ask to be a part of this. Liz didn't ask to be a part of this." He told Ali before taking another long puff on the cigarette which made the cherry at its top large and fire red.

"Carey?" Cale said weakly, Rent's behavior bringing back memories of his own captivity in Vietnam. "Ali, just tell us where they are." Cale told the man who did not respond. Cale's anxiety caused him to lean on the small square table that was held up by a single pole in the middle of the room, his weight causing the table to topple over. Rent grabbed the table before it fell and stood it back upright.

"Come on, what harm could it do? Tell me where the Austins are." Rent ordered. Cale watched him with interest, he didn't know what Rent was going to do next. Rent kept the cigarette in his mouth, approached Ali, grabbed the helpless man by the hair and yanked his head back, almost pulling the chair over. "Where are the Austins?" Rent yelled. He took the cigarette from his mouth and stuck the lit end deep into Ali's nose. Cale looked away. Ali screamed in pain. Rent removed the cigarette. "Aw, it went out. That's ok, I got a whole pack."

"I thought all you hicks liked to drive like this." Jackson

said casually after accidentally hitting a bus-stop sign. He was now halfway on a sidewalk and had slowed down a little in order to keep from hitting some of the pedestrians. He'd encountered a lot of traffic and was trying to slide through it. He'd scraped three cars so far.

"Not like this, oh my God we're going to die!" Owens clutched the handle above his door with both hands. The radio was reporting the firefight between the two men that were chasing each other down the street. Each transmission on the radio simply reinforced to Jackson that he was right and this was related to the terrorist attacks.

"Oh come on, I saw that tv show what was it, the Dukes of Hazzard." Jackson finally cleared the traffic, ran through an intersection and just barely missed a tractor trailer. "Let me ask you something? How come there weren't any African Americans in Hazzard county?"

"The hell if I know, keep your attention on the road man." Owens replied.

"I really wanna know, something like forty percent of the southern population is black and you don't see any on that show." Jackson said. "What did they do, lynch us all?"

"I don't know! I only watched that chick in the shorts—no no no no no!" Owens screamed when Jackson switched lanes into oncoming traffic. The cars coming at them began panicking and running into the other lanes to avoid them.

"It's because the south's still a bunch of racist bigots, can't even put a black man on a southern show, that's sad." Jackson turned down a perpendicular street, barely missing a SUV.

"Well if you let me live through this, I'll write them a letter and complain!" Owens responded.

The bullet hit Ron Jeremy right between the eyes. It had gone straight through the restaurant window and impacted the picture of the porn star with the management of the establishment that was hanging on the wall. It was one of two bullets that Muhammad fired from his revolver with the same poor aim that he'd used to fire the others. The second bullet or chronologically the first of this particular volley had struck the bottle of a hobo that had just sat down next to a building to sip his newly purchased whiskey. Luckily for Becca, not one of the four bullets that Muhammad had fired so far had even come close to hitting their target.

Ratib fired three more shots at Muhammad and though his aim would have been much better, he never took the time to take aim, thus all three shots missed. The two continued to chase each other down the street, both trying to find a good position to shoot from, but neither succeeding. Ratib decided to simply make a run for it, he headed through an intersection and was clipped slightly by a Dodge Stratus that was moving down the street. Both Ratib and Becca fell to the ground, but Ratib refused to let go of the little girl, his gun however slid a foot in front of him. Muhammad saw his opportunity.

Crossing the intersection, Muhammad pointed his weapon at Ratib so that he could fire his last two shots, and was hit head on by a Corvette. Muhammad flipped over the bumper and hit the windshield, his gun going off twice, firing its last rounds into the air. He came to rest on the ground next to Ratib and Becca.

"I just called the house. Ratib hasn't arrived yet." Aziz told Qudamah.

"There is a gunfight a few blocks from the house. They say on the police radio that it could link to us." Qudamah told him. "Something has gone wrong. Has anyone left the house?"

"No, they said everyone is there but Ratib and the girl." Aziz answered.

"This is not right." Qudamah picked up his cell phone, chose a number from his list and called it. The phone rang several times before a man answered.

"What?" The voice asked in a whisper, the sounds of the

North Police Precinct in the background.

"What is happening near the house?" Qudamah asked the phone.

"We don't know, two guys having a firefight is all we know, why?" The voice replied.

"Nevermind that, they must not be caught, you must make sure of that." Qudamah ordered.

"There's nothing I can do, I can't control the officers on the scene." The voice told him.

"You will find a way. Remember your wife and daughter's lives depend on it."

"No wait, we had a deal." The voice argued.

"And unless you do what you are told fully, the deal is off." Qudamah told the voice.

"There's nothing I can do about this!" The voice whispered into the phone.

"Perhaps you will be called upon to make a sacrifice." Qudamah pushed the end call button.

"Where are the Austins?" Rent spat into Ali's face. "Where are they?" Rent slammed the cigarette into Ali's other nostril which caused him to scream again. "Tell me where they are!" He left the cigarette hanging and hit Ali in the face with a closed fist. Ali blew through his nose and the cigarette fell out. Ali stared at Rent in defiance. "Alright, on to phase three." Rent opened the cutlery drawer and selected a black handled 8 inch Cook's Knife.

"Carey!" Cale said loudly so that Rent would hear him. "You can't do this!"

"Watch me." Rent replied sarcastically before turning to Ali. "Ok, you little bastard, here's the question, what's your answer. Where are the Austins?" Ali gave no reply. "Have it your way." Rent slammed the knife into the counter top and pulled it out again before using the indent he'd made to cut out a long thin splinter of wood. "So help me God, you're going to tell me where the Austins are." Rent grabbed Ali's right hand, extended his fingers out and shoved the splinter violently under the nail of his middle finger. Ali screamed in agony. "Tell me where the Austins are! Tell me now!" Rent yelled continuously while the man screeched.

"Carey!" Cale couldn't take it any longer. "Stop it!"

"If you don't like it, go somewhere else!" Rent snapped at the Senator. Cale decided to take Rent's advice. He took a cigarette from the pack, grabbed the lighter and exited the cabin through the side door.

"I'm not telling you anything!" Ali yelled, which angered Rent who used the splinter to peel the entire fingernail off. Ali's screams filled the cabin.

"Where are they?" Rent yelled at him as he grabbed another finger.

"Screw you!" Ali shrieked at his captor.

"Ok, but I like to spoon afterwards." Rent jammed the splinter under the fingernail and pushed it up. "Where are they? Now!" Ali only screamed in reply and Rent took the fingernail off. "Look, I got eight more but not a lot of patience, so what do you say, just tell me and I'll be on my way." Rent told him.

"Take them all off." Ali sputtered through the pain. "I will never betray my people. What you do to me here will make no difference when I am in paradise!"

"Ok, on to phase four. Rent dropped the splinter and grabbed one of Ali's fingers. "First I'm going to start with your fingers, then your toes, then your balls, then I'm going to start taking the skin off your palms, layer by layer. Believe me Ali, I'm going to make this last." Rent told him, breaking the finger. Ali screamed in agony as Rent twisted the broken finger around.

Ali's eyes rolled into the back of his head and his screaming slowly stopped. Rent looked down at the unconscious terrorist and knew that he'd overdone it. "Trust me you little worm, that won't help, your going to tell me where the Austins are."

"The mother is at the Perchman fishery on Seaview Avenue." Kicham's voice informed from the rear cabin door. Rent turned to see Kicham aiming a pistol at him along with two other men who were doing the same. "We took the children to our safehouse at 402 Mayfield. I hope that answers your question, but it won't do you much good because you won't leave this boat alive."

Jackson slid his vehicle around the corner and sped up, approaching the intersection, unaware that his suspects were there. Ratib grabbed his gun and struggled to get to his feet. Muhammad got to his knees and tried to orient himself. Ratib noticed the flashing lights in the grill of the unmarked police cruiser and launched two shots at it. The first shot hit a headlight, the second went through the windshield right between the two cops and ended up lodged in the back seat.

"Great." Owens muttered. Jackson twisted the wheel and sent the vehicle into a parked car. Ratib fired two more rounds at the vehicle, the first went through Jackson's window, past the two cops and through Owens window, the second deflected off the roof. Owens opened his door and crawled out of the car with Jackson hastily behind him. Ratib turned to run but was caught by Muhammad who struck him in the face with the butt of his gun. Ratib pushed Muhammad against the corvette, placed his pistol over his heart and fired three times. Muhammad died instantly and his lifeless body fell limp to the ground.

Jackson and Owens were moving up the street toward the intersection on foot, their weapons drawn, using various parked cars and other obstructions on the sidewalk as cover. Now that Muhammad had been dealt with, Ratib took off down the adjacent street with Becca still in his arms. Seeing his suspect on the move, Jackson yelled for the driver of the Corvette to call 911 and rushed after Ratib.

Ratib ran for two blocks, every so often firing a shot in the direction of Jackson and Owens who were steadily gaining on him. Knowing that escape was getting more difficult with every passing second, Ratib radically changed direction toward a department store supercenter that was near him. Jackson and Owens continued their chase in the new direction, hoping to get closer to Ratib, but fearing to shoot him because of the child in his arms.

Ratib crossed the busy street into the parking lot of the supercenter. He didn't feel the slide of his pistol click back when he fired his last round. The round failed to deter Jackson and Owens, they chased their suspect into the parking lot. Ratib decided to use the vehicles in the lot for cover until he could get to the store. Weaving from car to car, he made his way closer to the supercenter. His pursuers used the long straight lanes to run through, catching up quickly to Ratib and Becca.

Ratib turned and pulled the trigger on his weapon, only then realizing that it was empty. In desperation, he continued winding through the parked cars. He switched his pistol to the hand that was carrying the little girl so that he could fish another magazine out of his pants pocket. The hot muzzle made contact Becca's arm, burning her. Out of pain, she reached up and bit Ratib on the cheek. Ratib squealed and dropped Becca onto the hood of a sports car. Not fully realizing what he'd done, he continued running toward the store. Shoving the magazine into his weapon and activating the slide release lever, Ratib tried to take aim at the two cops who had split up and now had him in a crossfire.

Becca slid down the hood of the car and landed on her feet but lost her balance and fell on her rear. Jackson saw what was about to happen, lowered his weapon from Ratib and started at a full sprint. Ratib found Owens first and fired several shots in his direction. Owens saw the weapon leveled at him and jumped for cover behind the engine block of a car.

Realizing that he no longer had the little girl in his arms, Ratib probed the parking lot for her. Finding Becca just getting herself to her feet, he pointed his weapon at her and took careful aim.

Jackson rounded the set of cars, hoping to get to Becca before Ratib fired. The little girl was now within sight but not within reach. Becca turned to look at the man that would kill her, she smiled and Ratib fired four shots. Jackson used his legs for momentum and pushed himself off the ground, snatching the little girl like she were a fumble and cradling her in his arms, he dove. Jackson fell through the air with Becca in his arms and felt the whiz of the four bullets flying past him. He spun around and landed on his back, sliding to a stop.

Ratib turned and started running for the store again, his idea that if he could get inside, they would not be able to find him and he could sneak out a back door. By now, Owens was back on his feet and chasing his suspect. Ratib heard the sounds of sirens approaching and saw several police cars speeding into the parking lot. Seeing that Ratib no longer had Becca in his arms, Owens stepped out from behind cover and took aim.

"Jesse! We need him alive!" Jackson crawled with the little girl behind a nearby car. "We have to have him alive!" He yelled a second time, not knowing if his partner heard him.

Owens took up a good firing position with his legs shoulder length apart, knees slightly bent, gun out in front of him, elbows just barely unlocked. He could clearly see that directly in his line of fire, just past the running suspect was a six foot tall cage full of propane tanks. He considered for a second and decided it was worth the risk. Owens closed his left eye and squeezed the trigger slowly. He was concentrating so much on accuracy that the weapon surprised him when it discharged.

The bullet flew through the air in an arc at Ratib. The bullet arced up the it got closer to the running terrorist, then it began to arc back down and finally struck its target.

Ratib's knee exploded onto the sidewalk. The bullet continued flying and after hitting a bar on the cage holding the propane tanks, it ricocheted into the air. Ratib fell hard onto the sidewalk, just a few feet from the cage. Pain overtaking all his other senses, he looked around to see that the police cars had now stopped and several uniformed cops were running towards him. Owens quickly moved toward Ratib, keeping his weapon trained on his subject and praying that the newly arriving officers saw the badge on his belt.

"Throw that weapon away!" Owens yelled to his suspect. "Toss that weapon now!" Ratib heard him but didn't immediately comprehend what was being said. He lifted his head and saw Owens approaching him yelling, then the words began to hit him. "Toss that weapon, toss it now! Toss that gun!" Ratib realized that he was still holding his pistol, he thought very hard for a moment, said a prayer under his breath, then pointed the pistol at the propane tanks. "Take cover!" Owens yelled and jumped for a nearby car. Jackson pulled Becca close to his chest, covering her with his body.

Ratib emptied the rest of his magazine into the propane tanks. The first tank to explode set off all seven of the others in the cage, erupting in a huge fireball. The blast blew Ratib to bits and took a large portion of the wall it was next to with it. Shrapnel from the cage and the tanks plus large concrete chunks of the wall showered the surrounding area. A moment later all was silent, save for a few pieces of debris that soon fell to the ground.

Chapter 12:

"What's the status of the father?" Knox yelled to one of her officers. The police command room was buzzing with activity. In one corner, a trio of forensics officers were attempting to filter out Muhammad's voice and other background noises from the 911 tapes in order to listen to the conversation between Hakim and Ratib. On the other side of the room, several officers worked to try and determine the identities of all the parties involved in the shooting.

"His name is Hakim Rasheed, he owns several video stores in town." The officer replied to Knox. "He's at the hospital now, they're expecting him to pull through."

"What about the boy?" Knox asked.

"He was DOA." Another officer told her.

"Ok, I want units at the hospital to guard this Rasheed guy." Knox ordered.

"I've got my guys already there, tell them we're in charge." Bannister said, looking up from the laptop he was working at. The officer nodded and crossed the room to where a temporary radio dispatcher had been set up.

"I think we've got it." One of the forensics officers yelled to Bannister and Knox. "But it's all in Arabic."

"You," Bannister pointed to an officer, "get upstairs and tell my guys we need a translator down here." The officer nodded and left the room. Another FBI agent entered, this one holding a few stapled sheets of paper. The agent handed Bannister the papers, who skimmed through them. "There are three pages?" He asked his agent.

"Apparently they sent it out as an inter-office memo." The agent told him.

"What's that?" Knox asked.

"It's a list of Police Department employees who had access to Senator Cale's schedule today." Bannister informed. "There are civilians on this list." The FBI Assistant Director said in disgust.

"The Deputy Chief thought that it was better to let all of our unit commanders know where he was going to be." Knox said.

"Jesus Christ Bethany!" Bannister spouted in anger. "You put this list out for public consumption, everybody from the Chief to the psychiatrist knew exactly where the Senator would be and when." He told her forcefully. "You never put out a detailed schedule like this, never! Nobody non-essential below Assistant Chief should've known this information!"

"I didn't send it out Terry." Knox informed.

"Boy that's a relief." Bannister said sarcastically before turning back to his agent. "I want everybody on this list checked out head to toe. Then they should be double checked." The agent agreed and left the room. "Do we have an I.D. on the child yet?" Bannister asked Knox.

"No, DHS should be on the scene in a minute or two, we'll have them take her to the hospital and we'll draw blood. She isn't talking so we're going to have to find out who she is the old fashioned way."

"Keep an escort with her, I don't think they will but we don't want them taking another stab at her." Bannister ordered.

Rent tried to move his arms, but the quickties held them down firmly against the flimsy armrests of the director's chair. The irony of the situation was not wasted on Rent, who had just a few minutes before been torturing one of his captors in the same chair he was now in. Still unconscious, Ali was laying on the sofa where one of the Arabic men was taping up his fingers, he was having trouble breathing and had to do so through his mouth. The other Arab and Kicham seemed to be discussing something in another language. Rent couldn't determine which language. He was surprised that they were not beating him. He was sure that he was due some physical pain before he would be murdered. Kicham propped himself up on the counter and stared at Rent for a moment. A sour expression on his face, he picked his phone out of his pocket and dialed a number.

"You'll never believe who I found." Kicham said into the phone when it was answered. "Rent is here on the boat, we have him."

"How did he find you?" Qudamah asked. "Who else knows?"

"Nobody." Kicham responded. "They'd of taken us already if the police knew. He's here on his own."

"What about the Senator?" Qudamah asked.

"Cale's not with him, he must have killed him. If he'd let him go, he'd of gone to the cops and we'd know by now."

"I agree."

"What do you want me to do with him." Kicham inquired.

"I never would have thought he'd find the boat." Qudamah responded, beginning his answer. "He's too dangerous to try to control, kill him, leave him in the Sound."

"Of course, I'll call when it's done." Kicham hung up the phone. He turned to the man he had previously been talking to. "Take us into the Sound Samir." Samir nodded and left the cabin through the back door and untied the ropes holding the vessel to the pier. After going up the ladder he sat down at the controls of the boat, started the engine, and took the boat out.

Hiding under the tarp that held down the fishing equipment on the bow of the boat, Cale tried to be very still. He felt the boat begin to move and knew he didn't have long before they would either kill Rent or find his hiding place.

Jackson put another quarter in the machine and the little car started moving backwards and forwards, side to side. Becca turned the steering wheel on the large mechanical toy like a race car driver; a huge smile on her dirty face. A plethora of police cars surrounded them. Several officer's were wrapping crime scene tape around areas of the parking lot. Another officer was marking all the shell casings around the lot and circling the bullet holes in the cars. The Department of Human Services advocate arrived a few minutes before and was calling her office to determine if the child had been reported missing.

"Look, she drives like you." Owens, who was sitting on the bumper of a truck, said sarcastically. He had jumped for cover behind the engine block of a large truck and thus managed to escape the explosion with little more than a cut over his eye.

"Nobody's reported her missing." The DHS representative told the cops, approaching. "She still won't talk?"

"No, and I don't think there is anybody to report her. If I'm right, her entire family is missing." Jackson told the social worker. Owens got up and walked over to the trio, still holding the bandage on his head.

"Don't they take like footprints or something of these kids at the hospital?" Owens asked.

"Yeah, but if we don't know her birth date there's no way to find it, besides, do you know how many kids are born in Seattle?" The social worker answered.

"We don't even know if she's from Seattle." Jackson said. The quarter ran out and the toy car he was standing next to stopped moving. Becca stopped turning the wheel and turned to see what was going on.

"I'll make some calls, see what I can find out." The social worker stepped away and put her phone to her ear. Jackson turned and looked hard at Becca who was staring at Owens. He noticed she wasn't looking up though. She was looking at his waist which for the little girl sitting in the mechanical car, was about head level.

"Daddy." She pointed to the badge on Owens' belt. Owens turned to look down at the little girl. Jackson watched with curiosity, his mind working. "Daddy." She said reaching for the badge but too far away to grasp it.

"Oh God, not another one." Owens rolled his eyes. "Look kid, I don't care what your mother told you, I aint your daddy."

"Are you really that self-absorbed?" Jackson asked him. "She wants your badge." Owens took the badge off his belt and handed it to the little girl. Becca smiled at Owens and traced the badge's indented symbols with her fingers.

"I've got an idea, stay with her." Jackson told his partner.

"Whoa, wait man, I aint good with kids." Owens told him.

"Learn." Jackson turned to step away.

"But they have no souls!" Owens told him. Jackson stopped, shot Owens a look, shook the statement from his head, walked a few feet and put his phone to his ear.

"Records." An officer in the south precinct answered.

"Hey, it's Jackson, I need a favor." Jackson told his friend.

"Yeah, what's up?" The officer asked.

"I need to know who didn't show today. Is there anybody who didn't report for work?" Jackson questioned.

"Yep, we had a list, but I think they've gotten ahold of them all, there were only about four."

"They e-mail that list out don't they, do you have it?" Jackson asked.

"Yeah, hold on." The officer checked his computer, after a minute or so of search he pulled up a window with a revised list. "Yeah, there were four of them. They've gotten a hold of two, they say one is on vacation near Spokane, the other they haven't been able to find at all."

"Who?"

"Ah...Lieutenant Lewis Austin."

"Wasn't he going over to Personal Crimes?"

"I think so...He was due to take over today. I guess he didn't show up."

"That's gotta be it then, do you have an address for him?" Jackson asked, the officer gave him the information which Jackson wrote down on his notepad. He thanked the officer for his help, hung up and dialed Knox's number.

"Knox." The woman answered her cell phone.

"Hey look, I think this girl's father is a cop." Jackson told her.

"What makes you think that?" She inquired. Bannister listened next to her.

"Just a hunch, look I'm going to go check out a lead. I'll get back to you." Jackson informed.

"Absolutely not, give it to the FBI, under no circumstances are you to go..." Knox took her phone from her ear and looked at the display. "He hung up on me." She said aloud.

"I don't think he was asking your permission." Bannister laughed and went back to work. "I like that guy."

"Jesus Christ! Shoot me already, but don't make me listen to any more of this idealistic bullshit!" Rent yelled from the cabin of the moving boat.

The boat was now firmly in the Puget Sound, Samir, it's driver was watching the sky in awe. He had seen some beautiful sunsets before, but the one that was now directly in front of him was too beautiful for words. Seattle's almost permanent cloud cover was giving way on the western horizon to the setting sun, causing the horizon to fill the air with a bright orange glow that combined with the ever blackening clouds directly overhead.

"What?" Kicham replied. "Would you rather watch American Idol? It's time this country learned that it can't impose its morally decadent values upon the rest of the world."

"Oh please tell me that your argument isn't that America oppresses you because we won't allow you to oppress others. Please God tell me that's not your excuse for this crap!" Rent returned. Kicham laughed and turned to the other Arab in the room, Yushua and said something in Arabic which made him laugh.

"You have no idea what oppression is my ill-fated friend." Kicham told Rent. "You sit in your well constructed home. You want not for basics like food and water and clothing, not knowing and not caring that a continent away, your government's policies keep in power a Zionist regime that commits genocide by starving millions of Palestinians. A regime that laughs as they wash their cars while people of the book die of dehydration because their oppressors refuse to repair wells in their areas of the country. Americans don't care what happens to those people, all Americans care about is taking our oil. Any government that stands up against Israel or America is labeled a terrorist state and that excuse is used so that your government can bomb innocent people."

"We don't have to bomb your countries to kill your people," Rent shot back, "you do a good enough job of that yourselves. You gas the Kurds or lock girls in a school that's on fire because they don't have on the appropriate clothing to go outside. Your people do that, not mine. Don't you dare accuse us of human rights violations until you police your own backyard." Rent thought for a second and continued. "As far as Israel goes, you never wanted peace with them, from the moment they became a country you attacked them. They give you back land and you attack them, they make concessions, you want more and you attack them. You just don't get it do you? There's no peace in that region because you don't want it!"

"Liar!" Yushua crossed the cabin and struck Rent in the face with an open hand. "Zionists murdered my aunt, her husband, and her children while they slept when they sent a rocket into an apartment building to kill a Hamas leader!" Kicham grabbed Yushua by the arm and pulled him away from Rent.

"No my friend, we are better than that." Kicham told

Yushua. "We will not stoop to his level."

"Maybe if your leader hadn't purposefully taken cover behind innocent women and children they would still be alive." Rent replied angrily. "When somebody threatens me, the last thing I do is hide behind human shields! The Israelis are only defending their land."

"Land that they stole in the first place. We didn't attack them in sixty-seven, they attacked us. They wanted the land, they got it. Now they give back a minuscule piece of that land and we're supposed to thank them on bended knee? I don't think so."

"They attacked your invasion forces massing on the border in sixty-seven, you wanted war then and blame them for it simply because they fired the first shot. They have a right to defend their nation."

"But it's not their nation! That land is Muslim, it was stolen from us by the nations of the west and given to the Zionists who would kill every Muslim in it if they could." Kicham informed.

"Shoot me please." Rent rolled his eyes. "Here's something..." He said, yelling at Kicham. "They aint gonna leave, get over it!"

"And you wonder why we attack you." Kicham replied flatly.

Ali opened his eyes and saw his friends gathered around. A feeling of gratitude swept over him when he noticed Rent quicktied to the director's chair.

"I know why you attack us. That's no big mystery..." Rent replied.

Cale tried to formulate a plan in his mind. He knew the first thing he had to do was get back to Seattle. He didn't want to get too far out into the Sound because he knew that Rent was tied up and even if Rent was free, they were outnumbered two to one. Cale felt the raindrops begin to fall on the tarp that was covering him. He poked his head out slightly and looked up at the flybridge to see Samir working quickly to erect his rain canopy. It wasn't long until the clouds burst and a steady downpour of rain hit the rocking boat. He slowly searched the fishing equipment he was hiding with until he found a long spear gun.

"We are fighting a war for Islam, we're fighting against America and Israel and Britain and any other nation that would destroy the true faith." Kicham informed Rent.

"If that's your excuse, then you go ahead and use that." Rent replied. "But anybody with half a brain can see right through it. This isn't about your religion, this is about power and control. You like putting fear into people, it makes you feel good. You like killing people, it makes you feel powerful. Your religion is just your excuse."

"And your excuse for blasphemy is your ignorance of what is happening around you in the world. Your country trashes Islam every chance it gets. Your comedy insults the true faith, your movies and television make all Muslims out to be evil terrorists. Your news channels show pictures of dead Muslims without regard for their dignity. Your government condones cartoons printed of the sacred prophet. Everything about America is designed to attack Islam, and you hide behind your veil of ignorance." Kicham told Rent.

"No dipshit," Rent returned, "that's what you don't get, a lot of other Muslims do get it but you like to use it as an excuse. We have free speech in this country and that means–get this you're gonna love it–you can say whatever pops into your stupid retard head. We don't censor and when that does happen, usually by people like you who want control and power, we fight it. What this means for you is that you need to thicken your sensitive little skin up, because people are going to insult you. That's the way the world is."

"And what you don't get is that Allah's soldiers will not allow you to blaspheme our faith." Kicham retorted.

"Quit blowing smoke up my ass." Rent told him. "The reason you do what you do isn't because you've been slighted and it isn't because God told you to do it. It's because you're a psychopath. That's what terrorism is, Zarqawi, Bin Laden, you, even Timothy McVeigh and Eric Rudolph, it's all about the killing and power. All you people do is use religion, or anti-government sentiment, or abortion, or revenge, or whatever weak excuse you can find to hurt people, because that's what makes you feel good. You're psychos, the only difference between you and guys like Bundy, or Dahmer is that God is your excuse."

"That's the extent of American propaganda. We could show you unequivocally the atrocities committed in your name and still you would not believe us, who is really the one who is brainwashed here?" Kicham asked. Ali finally got up, crossed the room in front of Kicham, put his head in the sink and began splashing cold water in his nostrils. "What are you doing?" Kicham asked.

"He put cigarettes up my nose." Ali said through his mouth. "It hurts."

"Gotta love it." Rent snickered. "It's the gift that keeps on giving."

"Yes, that's American morality." Kicham commented.

"Maybe I should've been more like your brethren and just cut off his head?" Rent returned.

"We do what must be done in Allah's name." Kicham responded, slightly angry.

"Now who's the brainwashed one?" Rent retorted, now very

angry. "You kill because you choose to. If you really wanted to influence political change you'd take your ass downtown and vote like everybody else! No, this is about power and control, the power and control over people's lives, to hold their fate in your hands and dictate to everyone what is going to happen, that's what you're after! You're like a pedophile, just another monster trying to get its fix. You're little men with little recourse, who toy with people's lives for your own personal gratification!"

"Well in a few minutes, I will get my fix then." Kicham said, unofficially ending the conversation.

"Good news." Bannister said, entering the police command room where Knox was standing. "Our suicide suspect's hand was found about a block from where he blew himself up, my guys think they may get quality prints from the two fingers still on it."

"That's morbid." Captain Carrasco said, looking up from some maps.

"But in the anti-terrorism line of work Captain, it's a huge lead." Bannister returned.

"How long until we know something?" Knox asked.

"Depends on whether we have his prints on file in Washington, my guess is that he's another sleeper like the others."

"Do you know what kind of training these sleepers get?" Carrasco asked.

"It depends, some like to try their hand at civilian stuff like shooting and hunting. Paintball is big with them. Others take to technical stuff like bomb making. It's all in their spare time of course and most of the more notable hobbies might have stay under the table, lest they draw unwanted attention. Like I said, it just depends. Getting an I.D. on this guy puts us one step closer to finding Al-Khalifa though. Any luck with Rent and Cale?"

"They've dropped off the face of the Earth." Knox told him. "We've got everybody we can out looking for them but it's unlikely we'll find them anytime soon."

"I hope to God that the Senator is still alive. If Rent kills him, it will mean a victory for Khalifa." Bannister speculated.

"Rent won't kill him." Carrasco told the two. "I've known him for years. He and Jackson were on my team for a while. Rent won't do it and you better believe that he had a good reason to do what he did."

"I hope you're right but I doubt it." Knox told the Captain. "Rent does what he wants, he always has, that's what got him in trouble in the first place. Despite what everyone says, any cop who'll plant evidence to secure a conviction is worse than the guy he's trying to put away. I think we should remember that."

"You never liked him very much, did you Bethany?"

Bannister asked.

"No she didn't." Carrasco answered for her. "That's why she had his union delegate pulled. She said that there was overwhelming evidence of Rent's guilt and that the department does not support cops who take the law into their own hands. Isn't that right Chief?"

"In a matter of speaking yes, Carey Rent didn't deserve to wear a badge. A cop has to be above reproach, Rent has a history of..." Knox stopped and nodded to Carrasco who got a call on his cell and stepped out of the room to take it. Bannister was interrupted when one of his agents handed him a manilla folder. "What is it?" Knox inquired of the folder.

"We've identified one of the floaters found by the locks." Bannister informed.

"Which one?" Knox asked.

"The tall one, the one missing her head wasn't in the system." Bannister said, looking at the sheets in the folder. "Her name is Alice McKay. It says here that her prints were in the system because she was Chief Rodger's secretary."

"Didn't she just get married to someone inside the department?" One of the officer's in the room asked.

"I think so." Knox answered. "This is her name from her first marriage, her new name must not have hit the system yet but I can't recall who she married?"

"I don't know, the only time I ever spoke to her was when I had to see the Chief, that usually meant I was in trouble." The officer added.

"I need her personnel file." Bannister ordered.

"All those files were in Police Plaza." The officer told them.

"Even if it survived, there's no way we could get to it." Knox continued. "What about Seacrest? He might have her psychological profile, that should contain some personal information and his office files are here in this building." Knox pointed to one of the lower ranking officers in the room. "Find me Dr. Seacrest."

The sunset sky's beauty equaled any photograph or painting known to man. The rain was free falling onto the Puget Sound. The wind was moderate but like most sun showers in the Seattle evening, this storm was peaceful, its rain fell straight down with the grace of millions of tiny dancers. The ocean waves remained calm and harmonious, absorbing the raindrops, and the boat rocked only slightly on top of them. The sun was a little more than halfway over the horizon, its orange beams reflecting off the raindrops making each a tiny prism. The rotating light of Discovery Park's lighthouse began whirling slowly in its usual circle, every so often beaming the trawler with its rays.

On the deck, still under the tarp covering the bow, Cale felt the raindrops and formulated his plan. He knew that time was running short and if he didn't act soon, Rent would be killed, then he would be found and killed also. Cale also knew that a forward assault would only get him killed faster, so he decided that his only viable option was to take the man who was alone on the flybridge driving the boat. To do that he would have to move to the aft of the boat undetected and climb the ladder before anyone knew he was there. He searched his mind for his military training and though it didn't include anything like this, he used what he could remember. He took the spear gun he'd found and started moving. Slowly he made his way out of the tarp, praying that no one saw him through the closed blinds of the windows.

Inside the cabin, everyone was beginning to calm down. Ali had stuck wet paper towels in his nose, which seemed to reduce the burning pain somewhat. Kicham was using the Cook's Knife to slice open a grapefruit to snack on. Yushua had sat down on the sofa and was watching Rent intently, savoring the prospect of watching him die. Rent remained calm. Knowing that he would sooner or later have to make a move to save his own life, he studied his prey.

Believing that Rent was secured to the director's chair,

Kicham had become complacent, he placed his gun on the portside counter next to the sink. Rent determined that should be his goal; to get that gun, or more importantly, to keep it out of Kicham's hands. Yushua still had his weapon in the belt of his pants, but Rent saw the hate in the man's eyes and determined that the gun wouldn't be pulled immediately. Yushua was thinking about hurting Rent and the first thing that would pop into his mind would be to hit him. Rent knew that was a gamble. Ali was standing next to the square table held up by the unsteady aluminum pole, his hands at his sides, he watched Rent with anticipation. Ali didn't appear to be armed and Rent observed that his left hand, the one with the bandaged fingers, was right next to the table.

Everyone listened to the sounds of the rain hitting the boat, and Rent noticed an uncomfortable silence sweep through the room. The distinctive clacks and clangs the raindrops made on the various textures of the vessel caused an almost tapdance type of noise that seduced everyone who heard it. Rent subtly moved his wrists to see if the quickties fastening him to the chair were completely secure. He noted that his right hand would be unable to escape but the tie around his left wrist was slightly loose, not enough to pull his hand out but loose enough that with some solid pressure he could probably get it free.

After the light from the lighthouse filled the cabin and dissipated one more time, Rent looked between the blinds and saw a human figure moving along the port side. Kicham was starting to bite into his grapefruit when Rent broke the silence.

"It's raining." Rent said in a very serious tone, which gathered the attention of the three other men in the cabin. Kicham looked at Rent but after a second of silence, turned back to his grapefruit.

The instant Kicham's eyes left him, Rent kicked the table hard into Ali's wounded hand. Ali jumped back toward the counter while clutching his hand. Yushua immediately started off the sofa. Rent's prediction proved true, he'd not yet thought about his gun. Kicham however, moved for his. Rent used the momentum from the kick to rock himself back in the chair, then forward onto his feet. Though the chair still forced him to stand bent over, he had enough balance to deliver a side kick to Ali who was not expecting it and fell back into Kicham before he could grab his gun. Under Ali's weight, both men fell to the floor.

Yushua was on Rent, and worse yet, he'd realized he had a gun. Yushua was close enough to Rent that when he tried to pull his weapon out of his belt, Rent used his right hand to grab his wrist and twist it, which flung the weapon across the cabin.

Yushua used his free hand to punch Rent mercilessly in the face. Rent absorbed the hits and allowed Yushua to push him and his symbiotic chair back against the aft wall and door of the cabin which broke the legs of the chair and allowed Rent to stand a little straighter. He propped the left armrest against the wall and struggled with all of his strength to yank his hand from the quicktie. Yushua struck Rent twice more in the face, which only made him angrier. Trying to free himself, he slammed his right knee into Yushua's groin, causing him to double over and back up. Rent turned his attention to Ali and Kicham who were getting up off the floor.

Folding his thumb into his palm and pulling hard, his hand shot out of the quicktie, taking several layers of skin with it. Yushua was reaching across the cabin for his gun, which had fallen onto the counter. Rent reached out with his left leg and smacked Yushua in the stomach with his shin, the force of which slammed him against the starboard side cabin wall.

Seeing that both Ali and Kicham had gotten to their feet, and Kicham going for his gun again, Rent broke the left arm off the director's chair and threw it at them. Ali saw the missile coming and easily sidestepped it, leaving it to find its intended target. Only mere inches from his gun, Kicham was struck in the face by the arm of the chair, sending him backwards onto the floor again.

Cale passed the aft door of the cabin. Seeing the mayhem ensuing inside, he determined to work fast. He placed the spear gun in his left hand and climbed the ladder, ready to fire at a moment's notice.

Onboard the flybridge, Samir thought he heard some commotion on deck and though he thought it was nothing, he left his seat and stepped out from under the canopy to go down the stairs. Bending over the stairs in preparation to go down, he saw Cale and grabbed his gun. Before he could point the weapon at the Senator, Cale shot him in the stomach with the spear gun. The force of the impact flung Samir back onto the flybridge and his gun slid forward to the driver's station. Cale dropped the empty spear gun and hurried up the ladder.

Yushua shook off the hits he'd taken and lunged at Rent again. Rent didn't give his opponent time to strike, he flung his right arm, which was still connected to the chair, around delivering the entire director's chair forcefully to the man. Yushua was entangled in the combination of the wood and fabric that the chair was made of. Once Yushua had been hit, Rent yanked his right arm away from him, which broke the arm of the chair away from the other section.

With the armrest of the director's chair still quicktied to his forearm, Rent used the piece of wood as a weapon, smashing it into Yushua's face, sending him reeling onto the sofa. Rent's left shoulder was then grabbed by Ali, who'd finally managed to make his way to Rent. Ali twisted Rent with his good hand and Rent willingly switched positions with Ali.

Knowing that Kicham was almost to his feet, Rent blocked one of Ali's punches with the piece of wood still on his forearm and slammed his left elbow into Ali's face in an upward arc. Using a front kick to push Ali to the aft of the cabin, Rent turned to find Kicham almost to his gun again.

Cale got on deck and rushed to the driver's station, past Samir who was holding the spear that was still in his stomach and screaming. He twisted the steering wheel to the right. The boat began to turn, causing Cale to lose his balance and fall against the side wall of the driver's station. Cale pushed the throttle to its max and the engine to suddenly jolted the craft.

Kicham reached for his gun again but felt the pull of inertia to the starboard side and missed the weapon. This gave Rent enough time to lunge for the gun and give it a swift push which sent it sliding across the counter until it dropped between the counter and refrigerator. Kicham saw the gun go out of play and changed his tactic to Rent, who he grabbed and delivered several hard hits to. He turned Rent around and threw him into the forward wall of the cabin.

The back of Rent's head smacked the large window that looked out at the bow.

The boat turned in a circle, Cale used the lighthouse for his bearing and attempted to point the vessel toward the light. The speed of the boat causing the rain to come sideways under the cheap canopy and hit Cale in the face, the old Senator didn't notice Samir, the spear still in his stomach, getting to his feet and approaching him.

Cale was completely surprised when Samir grabbed his shoulder, turned him around and punched him twice in the face. Cale fell against the console of the driver's station, and attempted to push off. When that failed, he punched Samir in the face and the wounded man fell to the deck of the flybridge, pulling Cale down with him.

Kicham delivered a powerful uppercut to Rent whose head hit the glass behind it again. Kicham attempted to come in from the side with a punch but Rent locked his arm up with his hands, forcibly bending Kicham's elbow, Rent threw him into the larger table, knocking the television onto the sofa.

Yushua'd untangled himself from the remains of the

director's chair but could no longer find his gun, apparently the boat's sudden turn had moved it, and it was no longer in sight. "Find out what's going on topside!" Kicham yelled to Yushua in Arabic. Yushua fished his way to the door and opened it, leaving the fight.

Ali jumped on Rent, pinning him against the forward wall and punching him furiously in the ribs. Rent locked his arms around Ali and pulled him closer to take power from his strikes and deliver a headbutt. Ali fell backwards to the floor but Rent was caught off-guard by a punch from Kicham.

A second punch came in but Rent blocked it with the armrest of the director's chair. He slid his right elbow over Kicham's left arm that had grabbed Rent's shirt and struck him in the face, sending him into the counter.

Samir and Cale wrestled on the ground until one of them noticed Samir's gun which was sitting peacefully in a corner of the flybridge. Cale elbowed Samir in the chest and grabbed the gun, only to drop it again when Samir smashed his fist into Cale's ribs. The gun slid aft on the deck until it hit one of the aluminum poles holding the aft ladder in place.

Cale broke free of Samir and quickly got to his feet. Approaching the ladder, he saw Yushua's head rise above the last rung. Instinctively, Cale delivered a kick to Yushua's face and he hurtled down to the deck of the boat.

The trawler sped anxiously toward the lighthouse. Cale picked up the gun but before he could turn around he was grabbed from behind by Samir who locked his gun arm up with his own. Cale began twisting and turning, trying to get the wounded man off his back, but with little success.

Rent broke a ceramic plate over Kicham's head, sending him yet again into the counter. Ali pushed off the cabin floor with his legs in a tackle maneuver and slammed Rent against the starboard side door. There was a loud crackling of wood when the door broke from it's position and opened, allowing inertia to deliver Rent against the outer railing of the vessel with Ali on top of him. Rent felt the sting of the large raindrops hitting his face.

The thin aluminum railing bowed at the weight of the two men. Not really knowing what to do next, Ali attempted to punch Rent, who blocked the blow with his left hand while reaching around and grabbing his long hair with his right.

Yushua was recovering from his fall, getting his bearings and pulling himself to his feet when he saw Rent and Ali fighting on the side of the boat.

Rent yanked Ali's head back by the hair and delivered a punch to his face, backing him up far enough that Rent was able to deliver a front kick and knock him back into the cabin.

Samir slammed Cale against the wall of the flybridge. The two were in a stalemate, Cale couldn't get Samir off his back and Samir no longer had the strength to force Cale to drop the gun. Samir slammed Cale against the wall again and the Senator felt all the air rush out of his lungs. Gasping, Cale looked over the side to see Rent kick Ali back into the cabin.

"Carey!" Cale managed to stammer out. Samir pulled back to slam him against the wall again. Rent looked up to see Cale hit the wall and drop the gun. Rent reached with his right hand and picked the pistol out of the air. Out of the corner of his eye, Rent saw Yushua coming down the narrow walkway towards him.

Rent spun around, putting his back to the cabin door and fired three shots into Yushua's chest, the force of which knocked him overboard. Rent turned to shoot the occupants of the cabin but was caught mid turn by Kicham who grabbed Rent's gun hand and slammed it hard against the aluminum railing. The force of the

strike caused Rent to drop the gun into the Puget Sound. Kicham
wrapped his arm around Rent's neck.

Seeing the gun was gone, Samir flung Cale across the
flybridge. Cale came to a stop by the port wall of the bridge just in
time to look and see where the boat was headed. The shoreline
around the lighthouse was laden with very large, uneven, rocks.
Cale lunged for the steering wheel to turn it but Samir was already
on him and threw several weak punches that connected with Cale's
face and kept him from reaching the wheel.

Ali saw the Cook's Knife in the sink and grabbed it while
Kicham and Rent fought. Rent still had his back to Kicham, who
was trying to get him in a choke hold. Using the armrest from the
director's chair that was still attached to his forearm via the quicktie,
Rent jabbed the back of the long piece of wood into Kicham's ribs,
causing him to lose his hold. Rent spun around and delivered the
back of his left elbow to Kicham's face. Facing Kicham, Rent
propped both his arms on the aluminum railing, lifted both legs and
double kicked Kicham in the chest, knocking him back into the
cabin.

Ali saw his chance and lunged at Rent. Kicham saw the

Cook's Knife and remembered that he had his own. Kicham reached into his boot and produced a 3 inch double edged boot knife. Rent saw Ali come at him with the knife and parried to the side. Ali's knife hand missed its target and lodged between the bowed aluminum guardrails. Rent grabbed the hand, yanking it up and locking it between the rails. He used his other hand to liberate the knife from Ali. Rent spun around and stabbed Ali in the eye.

Ali shuddered and without thinking Rent let go of both the corpse and the knife. Ali began to fall overboard but his fall was halted by his hand that was still stuck between the rails.

Samir was weak and becoming light headed. He didn't realize that Cale was no longer trying to fight him but instead trying to get to the steering wheel. Since he couldn't throw an effective punch, Samir resorted to grabbing Cale's shoulders to keep him from advancing on him. Cale's age was also preventing him from putting up an effective fight but he knew that if the two stayed deadlocked much longer, the trawler would hit the rocks.

The Senator looked down and saw the long spear still protruding from Samir's stomach. Cale reached out, grabbed the end of the spear and started moving it around the wound in wide circles. The incredible pain this caused made Samir double over in pain, giving Cale the opportunity to push his head between the rungs of the steering wheel and yank. The force of the wheel turning caused Samir's head to slam against the bottom of the driver's console and his neck snapped. The boat began to turn but Cale looked up and realized that it was too late; the boat was moving too fast and they were too close to the rocks.

Rent attempted to regain the Cook's Knife from Ali, but saw Kicham hold the small boot knife with both hands and jump at him. Rent turned and crossed his arms in an x shape over his chest, catching Kicham's arms and eventually stopping the blade at his skin.

The boat slammed against the shoreline at an angle and the bow flew up into the air only to come back down a moment later and smash against the rocks again. Forward momentum still taking the boat inland, it slammed against several smaller rocks until one of the larger one's punctured the port side bottom of the hull. With the large rock sliding through it, the vessel came to a very sudden stop.

Under the pressure, the aluminum railing completely buckled, causing Rent, Kicham and Ali's corpse to be thrown overboard. The boat sat for a few seconds, then succumbing to its own weight, it tipped over on the starboard side. Gravity yanked the starboard side of the vessel onto the rocks. The fiberglass stretched upwards and made all the glass on that side of the cabin explode before the cabin wall imploded inward. The boat shrieked upwards, then down again, struggling to find its point of balance. A second later there was only the sound of the rain falling against the fiberglass of the boat to break the evening silence.

Chapter 13:

Rent tasted the mud of the ground he'd fallen on. The rain continued unabated to splash down on him. He lifted his head from the watery mush of the mud and glanced behind him at the trawler that had toppled over. Next to him he saw Ali's corpse laying face up, the knife still in his eye. Feeling pain in all his extremities, Rent deduced that he hadn't broken any bones. He placed his hands next his chest and slowly pushed himself up. The mud rushed in underneath him. He looked at the evening sky, the sun was beyond the horizon but it's rays were still forcing the Puget Sound to glow a bright orange. Rent took a moment to allow the sight to seep in. The beauty of the sunset mixed with the dark clouds directly overhead and the rain bouncing off his skin made him think of his childhood.

Kicham's kick came when Rent got to his knees, and he was thrown back into the mud. Kicham bent over and grabbed him by the shirt. Kicham came down with his boot knife still in hand, attempting to stab Rent, who instinctively caught his knife wielding forearm.

Kicham used his strength to try to force his knife into Rent's chest. Rent used his to keep the knife from descending. Straining under Kicham's pressure, and realizing that gravity was working against him, Rent knew that he was going to lose. He lifted his right arm away from the Kicham's arm and reached out to Ali's corpse. Rent extended his fingers but couldn't quite touch his intended target. Finally, Rent lifted his right leg, threw it around Kicham's torso and pulled it toward the ground, propelling Kicham backwards.

Once free of the large man, Rent used his hips to slide closer to Ali and ripped the 8 inch Cook's Knife from the dead man's eye socket. Knife in hand, Rent rolled backwards ending up on his feet, and found Kicham ready to fight.

The two assumed solid fighting stances and circled each other very slowly several times while looking for the right time to make their moves. Kicham chose to keep his boot knife right in front of him, ready for defense or offense, Rent decided upon an underhanded grip in his strong hand.

Kicham came in first, the rain helping to telegraph his movements enough for Rent to see them, sidestep, move backwards and slash with his own knife. Avoiding Rent's blade, Kicham came back with his own, this time in a lunge that Rent barely avoided. Kicham extended his arm fully, swiped it upwards and caught Rent shallowly in the shoulder. Rent took a swipe of his own at head level but Kicham ducked out of it, allowing Rent to raise his right leg and catch him in the face with his foot. Kicham retaliated by slashing Rents face, which made a thick cut about an inch wide between his right eye and ear.

Rent stabbed his knife at Kicham who deflected it and locked Rent's arm up with his own knife arm. Rent reached over to Kicham's knife hand, grabbing it between the thumb and forefinger and twisting it. The boot knife came loose and fell to the ground. Kicham used his free hand to pull Rent's knife hand toward the inside of his wrist, making Rent drop his knife.

Seeing that his opponent was unarmed, Rent pushed forward with his legs and the two fell. They wrestled on the ground for a few seconds until Kicham climbed onto Rent's back. Rent reached behind him, grabbed Kicham's legs and fell backwards onto the ground. The force of the impact caused Kicham to let go and Rent quickly moved away from him.

Both combatants quickly got their feet, Rent moved in first this time, trying to land a series of blows, most of which Kicham blocked or deflected. Kicham pulled Rent close and sent a knee to his stomach. Bent over, Rent threw several rabbit punches into Kicham's ribs, which momentarily caused him to gasp for air. Kicham lifted Rent onto his shoulder and fell backwards in a suplex. Rent bucked his hips and tried to flip his way out of the move, though he wasn't entirely successful. The two hit the wet rain-soaked mud with a thunderous splash. Kicham got to his feet and turned to see Rent had beat him up. Using Kicham's surprise, Rent fired several punches to Kicham's face followed by a spinning crescent kick, knocking him down.

Looking forward from the ground, Kicham saw his boot knife laying in the mud and dove to grab it. Rent saw this and jumped for his own knife. A moment later the two men were again on their feet sparring with the knives. Kicham moved in first again, this time with a series of short slashes that seemed to go in every possible direction. Rent moved backward in an attempt to avoid the blade, eventually stopping it with the armrest of the director's chair.

Tired of being thwarted by the device, Kicham slid the knife up the length of the armrest, cutting the quicktie that held it to Rent's arm. Meanwhile, Rent had fired a jab into Kicham's face, backing him up enough for Rent to use his right hand to slash at throat level. Kicham ducked, and put a gash in Rent's right side, just below his ribs then used his other hand to sweep Rent's right leg out from under him.

Rent recovered quickly, getting to his knees, he parried Kicham's next slash and stabbed his knife into Kicham's right knee. Kicham fell, making both fight on their knees.

They both executed a series of slashes and stabs, but only made minor contact with each other until Kicham brought the back of his left hand into Rent's face and stabbed out toward Rent's chest with his right. The force of Kicham's backhand aided in Rent's parry of the stab and he locked Kicham's knife arm up with both his arms.

Bending Kicham's elbow with his own, Rent reversed the grip on his knife so that it faced up and slammed the 8 inch carbon steel blade up under Kicham's chin. The Cook's Knife cut through Kicham's head like butter and the tip broke the top of Kicham's skull, protruding less than a millimeter. Kicham's eyes went wide and fogged over. Kicham's head become a waterfall; blood poured out of Kicham's mouth, ears, and nose. Rent hastily unlocked Kicham from his grip, and leaving the knife in his head, pushed the dead man over onto his side.

Exhausted, Rent fell back into the mud and laid there, letting the rain hit his face. He stayed on his back in the mud with the rain soaking his body for several minutes before regaining the strength to get back onto his feet. Hurt and tired, Rent stammered over to the shipwrecked vessel. He carefully maneuvered his way over and around the thick rocks to approach the tipped side of the boat.

"Senator?" Rent looked around the wreckage. "Senator Cale?" He worked his way up to the flybridge. Propping himself up on some of the rocks and holding onto the side of the flybridge, he found Cale clinging to the horizontal wall. Cale was head level with Rent and carefully turned around to face him. "Are you alright?" Rent asked.

"I'm sixty-five years old." Cale responded in a childlike

tone.

"Are you hurt?" Rent asked.

"I'm sixty-five years old." Cale responded. He looked up to see Rent's bruised and bloodied face. "What the hell happened to you?"

"You're alright." Rent reached onto the flybridge and grabbed Cale under his arms. "Come on." He helped Cale off the flybridge and placed him securely on the ground between two large rocks.

"Carey, I've got to tell you something." Cale said solemnly after Rent let go of him. Rent turned to see what the news was. "I'm sixty-five years old." Rent rolled his eyes, and stepped to the front of the boat, looking inside the bow windows. After a moment's thought, he sat down on a nearby rock.

"I need you to crawl in there." Rent told Cale. "I need you to find all the guns and ammo you can." He said, clutching the wound on his side with one hand, and the wound on his shoulder with the other. "And a first aid kit–yeah–I could use a first aid kit." Cale complied by stepping carefully to the bow windows and looking in.

"Is there anything else, maybe you want me to make you a sandwich too?" Cale asked. "You know sooner or later you're going to have to start pulling your own weight in this thing."

"So what's the deal with this anyway?" Owens asked, observing the rain hit the windshield of the police cruiser the two had borrowed. The windshield wipers whipped back and forth, throwing the rain off the glass.

"Rent used to be engaged to Austin's wife." Jackson said from the passenger seat because Owens had insisted on driving. "He never really talked about it, but I think that when she left him it tore him up."

"And you think that's what they've got on him?" Owens deduced.

"It's just a hunch, but Austin didn't show for the roll call and we need to know why anyway."

"Look Dave, I feel you, I really do, but I've been blown up twice today already and frankly I'm getting tired of it. What's got you on this crusade anyway? I mean the way I remember it Rent got caught planting evidence, is he really worth all this?"

"Yeah he is." Jackson replied without having to think. "I went through the academy with him. We were partners for years. We came over to narco together. Rent and I weren't friends, we were brothers. When Marcy and I were on the rocks, it was Carey Rent who got us talking again, though that was probably him getting sick of me sleeping on his couch and eating all his food."

"Yeah well that's a far cry from his rep, which was pretty

bad." Owens remarked.

"That's because you didn't know him. Bottom line, my friend is in trouble and he needs us. We're all fighting the same war here." Jackson said. Owens pulled the cruiser next to the mailbox of the house. The two cops got out and made their way through the rain to the front porch, their weapons drawn but down at their sides.

Owens rang the doorbell several times. "Maybe his grandfather died and nobody got the message?"

"No, Austin's a career cop, we'd know if he'd suddenly left town. He'd make sure of it, especially today. Let's check around back." They stepped into the rain again and started making their way around the back of the fenced in house. Austin's two cars were still in the driveway and Jackson looked underneath to see if there was water under them, indicating whether or not they'd been moved.

"If I get blown up again, I'm putting in for a new partner." Owens threatened, rounding the corner to the backyard. "I've got broken glass." Owens said when the broken sliding glass door came into sight. Both men raised their weapons and entered the kitchen.

Inside, they saw Lieutenant Lewis Austin's body on the kitchen floor, blood spatter on the wall behind him and a half dried blood pool around his head. Rigor mortis was clearly visible by the stiffening of the muscles. The blood had completely pooled in the lower portion of the body leaving a dark red and purple discoloration of the skin from the ground to about a two or three inches in height.

Seeing both the rigor and liver mortis, the cops knew that Austin had been dead for quite some time.

"Damn, Lewis, I'm sorry man." Jackson kneeled next to the corpse, he hated to see any homicide, he especially hated it when a victim was a fellow officer. He snapped his fingers and Owens tossed him the radio that was on his belt. "Dispatch, N.S.1, 187 of an officer, we're at 1421 Sheldon. We have an officer down, say again 187, 1421 Sheldon we have an officer down, relation to terror attacks. Dispatch forensics and inform the FBI. Send officers to secure the scene." Jackson said into the radio. Owens covered the entrance to the living room. The dispatcher responded appropriately and Jackson hooked the radio to his belt. "Ok, let's clear the rest of the house."

"They know about Austin." Qudamah entered the room and told Aziz after hearing Jackson's call on the police radio. "They've also found the other bodies."

"Brewer's family already?" Aziz asked.

"No, the one's last night." Qudamah answered.

"I told you that we should have waited." Aziz spoke out of place.

"We needed to make the video." Qudamah reminded.

"If he doesn't know by now, he surely will soon. When he discovers what we've done, we will have no one on the inside. Worse, he will tell them what he knows." Aziz said.

"We must use him quickly." Qudamah said. "I planned for this, we must use him in such a way as to have him killed."

"I can't find Seacrest anywhere, they're telling me he went and got some dinner." An officer told Knox. Bannister stood next to her, not amused that the Seattle Police Department couldn't find a crucial member of its team.

"He left?" Knox sputtered in amazement.

"That's what they said."

"When will he be back?"

"They didn't say." The officer told them.

"Well I need that file." Bannister turned to one of his agents. "Go through his office and find that file." He ordered. The agent nodded and started out.

"You can't go through those files, they're protected by doctor-patient privilege." Knox objected.

"Not today they aren't." Bannister told her.

"I need to be present. We need to be able to say we took only what we needed." Knox followed the FBI agent out.

The clouds above began to disperse, stopping the rain and revealing the night sky. On the battered boat, Cale found Rent's and Kicham's pistols, though Yushua's still eluded him. He also found three full magazines in addition to the full magazines that were already in the weapons, and a cheap first aid kit, out of which Rent took some aspirin. Rent and Cale knew they needed more first aid measures and made their way to the sewage treatment plant at the edge of discovery park.

Rent figured that a night crew of only two or three would be on shift at the treatment plant and broke into one of the outlying offices. There he found a standard city issued first aid kit which contained exactly what he needed.

A few years ago, an experimental bandage had been developed for the war in Iraq, it was a trauma bandage meant to save the lives of soldiers that had been wounded by shrapnel from roadside bombs. It was a self-adhesive dressing made from chitosan. Its adhesiveness was conducive on the blood around the wound, the more blood, the more the bandage stuck to the wound. The city of Seattle had discovered that this very expensive bandage could be used in the civilian world better than on the battlefield and thus decided to purchase one bandage for every first aid kit bought by the city.

Rent had to raid three more offices and even had to sneak into the main section of the plant to get the number of bandages he required. Rent applied the bandages to the various knife wounds he'd received in his fight with Kicham. Cutting the last one into small sections to cover the smaller cuts. Though only a temporary fix, the bandages sealed his wounds with ease and the two decided to move.

During his search for the bandages, Rent acquired a long screwdriver from a tool box and used it to pry out the lock of one of the Sanitation Department SUV's. He used the screwdriver to pop the steering column and start the SUV. Unbeknownst to the plant workers, Rent and Senator Cale drove out of discovery park in one of their Suburbans, having broken into three offices and stolen over six hundred dollars worth of their medical supplies.

"This is falling down around us." Qudamah said in agitation after being forwarded to Kicham's voicemail for a third time.

"Perhaps he is out of range. Rent is surely dead by now." Aziz comforted his friend.

"Until Kicham tells us otherwise, Rent is still alive." Qudamah responded.

"What will we do with the policeman?" Aziz asked. "We

must use him."

"Yes, we must." Qudamah dialed another number on the phone. The familiar voice picked up. "The time has come for your mission." Qudamah told him.

"I want to talk to my wife and daughter." The voice demanded.

"You know I will not let you." Qudamah responded.

"I won't do anything without first speaking to them." The voice told him.

"That will be your decision, but they will find out that you gave me the information. They will find out that you worked with us, you will go to jail. Either way, your family will still die." Qudamah responded, knowing that the man would do what he was told. "Who is in charge there?"

"Bethany Knox has taken over the Police Department, but the man really calling the shots is an FBI Assistant Director named Bannister." The voice answered.

"Good, I want you to kill him." Qudamah commanded.

"But...I can't..."

"Kill him or I will sever your daughter's head from her body!" Qudamah yelled before hanging up his phone.

"Do you think he will go through with it?" Aziz asked.

"Absolutely."

The FBI agent and Knox climbed the stairs and started down the hallway toward Seacrest's office. On the way, they ran into Captain Carrasco, who was coming out of the bathroom, his face wet like he had just splashed water on it.

"What are you doing up here?" Knox stopped and asked, noticing that the FBI agent kept walking.

"Looking for Seacrest." Carrasco said, putting his cell phone back into his pants pocket. "Jackson just found Lewis Austin dead in his house. I wanted to ask the doctor if it had any connection to Rent."

"Damn, Lewis was one of our best." Knox commented. "Where is Jackson now?"

"Probably on his way here." Carrasco responded. "Where's Bannister? I need to tell him."

"He's downstairs in our command center working up some information." Knox told him. Carrasco nodded and went down the stairs. Knox continued on into Seacrest's office. Dr. Seacrest had a small office in the building where he saw the various police officers either for personal or professional reasons. He also maintained a larger office for his private practice somewhere else in town, but state law forced him to keep all his police related files in one of the buildings run and maintained by the department.

The office was small, it contained a desk, two large chairs for him and his patients, and two large filing cabinets on either side of the room. The walls held various pictures of personal significance to Seacrest and diplomas from the various schools he had attended. Knox had been in the office several times before, but this time she felt uncomfortable because of what she was doing.

The filing cabinets were locked and in the time that it had taken to talk to Captain Carrasco, the FBI agent picked both locks and was starting to look through the files. Knox glanced around at the walls, noticing the pictures of Seacrest with other psychiatrists and professionals. One photo of Seacrest standing with a movie star always caught her eye. She noticed that his doctorate from UCLA was also on the wall. Holding back her discomfort, Knox went through Seacrest's desk before turning to one of the filing cabinets and starting in its top drawer.

Rent cut the lights and engine so the SUV could roll silently into the parking lot of the fishery. The building, which was located on the water's edge so that large fishing boats could dock and unload their cargo was dark now. Rent knew it had been abandoned for several years. Seattle's fishing industry had seen a major decline in the preceding decade and several of the large fisheries tanked in the more competitive marketplace.

"This is it?" Cale asked. Rent motioned for the Senator to hand him his gun. "How can we be sure they're here?" Cale asked. "How can you be sure that guy wasn't lying?"

"We can't." Rent checked the status of his Sig Sauer and placed it back in the holster on his belt.

"What's your plan?" Cale asked, not knowing what move Rent was going to make next.

"You read the bible?" Rent asked, ejecting the magazine from the Glock that Cale handed him.

"Yeah."

"Well the wrath of God is about to befall these scumbags." Rent thought of Dylan and became angry. He checked the magazine to make sure it was full, and slapped it back into the weapon, chambering a round. Rent opened the door quietly. "Stay here. Liz and I will be right back." He told Cale before gently and silently shutting his door and making his way to the building.

Outside, at the edge of the building, a young Arabic man named Fida, who was digging a shallow grave in which to bury Dylan Austin watched Rent leave Cale alone in the SUV and start toward the building. Not knowing exactly what he should do, Fida took a pistol from his belt and approached the vehicle.

Dr. Michael Seacrest showed his Police Department identification card to the officer at the front entrance of the North Precinct. The officer nodded, and checked a list of civilian employees that were designated important enough to be allowed inside the building. Finding Seacrest's name, the officer waved him through. Seacrest passed the desk, and another officer approached him.

"Dr. Seacrest?" The officer, a Sergeant, asked.

"Yes." Seacrest answered.

"Chief Knox is looking for you. I think she's in the downstairs operations room." The Sergeant told him. "She indicated it was important."

"Alright thanks." Seacrest told the officer and headed in the direction of the room.

Fisheries like the Perchman Fishery were commonplace in Seattle. Abandoned ones often became the playgrounds of teenagers or the homeless. Qudamah chose the fishery for two reasons: first, it was very close to the Ballard docks and would afford Qudamah an easy escape to the boat. Second, the fishery gave Qudamah a sense of privacy, it was on a street that was rarely traveled because all the fisheries on that particular street were abandoned.

Sajid, a young, enthusiastic college student who was born and raised in Connecticut liked the spacious and lonely feeling that the building provided. Sajid was the product of Muslim immigrants from Syria. His father owned and operated a small grocery in Bridgeport. Sajid's parents worked for years to provide the money necessary to send him to college. After a difficult search for the right school, he and his parents decided on UCLA, where he met Qudamah for the first time. Sajid's parents did not know what he was doing, nor did he believe they would approve. To Sajid, his parents had become the enemy, no longer did his mother wear the hijab, the traditional garments worn by Muslim women. Instead, his parents had become "Americanized" which angered Sajid. He had come to believe more in his religion than anything else.

Sajid had been given burial detail with Fida. They decided that it be only appropriate to dig the child a grave rather than throw him in the bay, the course of action suggested by Aziz. Through course of lively discussion, they'd gained permission to bury the boy outside the fishery but only after night fell. After digging for fifteen or twenty minutes, Sajid needed to use the restroom and on his way back, he decided to get himself and his compatriot some tea.

Sajid stepped down the stairs to the ground floor carefully with the two full coffee cups of tea and rounded a corner to the exit where he found Rent, moving silently down the corridor, gun in hand and aiming straight at him. Sajid and Rent locked eyes and Rent saw that Sajid's hands were shaking nervously.

They both stood, staring at each other without sound or movement for over a minute. Sajid's mind was racing, he had been so startled by Rent that he didn't know what to do. Rent on the other hand, could only think of little Dylan Austin and throughout the time they stared each other down, his anger boiled hotter and hotter.

Finally, Rent slipped his finger inside the trigger guard of the Glock, fired one round through the coffee cup into Sajid's chest, then double tapped him in the head.

In the upstairs room where Esam and Aziz were taking down the laptops and preparing to destroy them in the furnace, Qudamah was again attempting to reach Kicham on his cell phone. The three men heard the shots and each grabbed their pistols. Qudamah moved to the door and looked out, seeing nothing in the hallway, he moved back into the room to think this development out.

"The police have found us!" Esam screamed.

"No, we would know it, there are no lights, there are no men!" Aziz said, peering out the window that overlooked the road.

"It's Rent. It must be." Qudamah said, figuring that Rent somehow escaped Kicham. He looked around the room and saw the other two men looking to him for leadership. "Aziz, take the vest to the car. I will get the mother and meet you there." Qudamah ordered. "Esam, kill Rent!" Esam nodded and turned to Aziz who opened a footlocker that was on the floor and tossed him an AK-47, followed by two magazines. Aziz took an AK for himself, along with several magazines.

Esam left the room first, his rifle out in front of him as he moved down the hallway. Qudamah left next and followed Esam while Aziz took the explosive vest and moved in the opposite direction.

Rent entered the processing area of the fishery with his weapon out in front. He moved carefully between the various machines and pits used to process the many fish that went through the facility. He saw the set of stairs at the back of the processing center and moved toward them. Esam came down an adjacent set of stairs. Rent heard the footsteps but before he could turn his weapon to face them, Esam began firing.

Rent ducked for cover behind some machinery and returned fire at the first opportunity he got. Esam was moving very quickly between the machinery, taking cover everywhere he could. Hearing the silence between shots, Rent crept about the processing area, switching on every piece of equipment he passed.

Aziz put the explosive vest over his shoulder and climbed down the ladder leading to the gravel parking lot that contained the large white van. The young terrorist quickly placed the vest inside the sliding door, got in the driver's seat and started the vehicle.

Esam came up behind Rent and started firing. Rent dove over a workbench and returned fire. Rent dashed to take cover behind some of the larger processing machinery. Esam maneuvered himself to take more shots at Rent. The former cop threw himself backward onto the long conveyer belt that he'd turned on. The belt moved Rent away from Esam, who took cover to avoid Rent's fire.

Liz had been awakened by the gunfire. Hoping against hope, she got herself to her feet and not knowing what was happening or what she could do, she backed herself up against the back wall of the room. Qudamah flung the door open and ran to her. She resisted at first but Qudamah threatened her children, took her by the arm and led her out of the room.

Rent ran along the conveyer belt shooting. Esam was sporadically taking cover behind the machines and hastily returning fire at Rent. Rent felt his slide click back, tossed the Glock away and jumping from the conveyer belt, he took his Sig Sauer from its holster. Esam saw him jump and fired several times.

Esam saw that Rent was moving to take cover behind several large machines that were next to a linoleum pit was used to clean fish. Rent ran to the cover, and Esam emptied his magazine at him. Rent returned by emptying his own magazine at Esam. Under cover, Rent ejected his spent magazine and replaced it with another. Esam took cover behind a pillar and did the same. A moment later, they were firing at each other again.

Fearing a stalemate, Rent looked around for something he could use. He saw the large linoleum pit and a water spigot attached to the wall. Esam fired another short volley at Rent and instead of returning fire at Esam, Rent sent two rounds into the spigot, causing it to burst water all over the linoleum.

Rent took two shots at Esam, and when Esam left cover to return fire, Rent used his legs to push himself off the machinery, onto his belly and across the linoleum. Kicking out with his right leg, Rent went into a spin, hydroplaning across the pit.

Seeing his chance, Esam moved from his cover and let slip several rounds but none hit the spinning Rent. Rent whirled around and loosed five rounds of his own, two of which struck Esam in the chest. Esam fell to the ground, his weapon thrown several feet behind him.

Rent jumped to his feet. Walking past Esam, he casually fired two more rounds into him.

"Carey!" Rent heard Cale yell before he got to the stairs. Cale and Fida were in the processing center, about 15 feet from Rent. Fida was standing behind the old Senator, a gun to his head. Rent instantly turned and drew down on the two.

"Drop your gun, or I'll kill him!" Fida yelled at Rent. "Drop your gun!"

"Just cool out." Rent replied without lowering his weapon.

"Drop your gun, or I kill him now!" Fida yelled, almost hysterically.

"Ok, I'm dropping my gun." Rent lowered his weapon, then quickly raised and fired a single shot into Fida's head. The impact threw Fida back and left the bewildered Senator standing alone. Rent didn't say anything, he turned and ran up the stairs. Cale turned around, took Fida's gun, and searched him, finding a cell phone.

Inside the makeshift control room, Rent saw that it was empty, he heard the roar of an engine outside and looked out a window to see the white van. He frantically looked around, the drop from the window was too high for him to jump, but there was a thin tin roof that was under the window of the next room. Rent grabbed a chair, and after kicking in the door of the adjacent room, he threw the chair out the window.

The first thing Qudamah and Liz heard when they came out of the building was the breaking glass hitting the tin roof above them. Rent jumped from the window onto the tin roof that was held up by wooden pillars and covered nothing but the ground. Qudamah shoved Liz into the back of the van and slammed the sliding door shut before taking several shots at Rent. Undeterred, Rent started running along the tin roof.

"Go!" Qudamah yelled and jumped into the passenger seat of the van. The vehicle spun gravel with its back tires. Rent ran along the roof chasing the van until he came to the roof's end. Rent jumped, hoping to land on the van, but the vehicle was slightly ahead of him. Rent's feet hit the ground hard behind the van, and Rent went face first into the gravel.

Rent looked up from the ground and watched the van speed off onto Seaview Avenue. Slowly, he pushed himself to his feet. He watched his hope fade with the van. He holstered his weapon. Rent stood, staring into the night. Cale emerged from the building and walked up behind him.

"That's it." Rent said solemnly. "It's over, we've failed."

"Not yet." Cale replied, holding Fida's cell phone out to Rent. "We can still negotiate." Rent turned to look at the obstinate Senator.

Carrasco came to the door of the command center at exactly the same time Seacrest did. Politely, Carrasco stood aside and motioned for Seacrest to enter. The two entered the room and saw Bannister in the back giving orders to some agents. The two men crossed the room towards Bannister.

Upstairs in Seacrest's office, neither Knox nor the FBI agent found the file they'd been looking for. After finishing searching his filing cabinet, the agent began to look around the office for anywhere else the file might have been kept. Knox continued looking through her cabinet, thinking of Seacrest's words before the briefing. She'd asked him if he still had Rent's file, and he'd replied no, he'd also said that Al-Khalifa knew exactly what to look for in the men he'd selected. She looked through the file names, and these statements began to haunt her, though she didn't know why.

The FBI agent located Seacrest's briefcase, put it on his desk and opened it. He looked through the various files inside, picking out the last one and opening it.

"Here it is." The agent said. "What's it doing in here?" He looked through the papers inside the folder. Knox stopped and stared at one of the files in the filing cabinet. "Hey," the agent said, looking up, "you know who she's married to?" The agent stepped over to the acting police chief with the file in hand.

"Seacrest!" Knox exclaimed, everything coming together. Knox immediately turned and ran out of the office, her cell phone in hand, dialing Carrasco. The agent looked closer at the file she'd been staring at: **Rent, Carey.**

"I need to talk to Bannister." Seacrest told Carrasco when they approached Bannister at the same time.

"Alright, go ahead." Carrasco capitulated, not knowing what Seacrest was planning on doing. He took a few steps back and started looking at some reports. Seacrest moved toward Bannister from behind.

Carrasco's cell phone rang. He picked it out of his pocket and put it to his ear. "Hi honey." He said, thankful to hear his wife's voice. "No, I just wanted to make sure you and the kids were ok."

Frustrated that she couldn't get through to Carrasco, Knox ran down the stairs and past several officers.

Ignorant that Seacrest was behind him, Bannister continued his dialogue with the agents. Seacrest reached into his pocket and pulled out a .380 automatic pistol. He walked up behind Bannister and raised the pistol.

Chapter 14:

Seacrest raised the weapon to the back of Bannister's head, closed his eyes and pulled his trigger finger inward.

"Drop that weapon!" Knox yelled from the doorway, her sidearm drawn. The entire room jumped in surprise before drawing their own weapons, most finding the threat. Bannister didn't move, he stared straight ahead. "Michael, I know about your wife and stepdaughter." Knox moved across the room, keeping her weapon trained on Seacrest. "I know you knew Khalifa from UCLA."

"I have to do this." Seacrest said, more to reassure himself than Knox. "You don't know."

"I know you gave Khalifa Senator Cale's schedule, you gave him a copy of Rent's file. I know you're married to the Chief's secretary. I know Khalifa took your family Michael." Knox told him. "And I know he told you to do this, but you don't have to."

"I can't lose Alice, I just found her, I can't lose her." Seacrest's hand was shaking.

"I know Michael, I know how much you love her. I know

how much you love your stepdaughter. Khalifa is using you, he's been using you for a long time, even before he kidnaped Alice and your stepdaughter."

"He said he was collecting research across the country on people who had experienced debilitating loss. I didn't know what he was planning." Seacrest tried to justify his actions.

"I believe you Michael, put the gun down, you don't have to do this." Knox said. The tension in the room reached an apex.

"He'll kill them if I don't do this. Please, I can't lose them." Seacrest argued.

"Michael, it doesn't matter now, we found them." Knox told him.

"Oh God they're dead, oh God no." He started saying.

"Michael, you need to stay calm!" Knox pressed, trying to salvage the situation. "You're not going to do them any good if you do something rash!"

"He wouldn't have released them alive. I've killed them!" Tears streamed down Seacrest's face.

"Yes Michael, they are gone. That's why you can't do this Michael, everything you've done up to this point has been done for a reason, but not this, not any more." Knox told him. "We need to know what you know. It's the only way we can help the people he's still holding hostage. I know I'm getting through to you Michael."

"I don't know anything." Seacrest said.

"Alice wouldn't want you to do this, she wouldn't want you to sacrifice everything now. There's no point in it. Put the gun down. You know she loved you and she wouldn't want you to do this. Michael, do it for her." Knox said. Seacrest knew that she was right, his new family wouldn't have wanted him to do this.

Slowly, he lowered the pistol. Carrasco rushed him, grabbing the weapon from his hand and throwing him on the floor. The other officers charged in and handcuffed him. Bannister let out the air he'd been holding in his lungs since the situation began.

When Seacrest had been secured, Knox ordered him placed in an interrogation room. Leading him out the door, the officers passed Jackson and Owens, Jackson holding a small portrait of the Austin family.

"What's that all about?" Jackson asked, Carrasco informed him of the past few minute's happenings.

"You!" Knox yelled, seeing Jackson. "You're not about to be on patrol, you're about to be unemployed!"

"Now isn't the time Bethany." Bannister told her, still a little shaken. "What have you got?"

Calleigh Austin sat on her knees, handcuffed to a radiator in the upstairs master bedroom of the house. She'd cried so much her eyes could no longer create tears. The six year old girl looked around the room seeing the bed, the chest of drawers and the night tables so common to bedrooms. On the bed sat a vest with very large pouches that Calleigh didn't understand were filled with plastic explosives. Looking up at the window, she reached up and pulled on the cord to the blinds which lifted them and revealed the cloudy night's sky. She sat back down and stared out the window. She saw out the window, several more sleeper agents coming through the gate.

She didn't know what to think when the lock clicked and the door slowly opened to reveal Mustafar, the man who had taken her to the house from the fishery. He entered the room slowly while discussing something in Arabic with another man. He placed a small steaming TV dinner on top of the radiator along with a plastic fork and tossed a can of soda into her lap.

"Eat." Mustafar turned and locked the door.

Bannister looked around the room, Knox, Jackson, Owens, Carrasco, and FBI agents encircled the large table in the center of the room and were all trying to talk to him at the same time. Bannister tried to appease them for a few moments by listening but was quickly overwhelmed.

"Ok, hold on." Bannister said loudly, everyone continued talking. "Hey, shut up!" He yelled, soon the room was quiet. "Ok, let's lay this out. According to what Seacrest has just told us, Al-Khalifa used his contacts to compile research from other psychiatrist's files for the past year or so. This enabled him to pick and choose which people to use for his plan. We also know that sometime before that, he was recruited into the splinter sect of Al-Qaeda by Kicham Baday."

"Senator Cale's visit to Seattle has been on the books for almost six months now. I think it's safe to assume he was just waiting for it." An FBI agent told the table.

"Khalifa needed someone to assassinate Cale, but he couldn't use any Joe Blow, he needed someone with the training and moxy to get to the Senator." Jackson interjected.

"Enter Michael Seacrest, he knew and trusted Khalifa from his time at UCLA. He'd sent in the research material along with the other psychiatrists. Khalifa must have used that to choose Rent to do the job." Knox added.

"Senator Cale's detailed schedule was sent out three days ago, that must have been when Khalifa grabbed Seacrest's family. Next he made the tape and sent it over the internet to Al-Jazeera." Carrasco told them.

"Once the other sleepers had been activated, Al-Khalifa used them to start grabbing the families. Atlanta, Chicago, Utah, and three more besides Seacrest's here in Seattle, Jason Brewer's, Lynn Rowan's, and Lewis Austin's." Bannister said.

"He kills Seacrest's family early, we don't know for what reason, but keeps the others alive." Jackson contributed.

"Right because he probably knows that he has to kill or have Seacrest killed. Either way, it's useless to keep his family alive, just more hostages to feed and watch." Knox said.

"Lewis Austin must have been last, probably this morning. He kills Lewis and takes the family to make contact with Rent." Jackson added.

"He tells Rent he has to kill Senator Cale." Knox said.

"But Rent chooses to kidnap him instead, probably to buy time." Jackson responded.

"Jason Brewer decides he can't complete his assignment and hits the fence." Bannister told them. "But Lynn Rowan does complete her assignment and attacks Police Plaza, where because of Seacrest's intelligence, Khalifa knows that the FBI has set up shop."

"Now the youngest Austin escapes and is chased by our unidentified terrorist. Jackson and Owens corner him and he commits suicide rather than be caught." Carrasco added.

"Only we find Seacrest's family in the bay, Khalifa finds out somehow, panics and orders Seacrest to kill the head FBI agent on the scene." Knox told them.

"Exactly." Bannister leaned on the table. "Which means

that he wanted Seacrest out of play and that means that Seacrest can hurt him somehow."

"If he knew anything, he'd have told us." Knox said.

"Not if he doesn't know it's damaging." Bannister told her. All talking stopped when the sound of a cell phone ringing resonated around the room. Jackson looked around, slightly embarrassed. He picked the phone out of his pocket and put it to his ear.

"Jackson." He said.

"Dave it's me." Rent said over the phone. he'd parked the SUV he was driving on a small grassy patch just off the street, overlooking the city. Cale stepped around the vehicle and Rent put on the speaker phone so both could talk and listen.

"Carey where the hell are you?" Jackson said loudly into his phone, getting the room's undivided attention.

"Come on Dave, I'm not going to tell you that." Rent sat the phone down on the hood of the SUV.

"Ok, I'm putting you on speaker." Jackson told him.

"No, don't do that." Rent stammered.

"Carey, you're on with Terry Bannister of the FBI, Captain Carrasco and Chief Knox." Jackson placed the phone on the table and the others gathered around.

"Thanks Dave." Rent said sarcastically.

"Mr. Rent, this is Terry Bannister, Assistant Director of the FBI. Is Senator Cale alive?"

"Yes, I'm here." Cale told him. "I'm with Rent on my own volition."

"I understand Senator, but you must know that you're under duress and we can't consider you credible." Bannister informed.

"That figures." Cale responded.

"Look, Mr. Rent, we know about the Austins." Bannister took a few seconds to think the scenario through and decided that he had to make Rent at least believe that they could work together. "This has been orchestrated by a man named Qudamah Al-Khalifa. He's a psychologist from UCLA and plans to use the attacks to take control of Al-Qaeda."

"That fits, you need to send your men down to discovery park, a guy named Kicham Bradley and his crew are down there. They had kind of a bad day. There's more at the Perchman Fishery off Seaview. Their day wasn't much better. Jason Brewer committed suicide in the abandoned Rhine apartment building in Pill Hill" Rent informed.

"Understood." Bannister noted, sending an agent to investigate Rent's claims with a nod. "Mr. Rent, because of the circumstances, I can assure you right here and now that if you bring Senator Cale in, you won't face any charges for his abduction. Mr. Rent this is a one time offer."

"I got you, but we can't come in yet, they've killed Dylan Austin and they still have Liz and the two daughters, we'll come in once we get them back." Rent stated.

"Carey, we got the youngest daughter, she's safe." Jackson told him.

"Thank God, but they've still got Liz and the other daughter. We know where the kid is, but this Khalifa guy got away with Liz. He's in the wind." Rent told them.

"Where's the child?" Knox asked.

"We think she's at 402 Mayfield. That's what I was told but we don't know for sure."

"Check it." Knox pointed to one of her officers.

"Mr. Rent, you need to bring Senator Cale in. If he's in danger, Khalifa may still be able to salvage his plan, but if he's safe Khalifa most likely won't be able to garner the support he needs to take over the organization." Bannister told him.

"Yeah and the moment he's safe, Khalifa kills Liz. I won't risk that, do you understand?" Rent argued.

"If he's in the wind Mr. Rent, he means to make his escape, surely you know that." Bannister came back.

"I can still draw him out." Cale entered the debate. "But we're going to need you to secure the child first."

"There's a slight problem with that Senator. We think they plan to blow that house up when the time is right, if we rush them, they'll do it." Knox told them.

"We can do it Senator." Carrasco contradicted. "We'll get

her." Bannister turned and stared at the SWAT commander.

"How are you going to draw him out and where?" Bannister asked the phone.

"Nope, can't do it, if he even thinks we've involved you, he'll kill Liz and take his chances. We can't corner him like that, he's holding all the cards." Rent shot back.

"Don't you dare go rogue again Rent. We'll handle this." Knox yelled into the phone.

"Bethany?" Rent's tone nice and caring. "Stick it up your ass." Knox's face flustered with anger. "Dave?" Rent asked.

"Yeah I'm here."

"The youngest daughter, the one you found, what's her name?" Rent asked.

"We don't know, the only word she'll say is daddy." Jackson responded.

"Ok." Rent replied, disappointment in his voice. "We'll try and draw him out, get that kid." Rent hung up. Jackson saved the number Rent called from.

"Don't make promises you can't keep." Bannister sternly lectured Carrasco. The officer that Knox sent out of the room ran back in with a sheet of paper in his hand. Knox took the paper and read it carefully.

"402 Mayfield is owned by Dr. Michael Seacrest, and it's only a few blocks away from where Jackson found the little girl."

She stated aloud.

"That's it." Bannister noted. "Ok, I want all available units to surround this place. I want it clamped down tighter than a pair of nun's panties, nothing gets out, got me?"

"No! Don't do that!" Carrasco almost yelled.

"What then?" Bannister asked. Everyone's attention turned to Carrasco.

"Listen, he doesn't want us to know about this place yet, that's why he took Seacrest out of play. They aren't ready for us, when they are, you better believe they'll call and let us know. That is unless you surround them with lights and sirens. When they see that, they're just going to play us for time before they blow themselves up, just like in Atlanta." Carrasco told them.

"Do you have a better idea?"

"We cordon off no closer than five blocks so that they don't know we're there, then we send my team in." Carrasco suggested.

"With all due respect, I'm sure you're a competent commander, but if we were to do that I'd prefer an FBI team and we don't have one." Bannister told him. The Seattle officials stopped cold, it was the first time they'd heard Bannister say something they knew to be wrong.

"Captain Carrasco is one of the best SWAT commander's in the country." Knox told Bannister.

"He trains your Hostage Rescue Teams twice a year at

Quantico." Jackson added. Bannister stepped back a moment to think about the new information.

"You wanna throw a surprise party?" He asked Carrasco.

"That's exactly what I want." Carrasco responded.

"What's your plan?" Bannister rubbed his chin with his good hand. Carrasco detailed his plan for the room. "That's never before been done by a civilian SWAT team." Bannister said after Carrasco finished.

"We always knew it was a possibility, we've trained for it." Carrasco answered.

"If you fail?" Bannister asked. "You know what happens if they get to their bomb before you stop them."

"I'll take only volunteers." Carrasco said.

"I'll be the first to volunteer." Jackson told them.

"What about you?" Carrasco asked Owens. "You're a reserve member and my team is still short.

"I'm in." Owens said, looking at Jackson. "What the hell, right?" Jackson nodded his approval at Owens' decision.

"Get everything together. I'll have to get authorization from Washington." Bannister concluded.

The van moved through traffic at average speed. Neither

Qudamah nor Aziz wished to draw the attention of law enforcement, thus Aziz was very careful to obey all the traffic laws. During the trip, Qudamah went into the back of the van and used a pair of handcuffs to secure Liz to the sliding side door. The van was silent, with only the sounds of the police radio that Qudamah had in his lap to break the harmony of the outside traffic.

"What are we going to do now?" Aziz asked after several minutes of Qudamah's meditation.

"We will make our escape. The plan has succeeded." Qudamah looked out the window.

"What of Kicham, we have to assume he is dead and we can no longer use that escape route." Aziz asked.

"We must, yes. But it will have no bearing, drive north. When we reach the border we will order our men in the house to wage their war." Qudamah responded.

"And until then, if Rent goes to the cops they will find us before we are ready?" Aziz's question caused Qudamah to stir. The decision facing the professor was whether he could take a chance at getting caught. He had the explosive vest in the back, but did not wish to use it on himself unless absolutely necessary. He also had Liz, but he wished to use her to bargain with if he was found. Qudamah searched his mind for a solution. Suddenly, he was snapped out of his thoughts by the sounds of the police radio, the voices giving him an idea.

"The police will have more to deal with than us." Qudamah assured his friend before lifting the police radio, pushing in the button and speaking. "Attention Police! Attention Police! I am Qudamah bin Salman bin Abdul Aziz Al-Khalifa. I am responsible for the attacks on this imperialist nation today. I have taken the families of Americans to show all citizens of this country that no one is safe from Allah's wrath..."

Knox jumped when she heard the statement come over the radio. Bannister had left to join the SWAT team making Knox the ranking officer. She rushed out the door of the command center and ran down the halls to the temporary radio hub set up after the explosion at Police Plaza knocked out communications.

"As you can see, your own citizens are committing these terrorist acts, they do so under Allah's orders and they wage war against their own country. No child is safe, no parent can be ruled out a potential terrorist..." Qudamah was saying over the radio when Knox ran into the room.

"Shut him off!" She yelled.

"I can't, not without shutting the entire system down." A technician told her.

"The media monitor our radios, shut the whole system down!

Do it now! We have to shut him up!" Knox screamed at him.

"It's not that easy, you can't just..." The technician argued.

"Do it now!" Knox yelled again and reached behind the tables, shutting off the power strip they were using. Simultaneously, all the computers went dead.

"There is no place you can hide from Allah's will, there is no safe pla..." The transmission abruptly stopped.

"Contact all officer's by cell and land line, tell them to switch to the alternate frequencies." Knox commanded.

"There is no alternate frequency." The technician told her.

"What?"

"The system we had to set up can only be operated on one channel." The technician told her in an aggravated tone. "We had to rig the repeaters across the city to work independently of the main network, once the network is terminated, like you just did, the only way we can regain radio communications is by rebooting each individual repeater by itself."

"How long will that take?" Knox asked, her worry growing.

"A couple of hours, at least." The technician replied.

"The news outlets are going live again." An officer entering the room told Knox. "I think they're spilling it."

"Get everybody you can find," Knox turned to the officer, "put them all in riot gear and get ready for deployment."

The three vans of SWAT members, including reserve team member Owens and former member Jackson set up about a block and a half from the address. Officers were sent out to set up observation posts and fiber optic cameras to look at the house. The FBI sent the blueprints of the house to a laptop computer while the vans were en route and Carrasco was using the diagrams to design his entry plan.

Every available officer was used to attempt to cordon off a five block radius around the house but there were still large gaps in the coverage. Even though radio communication for this operation was prohibited, the officer's on the edge of the cordon were left confused by the disabling of the police radios.

One of the SWAT vans that arrived was a state of the art command center, it was designed to hold three operators, though only one was needed, and only one was inside. The interior walls of the van were lined with monitors and computer equipment, and the operator positioned himself in the command chair. He began turning on the equipment.

The second van contained the gear necessary to make entry. The SWAT team members suited up in their usual black Battle Dress Uniforms, and picked out their individual equipment per a prepared list depending on the type of entry they would be doing. This particular entry mandated full body armor, a utility vest on top of that, kevlar helmet, balaclava, side drop holster, three point sling, Nomex gloves, and LASH communications equipment. Flashlights were attached to both the MP-5 submachine guns they would be using and their Smith and Wesson tactical pistols. Carrasco used his key–he had one of only two–to open the cages that contained the silencers for the MP-5's. Another officer handed them to the teams waiting outside the van. Over and above what was dictated on the prepared list of equipment, two grappling hooks with ropes were also ordered by Carrasco.

Two sniper positions were set up on nearby houses to overlook the target house, these teams were designated Charlie 1 and Charlie 2, each team contained a sniper and a spotter.

When the teams were geared up, Carrasco led them to the assigned starting point behind some buildings, about a block from the target house. It was at this location that Alpha and Bravo teams went over the plan and made their final checks. Each team consisted of four men, Carrasco led Jackson on Alpha team, and was in overall command of the operation once it commenced. Bravo team leader led his team which included Owens but still reported to Carrasco.

Individual team members checked their gear to make sure that everything was operational before being checked again by the man next to them, and finally a third time by their team leader. The team members jumped up and down while their partners listened to make sure they emitted no noise and that all of their gear was securely fastened to their person.

They also checked their LASH systems–a communications system consisting of a device that wrapped around the throat and amplified vibrations made in the larynx, thus enabling the speaker to talk at the lowest possible whisper. The device sends the message loud and clear through the other headsets. The last thing done was to chamber rounds in all the weapons.

"HQ, Alpha, and Bravo teams ready for deployment." Carrasco said into his LASH, watching his teams line up in what was called the stick.

"Roger that Alpha one, standby." The officer in the command van told them. The officer checked and rechecked his systems. Bannister entered the van a few minutes later and stood next to the operator. "Would you like to listen sir?" The operator asked him. Bannister nodded, took a set of earphones with his good hand and clumsily placed them on his head.

"Can I talk to them through this?" Bannister asked.

"No sir, only I can talk to our team. We're completely autonomous from all systems. We even have a coded channel with our own repeater." The operator answered.

"Alright, I've got approval from Washington. It's a go. Whenever they're ready." Bannister told him.

"Yes sir." The operator said, flipping a switch. "All teams we have a green light, report status."

"Alpha and Bravo teams ready." Carrasco replied.

"Charlie 1 ready."

"Charlie 2 ready."

"Status acknowledged, all teams begin operation on Alpha 6's mark." The operator ordered. Carrasco took his place at the front of the stick. He reached back with his right hand and slapped the man behind him, who sent the slap to the man behind him until the slap reached the last person, and that person sent it back up the stick until it got to Carrasco.

"HQ, teams are moving to infiltration point." Carrasco said, leading Alpha and Bravo teams down an alley. The teams moved slowly toward their target, weaving in and out between the buildings until they got to the street next to the walled in house. The teams separated, going in opposite directions around a building across the street from the house. The street was carefully checked for hostiles. Both teams crossed and took cover directly behind the wall, moving to a predetermined point. "HQ, Alpha and Bravo at infiltration point." Carrasco said after the teams met up. Bravo leader dropped his MP-5 which was held in place on his chest by the three point sling and cupped his hands so that Carrasco could step into them. Bravo leader lifted him up to the point where Carrasco's head could see over the wall. Carrasco slipped on his night vision goggles to look over the wall. Seeing no hostiles, he scaled the wall, jumping to the other side and taking up a firing position on the ground.

"Clear for infiltration." He said into his LASH radio.

Each team swung their grappling hooks over the wall and one by one they came over, each assuming a firing position on one knee on the other side. After everyone was over the wall, the last man on each team jumped up and knocked the grappling hooks back over to the street side of the wall. Both teams lined back up in their respective sticks and gave the slap.

"Alpha and Bravo teams moving to standby positions." Carrasco told the operator and the teams separated again. Carrasco's team moved to the front of the house, while Bravo team approached the rear entrance. Before either team came in sight of their destination however, they stopped and took cover on the side of the house. "Alpha at standby position."

"Bravo at standby position."

"Roger that." The operator acknowledged. "Charlie team, clear your sights."

"Charlie 1, going sights hot."

"Charlie 2, going sights hot."

The sentry guarding the back porch lit his cigarette. A moment later, a round from the silenced sniper rifle ripped through his head and he fell to the ground.

"Charlie 2, sights are clear."

Two men stood on the front porch, both had AK-47's. The one on the right side of the porch turned to look around the front yard and wall just before he was struck in the head and fell. The other man saw this and started to raise his rifle and yell, but before any sound could leave his mouth; he was struck in the head by a second round.

"Charlie 1, sights are clear."

"Roger that, we are free of exterior hostiles." The operator said into the radio. "Alpha, Bravo teams, move to entry points."

Carrasco sent the slap back and a few seconds later it was returned. The moment he felt the slap he began moving onto the porch. Covering his weapon everywhere he looked, he used hand gestures to signal the window before lowering himself below it and raising back to his feet when he got to the door. The other team members did the same and soon they were all in the stick next to the door.

"Alpha, ready for entry."

"Bravo, ready for entry." Bravo team leader said into his radio when his team was in position on the back door.

One of the terrorists in the upstairs bedroom casually walked over to the window to look out. Scanning the night filled yard, he noticed something at the bottom of the window, very close to the house. He leaned up against the window to see what it was.

"Roger that." The operator signaled he'd heard and understood the transmissions. "Simultaneous silent entry on my mark. Five second count." With his command, the SWAT team members got ready to move.

The terrorist stood on his tip toes to see what was directly below the window. His eyes widened when he saw one of the men assigned to guard the front porch laying on the ground with a hole in his head.

"Five..."

"Mustafar! Mustafar!" He yelled.

"What?" Was Mustafar's reply.

"Four..."

"They're here, the Americans!" The terrorist yelled, grabbing for his AK-47. Mustafar ran out the door, with the other terrorist behind him.

"Three..."

"They're here!" The terrorist yelled in Arabic, darting for the stairs. Mustafar slammed the door to the master bedroom shut behind him. "They're here! Fight them!" The terrorist started down the stairs. The four men in the living room heard their comrade's yells and remembered their weapons.

"Two..."

The men in the living room reached for their weapons and began chambering rounds.

"Commence entry." The operator ordered.

In the kitchen, Bravo team burst in, finding one terrorist inside, making a sandwich, his only weapon; a butter knife. Bravo leader put three rounds into his chest followed by two more into his head.

Alpha team exploded into the living room, each team member finding targets and unleashing a barrage of silenced bullets into them. Within seconds all four men in the living room were dead from multiple gunshot wounds. The team cleared the living room of anything still alive. The other terrorist ran down the stairs. He saw the SWAT team and lifted his weapon to fire but was first slammed by the team's bullets. His body flung itself down the stairs.

The two teams met in the center hallway that connected the kitchen to the living room before turning their attention to the second floor.

"Ground floor clear, no hostage." Carrasco told the operator. "Charlie team, status on second floor?"

"Charlie 2, no hostiles in sight." Charlie 2's spotter announced.

"Charlie 1, unable to determine, cannot see into master bedroom from this position, relocating." Charlie 1's spotter said and the pair began to move.

"Clearing second floor." Carrasco said. The teams moved up the stairs, first clearing the rooms on the east side, and getting to the master bedroom last.

During the process, their order became mixed up, but per their training they adapted. Owens reached the master bedroom first, therefore he would be the first to enter. Jackson represented Alpha team on the opposite side of the door, and Carrasco ended up taking position behind Owens. He gave Owens the slap. Owens reached out, turned the knob of the door, threw it open, entered the doorway, and was shot in the throat.

Owens flew back and was caught by Carrasco, who pulled him out of the fatal funnel. Jackson started to move in, he intended to do so firing but stopped when he heard Mustafar yelling.

"I have a bomb, I will blow the girl!" Mustafar screamed. Jackson bent down and took a quick peek inside the door. He saw Mustafar and Calleigh sitting upright on the bed, a suicide vest on Calleigh connected by a cord to a button that Mustafar was holding down in one hand and the pistol used to shoot Owens in the other. "I have pressure switch, if my hand leaves this button, it blows the girl! Back up! Back up!"

"Ok, we're backing up!" Jackson backed away from the door. Carrasco took a bandage out of his utility vest and held it tightly on Owen's wound.

"Get him out of here!" Carrasco ordered three of his men, two picked Owens up. The third applied pressure to keep the bandage in place. Carrasco looked at Jackson, neither knew what to do next.

"If this button is released the girl blows!" Mustafar continued yelling.

Chapter 15:

The long haired news anchor popped on the screen. "We are sorry to interrupt your program. We have more breaking news on the terrorist attacks that have rocked our nation today." She began speaking. "Following the terrorist attacks in Chicago, Atlanta, Utah and Seattle, a claim of responsibility has been placed by suspected Al-Qaeda member, Qudamah Al-Khalifa. The claim of responsibility came over Seattle's police radio system and was followed by the radio going completely off the air. It hasn't been determined yet, whether the radio signal was pulled intentionally or if it fell victim to another terrorist strike."

"According to Al-Khalifa," the male anchor next to her began speaking, "the attacks have been orchestrated by kidnaping the families of Americans and forcing them to commit the attacks. Although these claims have not been confirmed by the United States Government, the public is already reacting with outrage. For more on the public response, we now go to our affiliate WRKT in Detroit Michigan and their correspondent. Mike, what is happening where you are?"

"Well Ron, there are serious problems here." The on-scene reporter commented. "About ten minutes ago we saw the eruption of several riots in and around the Muslim section of the city. Michigan holds a large Muslim community and it appears that that community is now under attack." The correspondent pointed behind him to the chaos on the street. Several fires were ablaze in the broken out storefronts of the once peaceful community. "Police in riot gear have arrived on the scene and though no one would talk to us, it is assumed that they intend to protect the Muslims here from the crowds."

"Thank you Mike, we'll be back to you shortly." The anchorman said. "Now we turn to our on-site reporter Jack Whisner in Seattle. Jack what is happening in Seattle right now?"

"Rioting has broken out in the International District here. Apparently the riots were in response to the announcement made on the Seattle Police Department's radio but it has quickly turned into a free-for-all. What is particularly puzzling is the lack of police presence in the area. It may have something to do with the fact that the police radios are completely offline. Shop owners have taken to defending their businesses with privately owned firearms. Behind me, there is gunfire, you may be able to hear it? If I had to describe the situation, it would be something out of a movie, there is complete lawlessness here."

"Jack, do you fear for your safety?" The anchorman asked.

"Absolutely, but the crowd seems to be ignoring us. We've seen several people pulled out of their stores and homes and beaten, the crowd appears to be targeting foreigners, specifically Muslim Americans. We can only hope that the police get here soon to stop this. Wait a moment..." The reporter put his hand to his ear so that he could hear better. "We are receiving reports that police in riot gear are arriving at the edge of the international district. The police radios still seem to be offline, but reports are coming in that they're moving into the area. We're going to try to find them, I'll get back to you."

"The scene is similar in other parts of the country." The anchorwoman started. "In Los Angeles, where there is another large population of Muslims, there are also problems, we'll go now to our reporter on the scene Reginald McCalley. Reginald can you tell us what is happening?"

"Yes Cindy, it's total pandemonium down here. I'm standing in front of one of the largest Mosques in the United States and as you can see, the crowd has set the Mosque on fire. Now we haven't had these reports confirmed, but we have been told that several of the congregants refused to leave the Mosque. We've also been told that the Mayor of Los Angeles just signed a declaration of martial law. Right behind me Cindy, the national guard is deploying in an attempt to disperse the crowd and allow the fire department inside to attempt to control the fire. I'll keep you updated."

"Thank you Reginald." The anchorwoman told him. "Though we haven't received any confirmation of the allegations from the government, the Department of Homeland Security has issued a bulletin stating that all Americans should check the welfare of their families. For more, we go to our analyst, former counter-terrorism tzar of New York, Micheletti Santini. Mr. Santini, what can we expect in regards to our families?"

"Cindy, the American family is one of, if not the most important aspect of an American's life, right now we are seeing a wide variety of protective measures taking place to protect those families. I have heard reports that many Americans are gathering in public places, that they are barricading themselves in their homes and even that some are running to bomb shelters. What we must understand Cindy is that these weren't the families of prominent Americans that were kidnaped, these were the families of ordinary, blue collar, working class Americans and that is what is fueling this hysteria. In effect, it makes every American vulnerable."

"Mr. Santini, what can we expect in the next few days?"

"We can hope for more information on how this was allowed to take place. Hopefully the government will implement some anti-terror techniques that will help us, but overall, I'd say don't expect the hysteria to die down anytime soon. Starting tomorrow we will see an influx of gun sales, Americans will start arming themselves, we'll also see more and more breadwinners staying home to personally protect their loved ones. Again, and this might be wishful thinking, but hopefully the government can stop these riots wherever they occur because that in and of itself will go a long way to assuaging fears."

"Damn it, I can't find it." Cale told Rent. Rent was driving around the docks of the city, not so much trying to find the terrorists, but because the docks were relatively deserted.

"How many names are in there?" Rent asked.

"About six dozen. This guy was popular." Cale scrolled down the contact list on the phone.

"Did you look in the K's?" Rent asked.

"Yeah, it's not in C or K." Cale returned.

"Well how are you going to draw him out if you can't even find his name?" Rent asked. "Maybe we should use something different."

"Don't worry, I'll get him in the open." Cale continued searching the phone. "Wait, here it is, Qudamah, it's a Q. Sorry."

"Maybe you ought to stick with campaign finance reform. I'll talk to him." Rent reached over to the phone. Cale yanked it away.

"Watch and learn young Jedi." Cale pressed the call button

and put the phone to his ear.

"Fida? Did you escape?" Qudamah asked after only two rings.

"I'm afraid not. You're talking to Bob Cale." Cale responded professionally. Qudamah recognized the Senator's voice and sat up in surprise.

"So, Rent didn't kill you after all Senator. That will very bad for the family I am holding." Qudamah threatened.

"I haven't gone to the cops yet. But I will if that family is harmed." Cale told him.

"Then go, I no longer need you."

"You may not need to kill me anymore, but you do still need me."

"Oh, why is that?"

"Because I'm going right back to the Senate, and I'm going to have the ear of every politician, pundit, journalist, and general in this country. And do you know what's going to happen? Absolutely nothing."

"Good luck with that." Qudamah laughed.

"You don't seem to get my point. I intend to erase you from existence. I'm going to give Kicham your role. I'm going to parade his dead body through the streets for every American to see. No one will ever know you were even involved, and with that down, so go your chances of taking over Al-Qaeda." Cale informed.

"Really, you should watch the news more, my name is already out there. There are riots because of it." Qudamah defended.

"Yeah, but you made your announcement over radio and nobody can confirm who you are. Tomorrow morning you'll be the assumed name of some schmuck who died in a car accident tonight. Kicham Bradley made that call and he was killed during apprehension." Cale surmised.

"Really, truth in media doesn't seem to be your forte Senator." Qudamah said, still not believing him.

"C'mon, I'm part of the American government, there's nothing we don't lie about. Besides which, about ten minutes after I get to the cops, I start making calls to the FBI, CIA, NSA, and even the screen actors guild. They're going to put together some top notch evidence for me. Before I'm done, I'll have pictures of Kicham sipping brandy with Bin Laden."

"That's impossible, even for you." Qudamah argued, the possibility hitting him.

"You don't honestly think the we're going to let you take control of a major terrorist network do you? We can't, every legislator in the country will go along with me. This was Kicham's plan, using people Kicham recruited, and utilizing Kicham's new tactic. Kicham was acting under orders from the traditional Al-Qaeda leadership, and Kicham is now dead, end of threat, the

American people can sleep in peace." Cale informed. Rent stared at him, knowing that he was making this up as he went along.

"You cannot hide the truth from the people! They will know!" Qudamah's voice was showing signs of anger.

"The hell I can't. We do it all the time, it's no big deal. Hey, get this, I'm not even going to advocate attacking the Al-Qaeda leadership, instead I think we'll talk about state sponsors, and bomb Tehran or Damascus."

"We will punish you for that!" Qudamah told him, his anger obvious.

"Maybe Al-Qaeda will, but you won't because nobody'll know who in the hell you are!" Cale's voice was containing its own anger. "All anybody will know will be that Al-Qaeda did this with Kicham in operational command. You don't even factor in. Oh by the way, we're going to give you a teeny bit of a head start. However, sooner or later the entire platoon of CIA sweepers that we're assigning to take you out, they're gonna catch up to you and something tells me Osama hasn't got a room ready for you in whatever cave he's cowering in. You know, I'm willing to bet he's a little pissed at you."

"Perhaps you choose this option because Rent didn't have the guts to finish his assignment." Qudamah responded, his anger overflowing.

"That's pretty hypocritical coming from somebody who

kidnaps women and children for a living." Cale responded quickly. "Perhaps you could finish the job? No wait that would be dangerous for you and that's not your forte."

"You would never allow yourself in that position!" Qudamah didn't take the bait.

"That depends, unlike you, I am willing to die for what I believe, not just send others to die for me." Cale responded without hesitation. "All we want is the mother. Fair exchange? I'll show you what honor and courage really are."

"That is a trap!" Aziz said to his leader but Qudamah's anger overrode his senses.

"We shall see how an American statesman dies. Seattle Center, thirty minutes. We will finish this!" Qudamah yelled into the phone before shutting it off and taking the battery out in case Cale was lying and they were tracking the signal.

"I don't believe it." Rent exclaimed, turning the SUV around.

Cale smiled and stretched his arms behind his head in a gesture of victory. "Yep, I can piss anybody off." He said proudly.

The police moved quickly and closed in on the house, there were patrol cars surrounding it in every direction, an ambulance was on the scene. The SWAT vans were on the street in front of the house with Bomb Squad trucks next to them. The house itself was evacuated of all personnel except Jackson, Carrasco and the Bomb Squad. The Bomb Squad was setting up several pieces of armor and shielding in the master bathroom. Jackson was still on his side of the door with Carrasco on the other side. Jackson removed his body armor, utility vest and BDU blouse revealing his black T-shirt. He donned a standard issue bulletproof vest, pulling the velcro straps tight.

"You sure about this?" Carrasco asked him.

"That guy can't keep his finger on the button forever. We have to do this before the reporters have time to arrive or he'll blow it." Jackson replied. "You staying?"

"Absolutely, I'll be in right in front of the Bomb Squad." Carrasco assured.

"Thanks man." Jackson told his former commander. He stuck a wireless transmitter in his ear. "Testing, testing, you have me?" Jackson asked.

"We've got you." Bannister spoke into the radio. He examined the house from the doors of the SWAT command van. "You sure about this?"

"It's our only chance." Jackson replied, a bit aggravated that everyone was asking the same question. "Are we ready?"

"We are, we're a go, on your move." Bannister confirmed.

"What's Jesse's status?" Jackson asked with concern.

"He's on his way to the hospital, the paramedics say the bullet missed his artery but its still touch and go." Bannister replied. Jackson lowered his head and said a prayer for his friend. He closed his eyes and forced his mind back to the job at hand.

"Alright, do me a favor." Jackson asked Bannister. "If this goes south, tell my family that I did it because I would want someone to do it for them. They'll understand that."

"I will." Bannister replied.

"Listen." The Bomb Squad commander said into Jackson's ear. "The pressure switch he's got in there is probably a block on the detonator wire. That means the signal's already been sent from the control box to the detonator but the switch is blocking it from getting there. If anything happens to that button, if he releases it, or the cord is cut for some reason, the bomb will blow. You'll have no warning at all."

"No pressure." Jackson's sarcasm was unappreciated. "You can fix that right?" He asked.

"If we can get to it, we can bypass the wire and send the signal harmlessly to another device, but the circuit has to stay intact. It has to stay exactly the way it is right now. Understand?"

"Got it." Jackson told him. "You'd better get in there." The Bomb Squad nodded and along with Carrasco, moved to the master bathroom and got under a blast shield.

Jackson dialed a number on his phone and put it to his ear. "Ok, I'm going." Jackson spoke, and approached the door. Taking cover outside the door, Jackson yelled inside. "My name is Sergeant David Jackson. I'm coming in to negotiate, don't shoot me, you want to hear what I have to offer."

"Stay back, I want to talk to the press!" Mustafar kept his finger on the button.

"I'm still coming in, you want to hear this." Jackson slowly stepped inside the doorway, both his hands raised, his pistol in one hand, a cell phone in the other. "I'm putting my gun down very slowly." Jackson placed the weapon on the carpet.

"I told you to stay back." Mustafar kept his pistol trained on Jackson.

"You want to hear this. We want to negotiate."

"You do not negotiate."

"We do today, I have a deal you can't pass up." Jackson took small, slow steps across the room toward terrorist and hostage. "On this phone I have the President of the United States. He doesn't want anybody else to die. He is prepared to negotiate directly with you." Jackson said calmly, his hands still up.

"Your President would never do that!" Mustafar raised his gun, believing he was being deceived.

"He has the authority, he's under tremendous political pressure." Jackson stopped his forward movement. "Too much has happened today. He's on this phone and wants to negotiate this girl's release. He's prepared to give in to some of your demands. You've seen the President on tv, you know his voice. If you don't believe me, you can still detonate your bomb. What do you have to lose? Just listen to him." Jackson said, wearing his best poker face.

Mustafar still didn't believe him, but two possibilities entered his mind, one was that he might not have to martyr himself, which comforted him greatly. The second was if the President even conceded to a few of his demands, it would be a great victory. He still had the bomb and his pistol and decided it was worth the risk.

"Alright, slowly." Mustafar ordered. Jackson moved in very slowly. When he was close enough to Mustafar, he lifted the phone to put it to the man's ear. "Stop." Mustafar ordered. Jackson stopped cold. Mustafar thought for a moment, perhaps Jackson was trying to trap him. He reached out with his gun hand and took the phone in it. With the gun in the hand also, Mustafar was forced into an uncomfortable grasp on the phone, and had to prop it up on his ear. "Mr. President?" Mustafar asked into the phone.

Jackson lunged with both hands, wrapping up and holding in place the thumb that Mustafar was using to cover the button. At the same time, a sniper's bullet smashed through the bedroom window and ripped through Mustafar's head. The dead terrorist fell to the ground, taking Jackson with him. Jackson strained to keep Mustafar's finger on the button.

The sudden shock jolted Calleigh, and she began to panic. She tried to jump off the bed, but the cord connecting Mustafar's button to the vest held her in place. Noticing the cord, she struggled to free herself from it. Jackson turned to see her, but could not remove his hands from Mustafar's for fear it would set off the bomb. Jackson watched the cord inch slightly out of place and knew that Calleigh's next panic driven thrust would break the connection. Calleigh braced herself to push off the bed one last time. The scared little girl pushed herself up but Carrasco's large hands landed on her shoulders and slammed her violently against the bed. The Bomb Squad moved into the room and started examining the bomb.

"We walk from here." Rent told the Senator. He pulled the SUV into a parking space on the side of the road and turned off the engine.

"Do we go right in?" Cale asked, his nerves racking him.

"Dave'll call when the daughter is safe." Rent answered, his hate still driving him. "Look Senator." Rent said as he turned to Cale. "You didn't have to stay, it means a lot. If we don't make it, I wanted to tell you, thanks." Rent extended his hand.

"I'll gladly fight next to you anytime Carey." Cale took his hand and shook it.

Qudamah arrived at the Seattle Center and parked the van reasonably close. Aziz placed his AK-47 in a black gym bag along with a few other weapons and magazines. Inside the van, Qudamah was preparing Liz for the meeting. He very carefully zipped up a thick black jacket on her. They got out of the van and looked out toward Seattle Center.

A large fairground type area, Seattle Center was located in the middle of downtown. It previously played host to the World's Fair and was currently hosting the final night's concert for the Fremont Festival. It was famously home to Seattle's Space Needle, Experience Music Project or EMP, and McCaw Hall, Seattle's premier opera house among other notable Seattle tourist spots. The concert was being held in Memorial Stadium, adjacent to the Experience Music Project. The EMP was an extremely odd shaped building which some have referred to as looking like a melted electric guitar or a giant hemorrhoid and holds not only a huge music history museum but also its own concert hall and a science fiction museum. Across from the EMP was Seattle's Space needle, one of the defining characteristics of Seattle's skyline. Between the larger buildings were various amusement park type activities, games, small rides, restaurants and outdoor tables.

The Fremont Festival's concert in Memorial Stadium

brought out hundreds of Seattlites and tourists. Since the concert raged since dusk, few attending it had heard the news of Qudamah's claims, and almost all were trying to forget the terrorist attacks earlier in the day. Because of the relatively low concern for problems at the concert and the riots, all but three police officers were called off the concert, leaving mainly the private security to deal with any problems.

The concert wasn't the only happening at Seattle Center. The final night of the Fremont Festival drew the vendors, make-up artists and street urchins working the festival for one final party. Thus the entire grounds were filled with people, forcing most of the businesses there, like the EMP, to remain open, at least until the concert was to end in the early morning hours.

Qudamah conversed with Aziz for a few moments, running through their plan before Aziz went off on his own toward the concert.

"You remember what I told you?" Qudamah turned to Liz. She nodded back. "If Rent does not die, your children will." Liz nodded one last time.

Seattle center was swarming with people. Most were unaware of what was going on in other parts of the country. Some, the ones answering their cell phones, were picking up their things and leaving. Rent and Cale stood on the east side of the EMP building, the area was relatively secluded and Rent knew that he could stay there undetected until he got word from Jackson. Both men were understandably nervous, the stress of the day's events was weighing heavily upon them both.

"We're late." Cale stated after looking at his watch.

"We wait for Dave." Rent replied. He took another look around the corner. There was a small courtyard that led to some stairs leading into the larger Seattle Center courtyard, of which the EMP was just one anchor.

"Won't they know something's wrong?" Cale asked.

"He's come too far to be scared off now." Rent told him.

"I haven't." Cale responded, Rent looked at him and a slight grin brushed over his face.

The cell phone rang. Cale handed the phone to Rent.

"Yeah." Rent answered ambiguously.

"Carey, we got her. It was hairy, but she's going to be alright." Jackson told him.

"Ok, Seattle Center, we're doing it." Rent slipped the phone into his pocket and turned to look at Cale. The old man nodded and they stepped out from around the building.

Rent and Cale went side by side, marching purposefully through the lower courtyard. The north anchor to the upper courtyard was Memorial Field, where a guitar soloist started. The music echoed off the large buildings, using their designs to send the sounds directly into the courtyard. They made their way up the stairs into the larger courtyard. Rent searched for targets, Cale was similarly looking around, but was amazed at all the people who were still there. Throughout the courtyard, vendors were selling everything from t-shirts to jewelry to hot dogs. People were lined up at the various kiosks to sample or view different products, oblivious to what was happening in the world around them.

After one pass through of the courtyard and not seeing Liz, they doubled back closer to Memorial Stadium where more people were congregating. Rent's hope was that he could spot them before they spotted him.

Inside the stadium, a security guard was blocking the entrance to the stairway that led to the upstairs balcony. The door was in a secluded hallway and though the security guard saw some people, they were few and far between.

Aziz caught the security guard's eye when he came walking down the hallway at a very quick pace. Because the hallway led to some bathrooms and another corridor that people used to get to their seats, the security officer did not intend to stop the man coming at him.

"Have a nice evening sir." The security guard nodded when Aziz was close enough.

"You too." Aziz told him with a smile, pulled out a .22 caliber pistol with an attached silencer and shot him in the head. Aziz placed the pistol in the gym bag and went up the stairs.

"There she is." Rent said to Cale after spotting Liz Austin at a distance. Liz was between the Children's Museum and Memorial field. The two extremely large buildings were about a hundred meters apart and between them was a large grassy park with a few trees where people were sitting and talking while they listened to the music coming from the stadium. Liz was standing alone in the park, looking around. "That's not right. Why would she be alone?" Rent asked himself.

"Yeah." Cale centered in on Liz, her appearance gave him a striking revelation. "Oh my God." He said aloud, causing the revelation to strike Rent also.

"It could be a bluff, draw us out to take a shot." Rent theorized.

"Either way, we're screwed." Cale acknowledged. Rent nodded agreement.

"Stay here and cover me." Rent told him. "I'll have to take

her by surprise."

"Yeah." Cale grasped the gun in his pocket and watched over Rent.

Using the cover of some trees, Rent slid his feet down the small embankment and stopped at the last tree. Liz was still looking around and Rent carefully stepped to a closer tree when she turned her head away. Moving up, he quickly jumped behind another tree when Liz looked in his direction. A few seconds later, he poked his head out to see if she was still looking his way, she wasn't. Rent started toward Liz again, walking quickly but not running for fear she might realize he was there.

On the edge of the courtyard, Cale stood staring at the woman. He continued to grasp the pistol in his pocket. Out of nowhere, he got the feeling that someone was watching him. He turned his head to look at the crowd and saw Qudamah pull out a large pistol. Cale drew his own but knew he wasn't fast enough and moved laterally, ducking down.

Qudamah's first shots missed Cale and hit one of the windows of the Children's Museum. The people in the courtyard burst into hysterics, everyone began ducking for cover or running to get out of the area. Cale didn't want to return fire because of all the people in the background, but Qudamah was not so squeamish and fired several more shots at Cale.

Upon hearing the shots, Rent dashed at Liz. Liz turned her head to the direction of the shots and saw Rent out of the corner of her eye. She turned toward him, unzipped her jacket to reveal a suicide vest, and flipped the switch arming the bomb. An onlooker saw the vest and screamed. Liz said a prayer for her daughters and reached to push the button.

Rent closed his eyes, hoped for the best, and tackled her. He grabbed both her arms and pinned them to the ground. Liz struggled furiously.

"The girls are OK!" Rent screamed at her, but Liz didn't seem to understand him. "Listen! The girls are safe, Dave Jackson just got the second one, they're safe Liz, they're safe!" Liz suddenly stopped struggling.

"Oh thank God." She cried out. Rent released her arms and started looking at the vest.

"We have to get this thing off you." He told her.

A member of the crowd attempted to subdue Qudamah's firing, but was shot for his trouble. That man's failure caused everyone else in the crowd to cower and take cover; no one was going to try to stop Qudamah now. Seeing the Senator hiding behind a kiosk, Qudamah returned to firing at him, this time running out of ammunition and reloading quickly. Missing Cale but hitting several bystanders, Qudamah became angry and started making his way toward the Senator, firing wildly.

"You're sure he didn't connect any wires after he put it on you?" Rent asked.

"No, he just zipped it up." Liz replied.

"Ok, here goes." Rent pulled the zipper down slowly. He stopped about halfway down when he saw a large man running at him from his right side. Rent let go of the vest, pulled his pistol and pointed it at the stranger.

"Wait, I'm a Marine, I can help." The young man exclaimed loudly, his hands in the air. Rent sized him up, nodded and unzipped the vest. Thankful it didn't explode, he took the vest off Liz, carefully looking for tripwires. The vest secured, he handed it to the Marine.

"Take this into those trees, there isn't anybody there and the trees will absorb most of the blast if it goes off. Don't let anybody in there. Understand?" He ordered forcefully.

"Yes sir." The Marine obeyed.

"Stay here!" Rent ordered Liz. Rent jumped to his feet and

ran toward the gunfire.

"Carey no, don't leave!" Liz yelled. Needing Rent's presence to feel safe, she followed him.

Cale was splattered with shards of glass from the nicknacks on the kiosk that Qudamah was shooting. He knew he couldn't stay where he was and fired two shots high before leaving his cover. The shots didn't deter Qudamah. He reloaded his last magazine and fired at Cale, missing all three times.

Two more shots came at Cale and he tripped over a chair. Knocking a table over, the Senator fell to the ground. Qudamah moved up to the old man, a smile on his face. Cale looked forward from the ground and saw that he'd dropped his gun when he fell. He started to reach for it but saw Qudamah standing almost right on top of him. The terrorist lifted his weapon at Cale and looked the Senator in the eye.

"See Senator, you can't defeat us." Qudamah told him.

Rent jumped from the short stone wall next to the picnic area onto Qudamah, and the bullet flew harmlessly into the night sky. When Qudamah fell, Rent slammed his gun hand against one of the tables and the weapon was dropped.

Rent pulled his own pistol and put it to Qudamah's head, but was surprised when Qudamah reached up, twisted his hand and flipped him over onto his back, forcing him to toss his gun. The gun was flung several feet and landed just outside the eating area.

Qudamah was instantly on his feet and attempting to place his knee on Rent's chest. Rent reached up with his leg and kicked Qudamah squarely in the face, backing the terrorist up enough for Rent to get off his back and onto his feet.

Qudamah took up a solid fighting stance with both his legs further than shoulder width apart, he opened up his left hand and extended his fingers with his palm up, his right hand shaped like a tiger's claw.

Rent stood.

Rent came in with a punch that was deflected by a circular block. The block forced Rent off balance, and Qudamah came in with his back leg and delivered a kick to Rent's knee followed by a palm heel strike to Rent's face. Qudamah's attack only served to aggravate Rent. He grabbed Qudamah's shirt, pulled him close and delivered an elbow to his face. Rent followed his strike by spinning around and delivering another elbow to Qudamah followed by a barrage of punches to Qudamah's stomach and face. Rent ended the combination with a jump spinning sidekick. The kick connected perfectly with Qudamah's chest, sending the ailing terrorist into some tables that collapsed under his velocity and weight.

Rent started looking for his gun. He found it and saw that it was dangerously close to his opponent. Qudamah saw the gun, and lunged for it. Cale also saw this and grabbed his own gun. By the time Rent was halfway to Qudamah, the terrorist had attained the weapon. Qudamah jumped to his feet.

"Drop it!" One of the police officer's who was assigned to the concert aimed at Qudamah. Rent and Cale both froze. Qudamah looked up at the police officer.

Three AK-47 rounds hit the officer in the side and he flew back toward the small stone wall next to the tables. Qudamah turned and narrowly avoided two shots fired by Cale. Deciding to let Aziz have his chance at Rent and Cale, Qudamah retreated. Aziz continued firing from his perch on the balcony of the stadium.

The first few shots were at Rent, who dove over the stone wall for cover. Several more shots went to Cale but he slid behind a kiosk. Seeing that his two targets were under cover, Aziz started firing wildly into the crowd.

Qudamah ran along the courtyard until he saw a woman staring wild eyed at him.
He grabbed Liz by the hair and pulled the screaming woman along with him.

Rent looked up from behind the wall and saw Qudamah and Liz heading away from him. He tried to get back over the three foot stone wall but Aziz's fire kept him pinned. When Rent was back behind cover, Aziz emptied his magazine into other bystanders. Cale fired several rounds at Aziz through the cries of the wounded, but Aziz's distance made him almost impossible for the Senator to hit.

Aziz ducked down to change magazines, and Rent saw his chance. He signaled Cale with his hand to lay down fire and hurdled the stone wall. Aziz lifted his head, seeing Rent, the terrorist took aim at him. Cale began to fire. Cale knew he had little chance of hitting Aziz but his fire needed to be close enough to make Aziz put his head down.

Rent grabbed the dead cop's Smith and Wesson and went into a forward roll. Ending up on his knees, he propped one elbow on his knee to take careful aim.

Aziz returned a few shots to Cale. He turned to take aim at Rent and was struck in the face, just beside his nose, by Rent's bullet. The bullet had lost some velocity and came to a stop inside Aziz's brain, killing him instantly.

Rent turned to Cale. "You ok?"

"Don't wait for me!" Cale yelled, his old age preventing him from getting to his feet quickly. "Go Goddamn it go!"

Rent turned and ran after Qudamah and Liz with Cale trying to follow.

The terrorist fired several shots at his pursuer. None of the shots came close to Rent but several struck members of the crowd.

Rent attempted to fire back at Qudamah but distance, a populated background, a chance of hitting Liz, and bystanders running between them made returning fire an undesirable prospect. Rent knew he was gaining, Qudamah couldn't run very fast with Liz in tow, but they had a large head start and Rent was no longer in peak condition.

Qudamah headed, gun in one hand, Liz Austin by the hair in the other, into the Experience Music Project building. When the shooting started, the museum was just closing up, but people had swarmed inside looking for cover. Thus the lobby of the building was full of cannon fodder. Qudamah burst inside, randomly pointing his gun at the cowering civilians. After he crossed into the museum, he turned a corner and found himself very close to one of the EMP security guards. Out of instinct, Qudamah fired two shots into the guard's chest and the slide clicked back on his weapon. Realizing he had Rent's gun and he didn't have any spare ammunition for it, he dropped the gun next to the dead guard's body.

"Which way!" Rent yelled, entering the lobby for the EMP and seeing all the people cowering yet again. One of the women pointed toward the museum and Rent entered.

The music history museum was eerily quiet and not even Rent's footsteps could be heard through the maze of corridors. Rent stepped slowly, his pistol out in front of him, ready to fire at a moment's notice. He moved through the halls, glancing into every exhibit room until he came across the body of the dead security guard. He noticed the pistol next to the man and bent down to check his vitals.

Sure that the man was dead, he moved on. Slowly moving through the corridors he heard a sound in one of the exhibit halls, the "Jazz Hall." An exhibit was speaking, its computer activated by the motion sensor attached to it. Rent carefully entered the doorway. He checked the left side of the arch first, then moved to the right where he saw Liz, a lump on her forehead, cowering next to a guitar in a glass case. Rent reached his hand out to her, she looked up at him, her mouth open. Her fear making her unable to speak, she reached out with her index finger and pointed behind Rent.

Qudamah came out from behind a large exhibit and struck Rent with his elbow on the back of his neck, Rent began to turn, but Qudamah grabbed his gun hand and slammed it against the edge of a glass case before twisting it and throwing the gun. The gun bounced off the wall and onto the floor. Qudamah slammed his elbow into the back of Rent's head and wrapped his other arm around his chest.

Rent struggled to get Qudamah off his back and eventually did so by slamming his elbow into Qudamah's face a few times. Rent turned to face the terrorist, but Qudamah had wrapped one of his legs around one of Rent's, yanking it out from under him. Both men fell to the ground. Rent and Qudamah rolled around on the floor, each trying to obtain the upper hand. Liz watched in fear, knowing that there was nothing she could do to help.

Qudamah pinned Rent on the floor and came down on him with several punches before Rent grabbed him by the back of his neck, pulled him close and head butted him. They rolled around some more, Rent got on top, but Qudamah quickly rolled him off. Liz watched them roll over the pistol, they remained there for what seemed like an eternity before rolling away, leaving an empty space where the gun had been.

They rolled around for several more seconds, hitting and kneeing each other until Rent gained the upper hand by rolling onto his side and using his feet to push him away. He grabbed Qudamah by the shirt and pulled him along, eventually sitting him up and slamming him against the wall of the room.

Rent punched Qudamah in the face several times and slammed his forearm against the terrorist's throat, pinning him to the wall and choking him. Qudamah responded by putting the muzzle of the gun under Rent's armpit and firing twice.

Rent's eyes glazed over and all the strength suddenly left his body. Coughing and taking in a deep breath, Qudamah held Rent close to look into his eyes.

"Allah will not forgive you." He whispered to Rent before pushing him onto the floor next to the wall. Qudamah got to his feet, watching Rent and cherishing every moment. "But before you meet Allah, I want you to watch her die." Qudamah pointed the gun at Liz. Liz looked up at Qudamah with fear in her eyes, her hands shook and nausea enveloped her as she looked up the barrel of the gun. "This is the price of sin." Qudamah told her.

Three shots slammed into Qudamah's back and burst out his chest. Cale lowered his pistol and stepped through the doorway. Qudamah dropped the gun he was holding and tried to take a step. Spitting up blood, Qudamah fell into one of the glass cases. Spitting more blood, he rolled over and fell onto the floor; a dozen large shards of glass making their own wounds in his chest.

Liz ran to Rent.

Cale approached. Qudamah was staring at him, coughing up blood. With every breath, every heartbeat, more and more blood spurted from his wounds.

"Thank you." Qudamah smiled, his teeth stained with his blood. "Thank you for sending me to Allah."

"Give him a message for me." Cale raised his gun to Qudamah's head. "Tell him we're going to fight back." Cale fired a single round into Qudamah's head.

Liz cradled Rent in her lap. She took his hand in her's and tears ran down her cheeks. Rent was fading quickly and she knew there was nothing anyone could do. His breathing was becoming shallow and he'd turned pasty white.

Cale saw Rent laying in her arms. "What's the name of your youngest daughter?" Cale asked softly. Liz turned to look at the Senator in bewilderment. "He doesn't know."

"Rebecca." Liz turned to Rent. "Her name's Rebecca, we call her Becca." She told him, wishing he had more time. Rent smiled at her, he began saying something but did not have the strength to fully vocalize it. Liz leaned down to his blue lips.

"I...'m...I'm....s–s–sorry." Rent said with his last breath. Suddenly his grasp tightened around Liz's hand, he convulsed and his grasp gave way.

Liz brushed his hair with her hand. Cale wrapped his arm around her shoulders.

Epilogue:

Within twenty-four hours, all the riots were quelled by a combination of police and National Guard. The riots that occurred in Seattle ended up not being as severe as in Detroit or New York, but still caused millions of dollars worth of damage. Because of the quick governmental response in dealing with the riots and assurances from law enforcement agencies and politicians that the attacks were over, the American people's paranoia quickly settled into a low level state of fear.

Two more sleeper cells were discovered, the first in Houston Texas, the second in Los Angeles. The FBI quickly apprehended all involved without incident. The Utah cell was located in Salt Lake City and a tactic similar to Captain Carrasco's was used to secure the hostages they took. The cell in Chicago was never located, though the FBI office in that city maintained that the case would remain open and would be actively investigated until the perpetrators were brought to justice.

After news of the Seattle cell's demise circulated around the country, the President, joined by other prominent members of government, declared the incident to be a major battle in the war on terror. A battle won by the brave men and women of the United States of America. The President held up a picture of Qudamah Al-Khalifa and declared his attack foiled. His plot to gain control of Al-Qaeda was never made public.

Senator Cale was hailed a national hero, a member of the legislative branch who literally took up arms against the terrorists attacking his nation. Politicians made a bipartisan effort to make him the symbol of America's resolve in the war on terror. Senator Cale did not accept this recognition and though he used the attention to speak about moderation and assure the American people that they were safe, downplayed his role in the actual fighting.

Bethany Knox didn't remain the acting Chief of Police very long, within three days the City Council of Seattle hired a new Chief. The former Sheriff for Las Vegas was lured in with a considerable benefits package. Knox returned to her original position of Assistant Chief of the Criminal Investigations Bureau.

Against her explicit recommendation that he be fired for insubordination and disobeying direct orders, Sergeant David Jackson was promoted to Lieutenant and given full command of the Narcotics units.

Terry Bannister remained the FBI's Assistant Director in charge of Counter Terrorism. His unit was once more expanded and several domestic command centers were created in conjunction with the Department of Homeland Security to deal with crises that pertained to terrorism occurring on American soil. Though Knox was more or less forgotten in the incident, Bannister was portrayed as a competent leader who'd done an invaluable job of keeping things together.

Captain Manuel Carrasco's tactics in dealing with hostage situations involving suicide bombers became the mainstay of SWAT and Hostage Rescue units across the country. He was offered a full time position at Quantico, training Hostage Rescue Teams, SEAL teams, Delta Force, etc., but declined in order to remain in Seattle with the men that he trained and worked with.

The issue of what to do with Michael Seacrest became a very politically volatile issue. Many people felt his actions should not be punished because they were in defense of his family. Other people felt that part of his responsibility as a Doctor, a civilian contractor with the Police Department, and an American citizen was to put his country and the lives of fellow Americans before his family. When prosecutors decided to bring him to trial on conspiracy charges, people on both sides of the issue protested outside the courthouse. After a three month trial, he was found guilty and given a suspended sentence of fifteen years. He subsequently disappeared from view, moving to central Washington state to be close to his surviving family.

Jason Brewer's wife and son were found several days after

the attacks in the Puget Sound, both were shot once in the back of the head.

The Mayor of Seattle was brought up on impeachment charges for gross negligence in refusing to cancel the final concert of the Fremont Festival. The argument against him was that the concert provided an extremely likely target for a terrorist attack and that the five people who were killed and thirteen more that were wounded would have been safer had the concert been cancelled. The impeachment did not come to fruition because of the Mayor's abrupt resignation.

The memorial service for the fallen warriors in the attacks became a major media event. Occurring exactly one week after the attacks, people from across the country came to pay tribute to the men that died in their fight against the terrorists. Virtually the entire Seattle Police Department was in attendance, with only on-duty officers absent. Family members of the victims were seated in the front row of the massive church where the service was held. Also in the front row were various members of the Police Department and FBI, including Knox, Bannister, Carrasco, Jackson, and Owens. Owens neck was still wrapped with bandages because he'd broken out of the hospital to attend. Jackson aided and abetted.

The caskets were lined up in front of the pews. They were arranged from right to left in the specific order of: Chief of Police William Rodgers, Jason Brewer, Muhammed Rasheed, Lieutenant Lewis Austin, Dylan Austin, and Carey Rent. The caskets were closed with American flags draped over them.

"These men have been called heroes." Senator Cale said from the podium behind the six caskets. "That moniker does not give them justice. What do you call men who did what these men did? Men who made the ultimate sacrifice in defense of freedom, in defense of life? The word hero is not enough.

"One week ago we were attacked. I say we because this was not an attack only against America, it was an attack against humanity. The attackers meant to use our very own loved ones against us. They wished to erode the principles that we have built upon for so long. Principles such as freedom, justice, love, and righteousness. In the last week there has been talk about retaliation. The talk has been that war is imminent. Perhaps it is. Perhaps peace can never be attained. But I don't believe that. I believe that even though we were attacked, even though that attack was evil and malicious, even though many died in that attack, I believe that we will overcome. That no matter the attack, no matter the tactic, no matter their resolve, they cannot destroy the freedom we have built. War is not imminent, it has arrived, and we have time and again saw the challenge, faced it, and overcome in true American fashion. The war on terror has taken many turns, this is one of them. One week ago, our families became soldiers in it.

"I do not know what to call these men. Heroes? Too simple. Victims? When hell freezes over. Soldiers? Too ambiguous. The truth is that these men could be called many things, they fit into many categories. Not the least of which is heroes." Cale walked away from the podium and down the three steps to the caskets. He stood next to Chief Rodgers' body. "We have to look at these men with their humanity still attached. It's all too easy to label someone a hero and then forget the character of that individual. We must not forget that these were people like us, with all the frailties that humanity has given us. It's those imperfections of which they overcame that make what they did so special. That make the qualities that they exemplify, that they believed in, that they gave their lives in defense of, so important. Qualities like duty." He stood behind Chief Rodgers casket. He slowly walked to Jason Brewer's and stood behind it. "Sacrifice." He stepped to Muhammad Rasheed's. "Dignity." He moved to Lewis Austin's. "Loyalty." He stopped at the casket of Dylan Austin. Placing his hand on the flag covering the casket, he spoke Dylan's quality. "Innocence." With her son's word, Liz Austin, sitting in the front row with Becca in her arms and holding Calleigh's hand, began sobbing uncontrollably. Last, Cale stepped behind Rent, his voice breaking. "And for one. Redemption." Cale took a second to regain his composure. "Values that solidify a nation." He added.

"In the past week I have heard these men proclaimed casualties of war. When we look at them, when we pay tribute to the men whose force of will has saved so many, it is irresponsible to disregard the accomplishments they have made in order to make us free from fear. The sacrifice they made for their cause makes them so much more than that. But fighting to free us from fear is not what they died for. They died, not in defense of their country, but in defense of the values for which their nation stands. They died clinging to the values they held truest. The values our enemies hope to destroy with their deaths. That is not the definition of hero. That is not the purpose of a soldier. There is a word for which that definition fits. A word passed down to describe many who have made the ultimate sacrifice for their values. That word fits these fallen much more than it applies to those who would kill them.

"It is not right to say that these men are simply casualties of war, nor is it correct to say that they are just heroes. They are this nation's true believers. These *are* America's martyrs. I salute them." Cale raised his salute, followed by the entire crowd.

About the Author

Richard Hodgkinson was born and raised in Nashville Tennessee.
He served in the army but began his career in writing the moment he
discovered he could put words on paper. He currently resides in
Tennessee.

Coming Soon From Richard Hodgkinson

Kaylee

Wicked Lies

For more information, pictures, blogs, news, ordering information
and much more, go to

www.myspace.com/richardhodgkinson

www.ingramcontent.com/pod-product-compliance
Lightning Source LLC
Chambersburg PA
CBHW020256030726
47499CB00001B/217